THE MAGNOLIA CHRONICLES

KATE CANTERBARY

VESPER PRESS

Editing provided by Julia Ganis of Julia Edits.
Proofreading provided by Marla Esposito of Proofing Style.
Cover design and art by Qamber Design.

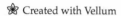 Created with Vellum

To all the women waiting for the world to evolve around them.

PROLOGUE

"THERE'S SOMETHING I'D LIKE TO DISCUSS WITH YOU, MAGNOLIA Lynn."

I watched my mother, waiting for some clue into the first-and-middle-name treatment. She reserved it for only three occasions:

1. Big Trouble. Even at thirty-four years old, I was subject to my mother's expectations. These days, it took the form of forgetting to call one of my seventeen aunts on her birthday, leaving the house with any part of my underwear visible, or walking my dog after nine o'clock at night. Per my mother, it was the witching hour for rapists and serial killers.

2. Big News. This often involved reporting on the health issues of people I barely knew. My Sunday School teacher's nephew was diagnosed with Lyme, our old neighbor—the one from the apartment building we'd lived in when I was an

infant—lost his glass eye again, my uncle Carl's sister-in-law had a suspicious mole and she was going in for a procedure, my father's second cousin in Philadelphia was cutting back on red meat on account of the gout. That type of news.

3. Big Asks. These were few and far between, due primarily to my mother keeping up with an *I can do it all* complex. That mindset made me sound like a mom-shaming monster but the truth was my mother asked for help once every leap year.

She would've mentioned any news on the car ride from my parents' home in New Bedford to Providence, the location of our annual post-Christmas, pre-New-Year's spa day. She would've disciplined me then too. This was an ask, one she'd waited to drop on me until we were swaddled in plush robes and kicked back in a dimly lit Zen room with cucumber-scented water in hand.

And it was a big ask. It had to be. There was no other reason for her to fixate on smoothing her robe and avoid my expectant gaze.

"What's that, Diana Leonore?"

She dragged the robe's belt between her fingers, repeatedly straightening it and rolling it into a cinnamon roll spiral. Still avoiding me. Then, "I've been thinking about my New Year's resolutions. Have you given any consideration into your resolutions?"

It was a good thing she was obsessed with her robe because I couldn't have repressed my eyeroll for anything.

I loved my mother. I did. If I didn't have a fond, affectionate, *accepting* spot in my soul for my mother and all her quirks, I wouldn't put up with her criticism of exposed bra straps and post-sunset dog walking. I'd skip all the girls' days spent at spas, nail salons, and Boston-area malls too. But I loved my mother and I accepted these gestures as her unique way of returning that love.

However.

I didn't love my mother's lifelong self-improvement quest. Perhaps it wasn't lifelong to her but she'd openly expressed dissatisfaction with her body all of *my* life. To twist and tangle matters even more, my mother and I had the same bodies. Exact same, right down to the one eyebrow forever intent on colonizing the hairless gulf between brows.

Five foot six inches, dark chestnut hair with wonky, inconsistent waves, honey-hazel eyes, bodies straight out of a Botticelli painting. No amount of Pilates, low-carb dieting, or celery juice could banish our soft, round bellies or thick hips. They were part of us just like our button noses and plump, pale lips, and we couldn't hate them away.

We were generous.

We were handfuls.

We were full-figured.

And I was all right with that. It took me years—*years*—to realize it, but my body was strong and capable. This body was the only one I had to see me through this life and it was the right one for me.

My mother wasn't there yet. In all fairness, she'd also brought three babies into the world—at the same time. She'd carried me and my brothers all the way to thirty-six weeks and then we'd weighed in between four-and-a-half and six pounds each. That was no small feat and for that, I indulged her assortment of health kicks. I went along with her, if for no other reason than to remind her she was so much stronger and more capable than she gave herself credit for. Even if I rolled my eyes about it sometimes.

"I haven't thought about resolutions, no," I replied. "I take it you have some ideas."

"One or two," she murmured. "Nothing too wild."

I reached for the glass of water seated on the table beside me. "Since we're chatting," I started, pausing for a sip, "why don't you share them with me?"

She shifted in her chair, tucked the robe between her knees. Modesty, very important to my mother. It made no sense that she loved massages where she laid on a table, fully nude, while a stranger rubbed out her knots. But no one ever said mothers had to make sense.

"Please listen to what I have to say before you get defensive."

Okay. So, this is a really big ask.

I made a cross over my heart. "I will try my best."

My mother drew in a breath, held it a moment, and took my hand in hers. "It's been months since things ended with Peter and—"

"Oh my god," I murmured.

"—and years since the unpleasantness with that other boy. I won't say his name because my blood pressure can't handle it but—"

"Oh my god."

"—it's time for you to make yourself a priority, Mag."

"Right, because I never do that." I gestured to the Zen room, the robes. "Never ever."

"Stop it," she chided. "You know what I mean. You work at your business, you work at your friendships, and you work at giving your dog a life of extraordinary comfort."

"Being the best dog mom is my most important job," I replied.

After a decade-long sigh, she continued, "I want you to commit to caring for yourself this year. I know you've had a difficult run with boys but I want you to give it a real shot this time."

"What do you mean, a real shot?" I sputtered. "I have given it real shots. Lots of shots. So many shots." I channeled my frustration into shaking my head hard enough to make myself dizzy. "I've put myself out there, Mom."

"You have," she said, a bucket of hesitance in her voice. "But—and don't bite my head off here—I don't think you were trying."

Everything I'd said about tolerating her extra-strength mothering was a lie and I wanted those statements struck from the record.

Not trying.

Not *trying*.

Was she fucking kidding me?

For fuck's sake, *not trying*?

"I doubt you see it that way," she said carefully.

I hit her with an *uh, you think so*? glare.

"And that's because you're not seeing it from my perspective, Mag. You aren't seeing yourself the way I do—beautiful, smart, amazing—and you aren't choosing men who see that either. You are choosing men who walk all over your kindness and abuse your generous spirit and treat you like you're disposable. Like a damn plastic straw." She wagged a finger at me.

Oh, great. Now it's the Big Ask and some Big Trouble. "Mom—"

"No," she shot back. "You are not a plastic straw, my girl. You're compostable."

I laughed before the tears started pouring down my face. That was the proper order of operations. If I didn't lead with laughter, I'd drown in my weak, tender spots. I knew this because I'd drowned there before.

"Compostable?" I asked, sniffling. "Like eggshells and apple cores?"

"Don't start with the eggshells," she replied. "You're no eggshell. You're tough like potato peels and artichoke leaves."

I thumbed open my imaginary notebook, pulled an imaginary pencil from behind my ear. "December twenty-eighth, the day my mother referred to me as a potato peel."

"So dramatic," she murmured.

"Please. Ash is the dramatic one."

"Your brother is moody," she argued. "Ash is temperamental, Linden is introverted, and you are, on occasion, dramatic."

Yes, my brothers and I were named after trees. I got off easy with Lynn as my middle name in honor of my great-grandmother but Ash Indigo and Linden Wolf got screwed. That was how it went with hippie parents.

They'd missed out on the Summer of Love but that hadn't stopped my parents from living the hippie life. They'd had the VW van, the long hair, the peace, the love, and the weed. And then they'd found three heartbeats.

I didn't know the precise sequence of events that followed but I knew my father cut his hair, took a job as a mail clerk, and started night school a few months before we were born. My mother had stayed home with us when we were babies before Mrs. Santillian became everyone's favorite substitute teacher in the New Bedford Public School district.

But they never abandoned their hippie lives, not all the way. They'd championed organic farming long before it was a widespread practice and when we'd moved from an apartment to a single family home, they commandeered the entire backyard for that purpose. My dad was an accountant now and—rather unbelievably—enjoyed the shit out of the tax code. And he still drove the VW van.

My mother tapped my wrist. "I've known each of you since the first time I saw your little faces on the sonogram. I knew who you were."

The fourteen-year-old version of me wanted to argue with this because how could she possibly know me before I knew myself? The thirty-four-year-old version knew how to pick battles.

"What do you propose I do with my dramatic potato peel self, Mother?"

She took a sip of her water, then another. Oh, this was going to be good. No other reason to stall for an entire minute. I glanced at the clock. I hadn't paid attention to the day's spa service itinerary, but I was certain we were due to start with some seaweed masks or pumpkin baths or salt rubs by now.

But I wouldn't put it past my mother to book an hour in the Zen room specifically for this conversation.

"I want you to let me set you up on some online dating sites," she said. "I'll pick out the photos and write the little descriptions, and I'll help you screen the matches." She tipped her head to the side. "I'll screen all of them if you'd like, but I figured you'd want a hand in this."

"Oh, I'll help," I replied. "I don't want to subject you to all those penises because there are going to be penises, Mom."

"Pfft." She waved a hand at me. "I've seen plenty of penises, thank you. I married a man, and I raised two sons. For years, I couldn't go a day without seeing at least two penises. *Years*, Magnolia. I doubt you remember it but your brothers would just whip those things out. It didn't matter if we were at the park or in the middle of the grocery store or Sunday mass." She made an exasperated sound, shook her head. "Penises are nothing new to me."

I pressed my fingertips to my eyelids. "I—oh, god—I don't want to put all of these things in the same category. Brother penis doesn't live in the same world as date penis. Separate and distinct categories, please."

"Whatever you want," she replied.

"Then—wait." I peered at her. "You want my New Year's resolution to be giving you control of my online dating profiles? That sounds like a project for you and a punishment for me."

"It is not a punishment," she argued. "But no, that is not the resolution I have in mind for you." She ran the belt through her fingers again. "This year, I want you to commit to finding someone who sees you the way I do—beautiful, smart, amazing."

"And compostable," I added.

"Compost is magic, Mag." A thin frown pulled her lips down. "Promise me you'll try."

"You just want to plan a wedding and start shopping for baby baptism gowns."

I didn't want to admit it to her or even myself but after attending twenty-two weddings over the past six years, I'd socked away enough plans of my own. I knew I wanted a beachy summer wedding on the southeast coast of Mass-achusetts and I had some ideas about ornamental cabbage centerpieces.

She lifted her shoulders. "That's a fringe benefit," she admitted. "Your happiness is the goal."

"And I'm finding happiness in a man? That's what you're telling me?"

Another shrug. "The happiness won't come from a man."

"No?" I challenged. "Then where is it coming from in this experiment?"

My mother grinned. It was the same grin she used when insisting she knew us as fetuses. She was right about that, about us. Ash's moods were volatile, Linden couldn't be more introverted if he tried, and I had a dramatic moment or two.

"You'll find out, my girl. You'll know."

I wished I shared my mother's confidence.

CHAPTER
ONE

MY DATE WAS PICKING HIS TEETH WITH A STEAK KNIFE.

It wasn't a quick thing either. No in, out, done. He was halfway to giving himself a root canal right here in the middle of the restaurant.

The best part was when he struck gold and dug out a bit of food. He'd give it a thorough inspection and then pop it back in his mouth. Maybe I was wrong about it being the best part. None of this could qualify as the best of anything. I didn't know how it could qualify as the best when it seemed like increasingly dark shades of awful. The dating world knew no connection to logic. This had to be the worst part.

He'd ordered the largest steak on the menu and requested it "blue and mooing." There was something about the purposeful wink he'd shot in my direction as he'd said those words, as if his capacity for red meat was somehow indicative of his penis size.

But I couldn't get past the dental exam.

I watched, my fingers frozen around the stem of my

wineglass, while he engaged in this ritual for full minutes at a time.

My first instinct was to drown the flames of this date with Pinot Grigio, but I was oddly entranced by this guy's knife-swallowing act. I didn't want to be caught unaware when he sliced off a chunk of his tongue.

In the two months since diving headfirst into the dating game, I'd learned one thing: it shouldn't be this difficult. The human race had millions of years of existence on its side, and it wasn't supposed to be so complicated to find a decent guy. That was all I wanted: a decent guy. I didn't need a prince, a white knight, a billionaire, an athlete, or even an architect.

Another thing I'd learned: I wasn't asking for much. I wanted a guy who knew how to wear a pair of jeans and fix a leaky faucet and enjoyed big family dinners on Sundays. I wanted a guy who returned text messages and remembered birthdays and never made shady comments about his exes being crazy clingers. He didn't have to be perfect. He could leave his dirty socks and underwear right next to the laundry hamper and keep porn on his computer. Hell, I loved porn and didn't even own a proper hamper.

And another lesson: I was convinced I'd met all the men metro Boston had to offer. There was the wandering millennials, the affluent assholes, the man-shaped children, the chronically misogynistic mansplainers. I wasn't positive where the knife swallower fit in this phylum but I knew these savage teeth-cleaning rituals met the criteria for automatic disqualification.

Next, please.

"What do you do, Margot?" he asked, his gaze trained on

the half-chewed bit of god-only-knew-what on the tip of his knife.

Since meeting him at the restaurant an hour ago, he'd managed to butcher my name into an endless string of nonsense. Maisey, Margot, Melanie, Mackenzie. Without my name and profile pic front and center on the dating app in which we'd matched, it seemed he was lost in the sauce.

Damn dating apps. As promised, I was going along with this crazy scheme of my mother's. She'd signed me up, loaded the photos, wrote the pithy profile, and breathlessly waited for me to meet the man of my dreams.

Easy enough, right?

Not so fast.

The presumed anonymity of the internet stripped back layers of formality and pleasantry—and humanity. This algorithm-fueled existence reduced many men—not all, but a good share—into vagina-seeking drones who led with their penises and defended themselves with a war chest of insults. Despite my mother's insistence she could survive a dick pic or twenty, I'd shielded her from all manner of messaging. It was the Wild West out there.

"Landscape architect," I said with a smile. I'd told him this during our first message exchange but I figured it was filed away with all the other useful information I'd shared.

Like my name.

He glanced at me and then returned his attention to the bar on the other side of the restaurant. He'd been eyeing the busty bartender since we walked in. "What is that again?"

"I design and build outdoor environments in residential settings," I replied. I couldn't scrub the smile from my face. Whether blessing or curse, I was a serial smiler. "I specialize in roof gardens and sustainable design."

"That sounds like good money," he said. "What do you pull in per year?"

Lord have mercy.

"I do all right for myself," I said, a stiff grin pointed at my dish of ravioli. "You're in the fire detector business, right?"

"Sure am." He plucked a sprig of rosemary from his plate, sniffed it, and tossed it down. It landed on the middle of the bright white tablecloth like an herbaceous casualty of this skirmish. "I was in Burlington today. Installed a whole floor on one of those new business parks. The building codes these days, I'll tell ya, they have a unit every few feet. Not that I'm complaining. More units, more money. And I've got a lot of units."

He leaned forward and wiggled his eyebrows as though the mere mention of cash would light my panties on fire. Unfortunately for him, money was good for heating my house but not my lady bits.

"Impressive," I said, forcing another smile. I took no issue with the pride he gained from his work or earning a comfortable living. It was the shallow arrogance soaking his every word and gesture. He was pleased with himself but got more jollies out of other people being pleased with him. "Really impressive. I love that for you."

He jerked his chin in my direction, a smug grin pulling at his lips. "Yeah, but I don't like talking about finances. That's pretty far down the road. I'm not interested in commitment. I'm not looking to wife anyone up, you know?" He lifted his rum and Coke, sipping while he stared at me. "You're cool with that, right? You're doing the casual thing, right?"

There was a long-suffering sigh gathering in my chest, a roll of impatient thunder. I managed a quick, "Mmhmm" and shoved a ravioli in my mouth. It was big and cheesy and delicious, and I took my time with it. To my mind, some tasty pasta could drown out the teeth-picking, name-forgetting, boob-ogling, commitment-dodging disaster of this evening.

There were no two ways about it—this was a disaster. He'd seemed fine in his messages. Funny and interesting, if not a little self-absorbed. But that was the trouble of chatting in an app: anyone could manage some amusing conversation for minutes here and there. Being affable and ordinary in person was a different ball game.

Dinner wrapped up without too many more comments about money or relationships, and I quickly shut down all talk of dessert. I didn't trust myself to share a slice of chocolate cake with this guy without wanting to gargle with muriatic acid. And let's be honest, I didn't want to share my cake.

The waiter cleared the table—including the steak knife, thank god—and left the check. Being the independent woman I was, I gestured toward it. "I'd be happy to pick this up," I said.

With a flippant shrug, he pushed the folio toward me. "Thanks," he said.

While I poked through my bag for my wallet, he snatched it back, opened it, and inspected each charge.

"I'm going to Aruba next month," he mumbled while he worked his thumbnail between his front teeth. Player really needed a dentist. "Me and my boys, we're all going." He tore his gaze from the bill and stared at my cleavage. "Ever been to Aruba? You might be able to pull off a bikini."

Aaaaaaaaand we're done.

As a rule, I wasn't fake. I didn't bullshit. I didn't go out of my way to make people aware that I disliked them either. I couldn't see how that helped anyone. But I wanted to smack this boy upside the head and tell him to find some manners. It wasn't that I couldn't take a compliment because that statement had no markings of a compliment.

"Wow," I panted, plucking my credit card from my wallet's front pocket. I didn't bother tugging my sweater up. If he was going to objectify my body, that was about him, not me. I wasn't hiding myself because he couldn't have breasts in his sight line without being disgusting about it. I tapped my card on the table. "I'll just get the waiter's attention for this and then we can be on our way."

"Nah, I changed my mind. It's on me," he declared, reaching into his pocket and producing a card of his own. He chucked it toward the center of the table. "What kind of man lets a chick pay?"

I blinked several times, not understanding this tug-of-war.

"We'll split it," I said, twisting my voice into that perky, breezy tone I used when my clients freaked out halfway through a project because their yard looked nothing like the pitch designs. I sounded perky and breezy but you can believe I rolled my eyes like a motherfucker.

The waiter appeared and I shoved the cards into his hands. "Here. Here you go. All set."

"Great," he drawled. "I'll be right back."

It didn't take long to process our payments, and I added a healthy gratuity to my total. This guy seemed the type to leave a forty-nine-cent tip and a pompous comment about the knives not meeting his sharpness standards.

"You're a sports girl, aren't you, Margene?" he asked, sliding his copy of the receipt into his wallet with care.

That he recalled this detail but not my name was amazing.

"A bit, yeah," I hedged. I didn't want to agree to anything.

"There's a bar around the corner." *Bahhhh.* His old-school Boston townie accent flared to life with that comment. "Good spot to catch the game."

Of course, I wanted to catch the game but there was no justification for spending another minute with this guy. With my luck, he'd get the wrong idea and stick his tongue down my throat. Couldn't have that.

"I wish I could." I stood and shrugged on my raincoat. "My dog has been home alone all day. I have to get back and take him out for a walk."

"You have a dog? What kind?"

I swallowed a sigh. My dog was in my dating app photo with me. Truly, he was everywhere. My holiday cards, my Instagram, my lock screen, my key chain. Everywhere. "A Boston Terrier," I said, moving toward the door. "He has some health problems and requires medication at a certain time, so I really should go. It was great meeting you."

He grabbed my shoulder—despite my obvious movement away from him—and pulled me into a one-armed hug. "Yeah, you're not too bad."

Not too bad. I couldn't tell whether he meant that as some sort of sarcastic endearment or he was being transparent about his assessment of me. "Mmhmm," I murmured, shaking out of his hold. My mother wasn't going to hear the end of it for swiping on this guy. "Thanks for, um—thanks."

We paused outside the restaurant, me pretend-busy with finding my keys and him tapping out a message on his phone. I smiled up at him, feigning some exaggerated frazzle as I rooted around in my bag. My fingers were folded around my keys but I wanted him to leave first. We couldn't walk together in painful, awkward silence until one of us reached our destination. Couldn't do it. I needed to be free of this man and I'd do whatever I had to do to make my escape.

"Okay, yeah," he murmured, flashing the peace sign. "I'm out."

He took two backward steps in the direction I meant to go. Forcing down a groan, I waved at him. "Have a good night."

Walking five minutes out of my way to get back to my truck was worth it. A few extra steps never hurt and it gave me a chance to burn off a bit of frustration. I ducked into a corner market and bought a black cherry seltzer for the thirty-minute drive from downtown Boston to my aunt's house in Beverly.

I'd lived there for several years but it was still Aunt Francesca's house. There was some whomp-whomp associated with being thirty-four and subletting from your aunt. It didn't matter that she'd moved to New Mexico or that I'd renovated the place from top to bottom. It wasn't mine.

It was quiet here in the suburbs and I liked it. I got my fill of the city during the day and I liked coming home to my quiet neighborhood. The driveway helped too. Parking in Boston was on par with an *Amazing Race* challenge, and there was nothing more comforting than a dedicated spot.

Slowing as I approached the stone bungalow, I noticed a string of box vans and pickup trucks on the opposite side of the street. People streamed in and out of the old Cape-style home, and every interior light was illuminated.

The house had been vacant for almost a year and neglected for several decades before that. It needed a ton of work. I knew because I lived across the street, but I'd also tried to convince my architect friend Riley to take it on as a pet project. He declined. He was busy working on multimillion-dollar mansions and centuries-old brownstones and didn't have time for a cookie-cutter Cape with wood paneling. Not that I blamed him. If given the choice between a high-budget roof garden in Beacon Hill and a tiny backyard redesign in Marshfield, I was taking the roof garden and I wasn't even going to complain about parking.

Now it looked like a team of flippers were fixing up the Cape. With any luck, they weren't tearing it down to the ground. More and more, house flippers razed houses rather than working with the original structures. They'd rip it all down, build on the old foundation, and leave the character and charm at the curb.

One of the men waved from the sidewalk. It was late, and though it was March and spring should've been springing, the temperature hovered around freezing. But he seemed immune to this cold snap in his jeans and hoodie. I lifted my hand in response before turning into my driveway.

I didn't have the energy for neighborly chatter tonight. Once the weekend rolled around, I'd bake some Portuguese sweet bread and introduce myself. With any luck, they'd spill the beans on their plans for the Cape.

CHAPTER
TWO

Dating App Guy 1: Hi, sweetie.

Magnolia: Hello.

Dating App Guy 1: Tell me something.

Magnolia: Okay…anything in particular?

Dating App Guy 1: What do you do for fun?

Magnolia: I'm all about the Sox, the Pats, the Celts, the Bs. I like gardening and beer. I like the idea of traveling but I don't do much of it.

Magnolia: What about you?

Dating App Guy 1: I like blowing my load all over your face.

Magnolia: Excuse you what?

Dating App Guy 1: Your face makes me think about blow jobs.

Magnolia: Oh, really?

Dating App Guy 1: You can't be cute like that and think I won't want to cum all over your face.

Magnolia: Thanks!

Dating App Guy 1: I want to suck on those big fat titties too.

Dating App Guy 1: Hello?

Dating App Guy 1: Sweetie? Where'd you go?
{ blocked }

————

THE WEEKEND ROLLED AROUND BUT I FORGOT ALL ABOUT baking. It was probably a blessing in disguise since my sweet breads only rose about half of the time. That seemed like a fair statement on my ability to function as an adult too: fifty percent meeting expectations, fifty percent blobbing around like thick, doughy uselessness.

I was loaded with the best of intentions but getting off the ground required more than intentions. And ducks. It was always about having ducks and they needed to be in rows or lines. I didn't know who decided we needed waterfowl to reach maximum adulthood but I had no ducks, no lines.

But that was only fifty percent of my existence.

That was how I saw myself: part-time muddles and struggles, part-time working my ass off and getting through it like a boss. That was the catch though—I was only getting through. Yeah, I crossed the finish line but it was one helluva challenge getting there.

And today, getting through took the form of sleeping late, eating peanut butter straight from the jar for breakfast, and then walking in circles around the grocery store. I didn't know what to get, but instead of figuring it out I frequented the cheese sample station.

The sword swallower hadn't reached out since our dinner four nights ago and that was fine. I couldn't endure another dinner dental exam but his silence stung, just a bit.

I knew it was absurd to reject him with one hand and also hold out the other with the expectation of being chased.

But that was my crazy view on the matter. I wanted to be wanted.

I wasn't sure when I'd collected that lofty attitude, since my entire romantic history resembled a highlight reel of dudes refusing me in sensational style. Even if we went back two solid decades to my freshman year of high school and my first "official" boyfriend, we'd find that pairing ended with him casually announcing he was dumping me because he'd discovered some other girl gave good hand jobs. And he liked hand jobs.

He hadn't given me a chance to show off my nonexistent handy j skills or even hinted at wanting one in the weeks we'd dated but that outrage was secondary. He'd already secured the services of another and determined I wouldn't—or couldn't—deliver. He hadn't wanted me.

All in all, that breakup hadn't dinged me as hard as the ones that followed. It'd wounded my pride and had shaken my confidence to the stump but it was a gentle preview of the road ahead.

Not unlike the bite of aged cheddar I sampled four times on my loop around the market. Each one ate a bit sharper, lingered longer.

And I kept going back for more. Choosing another cube as I smiled and thanked the clerk, and then wondering why I kept taking something that stuck on my tongue like a smoky, sweaty sock.

I didn't know what I was hoping to find by repeating this ritual with sword swallowers and immature hand-job enthusiasts and everyone in between. There was more to it than being wanted. But I didn't know what came after that.

I didn't know how it felt to be wanted and I didn't know how I'd handle it if I ever found out.

CHAPTER
THREE

Dating App Guy 2: Yummy.

Magnolia: …?

Guy Dating App Guy 2: You're delicious.

Magnolia: Thank you. I think…

Guy Dating App Guy 2: I'd eat your ass and cunt.

Guy Dating App Guy 2: Eat them like fuckin Thanksgiving.

{ blocked }

———

Dating App Guy 3: Hey what's up?

Magnolia: Not much. You?

Dating App Guy 3: Just chillin and trying to find a pretty lady.

Magnolia: Good luck with that.

Dating App Guy 3: Don't need luck. You're pretty and I found you.

Magnolia: There you go!

Dating App Guy 3: I have a boner.

Magnolia: Good luck with that too!
{ blocked }

————

Dating App Guy 4: Something about you just makes me think you'd give the world's best blow jobs.
Dating App Guy 4: If there was a contest for best head, you'd win.
Dating App Guy 4: You'd get the grand prize.
Magnolia: Yeah? What's the prize?
Dating App Guy 4: A pearl necklace.
{ blocked }

CHAPTER
FOUR

My date was on his fourth cup of coffee in forty minutes.

It wasn't even iced coffee. That I could understand. Not that I'd ever chugged four cups, but I could knock back a large iced caramel macchiato under the right circumstances. But hot coffee? No, sir. It took me forty minutes and an ice cube to *sip* hot coffee.

But this guy was a devotee of the Church of House Blend Hot and Sweet. He'd scooped a handful of Splenda packets from the courtesy bin after the barista announced our orders. Not a few packets but an actual handful of them. He then proceeded to deposit them on the center of the table we chose on the Boylston Street side of the shop. I'd ignored the small mountain of fake sugar then but now it seemed he meant to consume the entire quantity.

That and a whole pot of coffee in under an hour.

This was what I got for agreeing to a morning coffee date. Not that first dates qualified as proper dates. They weren't. They were interviews. Some of those interviews were more promising than others and they called for better locations, spiffier clothes, prime time slots.

Seven thirty on a Wednesday morning was the opposite of prime time.

He seemed immune to the temperature of his beverage, chugging away like it was tap water. He didn't even blow on it. No blow. Just gulp, gulp, gulp, gone. Then he slammed down the empty like a frat boy playing beer pong.

After the second cup, I started smiling and nodding my way through the conversation. He wasn't saying anything interesting. It was traffic, weather, and sports; basically, local talk radio. But I started wondering why he hadn't ordered a larger cup. This shop offered coffee by the pail, rendering four mediums illogical and wasteful in cups alone.

Unless he was killing time by scorching his mouth.

Or repeatedly leaving the table under the premise of ordering another cup while hoping I'd cut this nothing-burger short.

I was still nursing an Earl Grey latte. I preferred my tea iced and accompanied by an abundance of summertime, and this was neither. I wasn't sure why I ordered it though it was possible I wanted to come off as a touch high-maintenance today. A bit refined, like a woman who knew her teas as well as she knew her wines, her designer shoes, and herself.

I didn't have a sound explanation for it but I knew I wanted someone to look at me and my Earl Grey latte, and say, "Don't you see? She's different. You don't fuck with a woman who orders an Earl Grey latte. She knows something about the world. She's sophisticated. Snap this one up because she's in short supply."

Today, I wanted to be that sophisticated woman. The one

in short supply. I wanted the hamster wheel of online dating to slow down long enough for someone to see me as more than my age, location, and interests. I wanted to be someone worth getting to know. And then, I wanted to be someone worth treasuring.

I didn't allow myself this feeling often. But I still wanted someone to look at me like I was a brand-new kind of amazing. I'd thought this guy could do that for me. That I could be his brand-new amazing.

There seemed to be chemistry when we'd messaged, but none of that was present this morning. He didn't seem like the same guy who'd sent fun, flirty messages.

"I'm gonna grab another," he said, jerking his thumb over his shoulder. "Can I get you anything?"

I glanced down at my latte and shook my head, desperately trying to suppress the laugh threatening to burst free from my lips. Five cups. Five full cups of coffee. It was ridiculous. "No," I replied. "I'm fine. Thank you."

He shot me a quick smile and then strutted toward the counter. Objectively, the guy was attractive. Well-cut business suit, pleasant smile, decent hair. His fingernails were clean. All good things. But he was pounding coffee and yammering about road construction and he'd only managed a few cursory questions about me while we'd waited to order.

If my mother was here, she would've told me to play nice. Give the guy a chance. *Try.* "Throw him a bone," she'd crow. "Don't let him die on the vine."

And that was because she believed I was too tough on men. Yep, that was her new argument. After all my years of settling and not trying and accepting the plastic straw treatment, I now expected a little too much, a little too often. She had it in her head that I was working out my petulance by shopping for the perfect man, the one who checked all the boxes, and I wouldn't tolerate anyone found wanting. As of our last convening on my love life, she was pushing hard on fixer-uppers and letting someone grow on me.

I was tougher and my expectations were higher than they used to be. But as my mother had pointed out, I'd accepted less in the past and that was exactly what I'd received. I wasn't going down that path again and I didn't care if that meant I had to sit through one hundred shitty coffee dates in the process. I was going to find a good, honest, real man who required neither remodeling nor moss.

And people didn't change. I'd learned that lesson after dedicating far too many years of hard labor to the cause.

"The traffic on 95 in Needham is unreal," he continued when he returned. "They've been working on that project for damn near seven years. My sister got married, had a kid, and got divorced, all while those exits have been torn up. Unreal."

"Yeah," I replied, nodding. I wasn't positive, but I thought that construction wrapped up last year. I wasn't going to argue with him. Not when I could obsess over his coffee consumption. "It's quite a mess."

"The worst," he said, lifting the cup to his lips. "I plan my day around avoiding that area. It's a bitch." Before I could reply, he tapped the cup on the table and leaned toward me. "I don't know what your schedule looks like but I don't have to be anywhere until ten."

I shifted back on my seat to avoid the plume of his coffee breath. "Oh, well, I—"

He tapped the cup again. "My apartment's around the corner."

"That's—that's great for you," I said, confused. "I like this neighborhood. I worked on a project near—"

Another sharp tap of the cup. "You wanna come up?"

I blinked. "Excuse you?"

He tipped his head toward the window. "Do. You. Want. To. Come. Up."

I narrowed my eyes at his tone. What a snippy, snappy sonofabitch. "I have a busy morning," I replied with a bitter smile, the kind I reserved for my friends who claimed they often forgot to eat. *Pssh.* Lies and urban legends. "I should be going."

"All right, whatever," he mumbled as he stood. He pulled his coat on and shoved his hands into leather gloves. "Clearly, your loss."

"I'm sorry," I said, laughing. "What was that?"

"You should be sorry." He didn't bother looking at me. "You wasted my fucking time."

I pushed to my feet and crossed my arms over my chest. "Oh, really? That's how it is now? Because I'm not interested in having sex with you at eight in the morning after you've delivered the weather report and sports highlights? Or after you did lines of Splenda?"

"Not sure what you expected from this," he replied, "but that app is only for hooking up and your tits are all over your profile. If you're not down to fuck, you're sending all the wrong signals. You don't have to be a bitch about it."

For the record, my tits were properly contained. A girl couldn't wear turtlenecks every day but that didn't mean her tits had gone rogue. Nor was I being a bitch about anything.

But more importantly—"Who has a hookup on a Wednesday morning? That's just bizarre."

It was bizarre, and one of the many issues with the machinations of modern dating. Relationships weren't part of the program. It was fucking, not feelings, not forever.

In a strange sense, that was liberating. If I wanted to get some dick, there was plenty of it coming my way. I didn't have to pretend I was looking for anything more than one night—or morning, as it was—and I didn't have to go through a handful of nice, polite outings before getting some.

All of that was great. Truly. It was phenomenal that I could catch a different dick every day of the week and not think twice about it.

But I wasn't in the market for dick. Or, I should say, not *only* dick. I wanted the man connected to that piece, and I wanted that man to be one of the good ones.

Five-Cup Joe here—he wasn't one of the good ones. Not for me. Somewhere out there was a jittery gal who shot-gunned espresso and liked to bone down right after, and I was certain he'd find her. Godspeed to them both.

He snickered as he stepped away from the table. "I'll Venmo you for the coffee."

Shaking my head, I shoved my hand into my bag. "It was tea and here's five bucks. That covers it. Delete my number."

He pocketed the cash without meeting my gaze. "No problem."

I was almost content to let him go. Almost.

"Wait a minute." He glanced back at me, his scowl deep and impatient. "Why didn't you just order a larger coffee? Why five mediums?"

Not asked but also implied: Why are you like this?

His lips twisted into a reluctant smile. "I wanted the barista's number," he yelled across the shop. "I don't even like coffee."

I turned around, physically separating myself from him with the wall of my back. Even if none of this mattered, it still chipped away at me.

I glanced down at the table and the ruins of cups and Splenda packets. I debated leaving it all there because I wasn't about to Donna Reed this shit. But I couldn't do that. It defied coffee shop law and I wasn't about to disrupt the order of urban life by leaving a mess behind.

With a long sigh, I disposed of his trash and my unfinished latte. Once I was bundled up in my coat and scarf, I swung by the shop counter and gestured to the lone female barista.

"Don't worry," she called over the hiss of the milk steamer. "I gave him a fake number."

"Oh," I murmured. Had we been that loud? Or that obvious? "Thanks. I guess."

"No sweat," she yelled as she finished the order. "Can I make something new for you? Didn't seem like you were feeling that latte."

I stared up at the menu board. "Yeah," I said, nodding as I found my indulgence of choice. Earl Grey didn't make me sophisticated. I could be mainstream caramel and offer no apologies on the matter. "A caramel macchiato. Iced."

"You got it." I held out some bills, but she waved me off. "This one is on us," she said, nodding toward the other baristas. "Pablo live-tweeted the whole thing. It's the least we can do for you after providing us with enough entertainment to get through the morning rush."

I laughed to myself as I stepped away from the counter

but a not insignificant part of me wilted. I didn't want to be part of this joke anymore. I wanted to find that good, honest, real man and I wanted to find him soon. I couldn't endure this social experiment for eight more months.

CHAPTER
FIVE

Dating App Guy 5: Do you ever wonder about the Munchkins from *The Wizard of Oz* and the Oompa Loompas from *Charlie and the Chocolate Factory*?

Dating App Guy 5: Did they all live together because they were short in stature or were they short in stature because they lived together? Was it a recessive gene that turned into a dominant gene because they were either a small, isolated population or inbreeding?

Magnolia: Not sure. I've never considered it before.

Dating App Guy 5: That's cool. I like thinking about wild shit.

Dating App Guy 5: And pegging. I like getting bent over and plowed with a blue dildo the size of my arm.

Magnolia: Fascinating segue.

Dating App Guy 5: Would you tie me to a table and fuck me?

{ blocked }

———

Dating App Guy 6: Yo bitch.

Dating App Guy 6: You're fine as fuck.

Magnolia: Bitch? Really?

Dating App Guy 6: Shut up whore you should be thanking me for even messaging your ugly ass.

{ blocked }

———

Dating App Guy 7: Hi there. How's your day going?

Magnolia: Not too bad. What about you?

Dating App Guy 7: Happy the snow is melting haha.

Magnolia: Yeah, I was starting to forget what this city looked like under all the white stuff.

Dating App Guy 7: I thought we weren't supposed to see blizzards after St. Patrick's Day, you know? This freak storm stuff needs to stop #climatechangeisreal

Magnolia: True story.

Dating App Guy 7: Isn't it crazy how we're excited for snow every year but then after we have some we're like, not this again?

Dating App Guy 7: And we're all climbing the walls for summer but we're going to be hollering about the heat and humidity as soon as it's here.

Magnolia: Another true story.

Dating App Guy 7: So other than engaging in witty observations of weather's cyclical nature, what do you do with yourself?

Magnolia: I'm a landscape architect.

Dating App Guy 7: Then you really hate the snow haha.

Magnolia: After a while of it, yeah.

Magnolia: What do you do?

Dating App Guy 7: Dentist. Don't forget to floss haha.

Magnolia: Every night!

Dating App Guy 7: Can I ask you something? Or are you busy?

Magnolia: Just watching the Bruins slaughter Phoenix.

Magnolia: Go for it.

Dating App Guy 7: What's your muff like? Is it full and bushy?

Dating App Guy 7: If not…would you grow it out?

Dating App Guy 7: I like a big full bush. The kind that spills out the side of your underwear.

{ blocked }

CHAPTER
SIX

MY DATE WAS SITTING AT MY MOTHER'S DINING ROOM TABLE.

"This is Troy," my mother said as I stood frozen in the doorway. She popped up from her seat and joined me, wrapping her arm around my waist and gesturing toward him. "I thought this would be a great way for all of us to get to know him. Make it a little easier on you, you know?"

"Easier," I said, barking out a laugh. "This is easier?"

In all of my wildest dreams, I'd never imagined my mother would leap this far into my romantic life. This was several steps beyond swiping and proof that no good deed went unpunished. Not a one.

Agreeing to this experiment was a gesture toward assuaging my mother's concern for me. It wasn't something I would've adopted on my own and now I had to do it as performance art.

And do it while my brothers watched.

"Wait," my brother Ash said, holding up his hand, "I thought it was Trent. Since when are you Troy?"

"I thought it was Trevor," my brother Linden said,

shaking his head as he stared into his beer. "Fuck if I know what's going on here."

"And I thought it was Sunday dinner," I said. "Not speed dating."

"It's not speed dating," my mother argued. "There's only one of him."

"Trey," Ash yelled, pointing at the deer in headlights. That deer had the privilege of being my date for this gathering. What a treat for him.

"Travis," Linden replied, barely looking up from his beverage.

"Tristan," Ash continued, still pointing at the dude.

"Triton," Linden said.

"Truman," Ash replied.

"The two of you," my mother called, waving her hand at my brothers. "We have a guest. Stop being a-holes."

There was one thing I knew to be absolutely true about these men I'd shared a womb with: when presented with an opportunity to be assholes, they took it.

"Trace," Linden continued.

"Targaryen," Ash roared, as if throwing down some *Game of Thrones* made this shitshow more amusing.

"Trapper," Linden said.

"Tracker," Ash replied.

"Treat," Linden said.

"Tremain," Ash added.

"Tremont," Linden said.

My father walked into the room, took one look at the verbal food fight underway and turned right back around. Always predictable, my father. My parents were opposite sides of the same coin. She was outgoing and expressive. He could go days without speaking to anyone.

"Tripp," Ash said.

"Tron," Linden replied.

"Trotsky," Ash said.

"Now you're just being flaming a-holes," my mother said. She glanced to me with a sympathetic frown. "They were fine before you got here. They were talking about hockey."

"Hockey. The great uniter," I mumbled.

"Trader," Linden said.

That stopped my oldest brother. "What? Like, as in Joe?"

My date held up both hands as if attempting to keep the raptors at bay. "It is Troy," he said, sliding careful glances at my brothers before smiling at me. "Hi."

That single word packed many others in with it. There was "Holy shit, are they done yet?" and "What the actual fuck is happening?" and "Can this get worse? Please tell me it can't get worse."

"Hi," I replied, attempting to force a million apologies into that lame greeting.

"I'm Troy," he continued. "I didn't realize this was a family dinner and I thought, well"—he ran a hand down his face—"I thought you'd know about this. I thought I'd been talking to you. I'm sorry. This wasn't, I mean, it's not—"

"It's not your fault," I interrupted with more patience than I currently owned. "That's a fair assumption." I shot a mildly enraged glance at my mother before smiling at Troy. "Would you give us a minute?" I didn't wait for a response, instead yanking my mother into the hall bathroom and slamming the door behind us. "What the hell is going on?"

My mother seized this opportunity to tuck my hair behind my ears and rub a saliva-wet thumb over my chin. "I saw Troy on one of the apps and I liked his profile. He seemed like a good catch."

I rolled my hand in front of me, wanting more information. "Based on...what, exactly?"

She lifted a shoulder and then turned her attention to picking invisible things off my shirt. "Nice photos, nice bio, nice job. He likes dogs too."

"What does he do?" I asked.

"Real estate developer. He does very well for himself," she said with the type of self-satisfied head bob that told me I'd have to thank her for this injustice later.

"It's Sunday dinner," I started, "and you didn't mention we'd be having any guests today. Don't you think I would've pulled myself together a bit more if I'd known there was a dude coming to dinner?"

She glanced down at my tunic and leggings and then fingered the unwashed ends of my hair. "You're beautiful and perfect the way you are." She licked her thumb and ran it over my brows. "If he doesn't love you with a scraggly pedicure, then he's not the one."

I swallowed a sigh. "But I don't reveal the scraggly pedicure until date four or five, Mom. It's kind of like seeing each other first thing in the morning or acknowledging that everyone poops. It's not getting-to-know-you material."

She brought her hands to my shoulders with a tight smile. "Let's mix that schedule up a bit, shall we? Worst-case scenario, your brothers arm wrestle over the guy's name and he runs off like his hair's on fire."

"It would be awesome if there was something between respecting my schedule and my surprise date running from our home with his hair on fire." I gave her a manic grin. That I wasn't screaming at her was a victory. "So awesome."

"It's good to want," she replied with a shrug.

"So help me," I said, wagging a finger at her, "if I come for dinner someday to discover I'm a contestant on *The Bachelor*, I will put you in an old folks' home when the time comes. Maybe sooner."

"You'd miss me too much." My mother opened the bathroom door and gestured to the hallway. "Come on, now. Let's not leave Tiberius—"

"Troy," I interrupted.

"Whatever," she murmured. "Let's not leave him out to dry. Your brothers, they can be real a-holes when they want to be."

"Speaking of which," I said, stopping outside the dining room. "You're welcome to direct any of this matchmaking energy toward them."

She wrinkled her nose and shook her head. "They're young for their age. They're not ready for anything serious. But you—you're ready."

With that, she shoved me into the dining room.

"Hi," I said to him, drawing the word out into eight syllables as I planned my next move. I'd greeted the guy at least forty times now but what else was I supposed to do here? I exchanged a glance with Ash and Linden as I sat down beside Troy. They offered little more than innocent shrugs and shit-eating smirks in response. "How's it going?"

My date shifted toward me, smiling, and made a reasonable attempt at giving me a once-over without leering. Ten points to Gryffindor.

"Great, great," he breathed. "Sorry about the confusion. I thought—I guess, I didn't know—"

I held up both hands. "It's fine. Not your fault. Not at all. *You* have no reason to apologize." I pinned my mother with a harsh glare. "She knows what she did."

"Hush, you," my mother chided. "If nothing else, Trevor—"

"Troy," we chorused.

"—will get a home-cooked supper tonight. Young people don't get enough stick-to-your-ribs meals anymore. Not with all the delivery food and celery juice and chia seeds."

"Okay. Yeah. That's great," Troy said. "Great."

"Everything is great," Ash added from across the table. If the evening continued at this pace, I was going to strain my eyes with all this glaring. "Really great. The greatest."

I shot him a stare before turning back to Troy. "So, Troy," I started, "thank you for joining us today. I hope your family doesn't mind that we've stolen you from them for the evening."

"No worries," he said, laughing. "My parents live in Montana."

"That must make the Sunday dinner commute a lot longer," Linden said.

"Assuming you're beholden to a Sunday dinner routine," Ash added. "Clearly, we are, but we realize this might not be your way of life."

"What with the twenty-five-hundred-mile commute and all," Linden said.

Troy nodded as he considered this. "Yeah, we've never maintained that kind of tradition. I guess—"

"Because ranch life didn't allow it?" Ash asked.

Troy let out a startled laugh. "Oh, that's funny. No, I didn't grow up on a ranch. I'm actually from one of the biggest cities in Montana."

"Is that so?" Linden asked.

"No ranching, then?" Ash asked.

"The man said no ranching," Linden replied.

God help me. There was a reason first dates didn't take place at the family table.

"Common misunderstanding," Ash said. "Not all Montanans are ranchers. Some are city dwellers."

"Very common," Linden agreed.

"Perhaps the most common," Ash said.

"It happens," Troy said, laughing. Somehow, he was grinning. He hadn't bristled under a single moment of this ambush and I had to hand it to him. Putting up with this set of circumstances and smiling through it took a mile-wide sense of humor. He pointed at my brothers. "Excuse me for asking but—"

"No. We're not twins," Ash said.

"We're triplets," Linden announced. He patted his chest then pointed to me and Ash. "The three of us."

"Oh, great," Troy said. "That's so great."

"Really great," Ash added.

"The greatest," Linden said with a snicker.

My mother bustled into the room with my father in tow and set several platters on the table. My father glanced at the four of us, shook his head, and dropped into his usual seat. He motioned for Linden to pass the sausage. If I knew anything, it was that he'd eat, exit, and avoid the shit out of these hijinks for the rest of the evening.

"Dig in, everyone. I'll be back with the rice," my mother called.

We weren't horrible offspring for staying put. This was how my mother preferred it. She insisted on cooking and serving and she did it without any misplaced sense of duty. No, it was pure ego. She simply believed her food was better than that prepared by anyone else and she refused to eat—as she put it—"under-seasoned garbage." We didn't bother arguing over the matter anymore and we didn't dare insert ourselves into the preparations.

She'd stab any of us for doing it wrong.

The meal passed quickly, and I was damn thankful for that. We were too busy eating and praising my mother's food to engage in any common first date rituals. That, and my mother gave up liquor for Lent. She wasn't a practicing Catholic by most standards but she observed certain traditions to the letter. Giving up something for Lent, Advent candles in December, bringing my dog to church for a blessing on the Feast of Saint Roch. It seemed like a small connection to a faith she barely kept but couldn't do without, and I wasn't about to challenge that.

But a glass of wine would've helped a bitch out tonight, especially after my mother asked Troy how many children he wanted and what he thought of short engagements.

My brothers always came equipped with beer but they weren't sharing tonight.

Sometimes, they really were a-holes.

When we finished eating, my mother gestured to my brothers. "You're big, strong men. You can handle the dishes without your sister tonight."

Linden blinked at my mother before turning his gaze toward me. "We will collect on this debt at a later date," he said, pushing away from the table.

"Don't worry," I replied. "You will get your turn and I will cackle with glee as I wash those dishes and drink your beer."

Ash pressed his fist to his mouth as he snorted with laughter.

"I don't know what you think is so entertaining," I said, tossing a balled napkin in his direction. "You'll get your turn too."

"I will not," he replied. "Thanks, but I have no room for this bullshit in my life."

It was Linden's turn to throw a napkin at Ash. "Shut up," he barked. "You're on drying duty."

My siblings took their sweet time clearing the table while Troy and I traded uncomfortable smiles. They weren't smiles so much as eye crinkles and stiff lips, a tight, twisted expression that only certified the awkwardness of this setup.

When we were alone and I heard the sink water running in the kitchen, I shifted toward Troy. "I am so sorry about this," I said, my palms held out in apology. "My mom, sometimes she gets carried away and, like, loses her damn mind."

He drew a finger over his brows as he chuckled. "It's all good. It's great. This was great."

"You're lying," I blurted out with a choked laugh. "This was not great. It's all right to acknowledge that."

He shot a baleful glance at the empty table, tracing his brows again. "It wasn't as bad as you think. I haven't had a home-cooked meal like that in some time."

I blinked, looking him over and taking him in without the haze of surprise setup fury clouding my view. He was handsome. Easy on the eyes, if not a bit uptight. Maybe he wasn't truly uptight but his dress-shirt-tie-pullover-sweater combo read that way to me. And maybe I was judging this book by his cover but what was wrong about that? If the cover didn't accurately summarize the vibe of the book, it was the wrong cover.

"That—that's great." I cringed as Troy's favorite word passed my lips. "Mom's cooking is legendary. You know, she'd invite you back even if we aren't"—I pointed at the air between us, twining my fingers together as if that made sense—"if we don't. Because, you know. This isn't—"

"I get it. You seem great—"

"And so do you," I jumped in.

"But we don't have to—"

"Oh, god, no. No." I was agreeing too heartily but I couldn't stop myself. Under different circumstances, Troy and I might've shared an evening together but that would've been the beginning and end for us. We weren't it. Whatever *it* was, we weren't. We didn't have it. "But I'm serious when I say my mother would be thrilled to have you back for dinner."

He shot another glance at the empty table, the only evidence of the modest feast coming from stray bits of tomato rice, a chickpea on the loose, some chouriço grease stains on the tablecloth.

Troy was a nice guy. Sweet, kind. Better than many others would've been in the same situation. But being a nice guy wasn't the checkbox for me. Yeah, I wanted nice but I also wanted someone who'd take one look at this shitshow setup, grab me by the hand, and get the fuck out of here. Someone who put up with no more than two minutes of my brothers and their a-hole routine before giving it right back to them. Someone who recognized my family was important to me but knew when I required—deserved—breathing room from them.

Troy wasn't that guy. If he had any of those inklings, he hadn't acted on them. I could've grabbed him and made a run for it. But I hadn't. I'd waited for him to do it and it wasn't happening now. Nothing was happening now.

I couldn't help but see the lesson embedded in these events. If I wanted something, it was on me to take it. Waiting for a dude to read my mind was getting nowhere fast. I couldn't expect someone to show up for my unspoken needs. I needed to show up for myself.

"I might like that. Coming for dinner," Troy added, his words bashful. "We didn't have routines like this when I lived at home and"—he glanced down, away—"and this was great. Looking back, I realize now that your mom's messages were extremely focused on whether I was eating and sleeping well. I guess I liked that. It felt good." He laughed to himself. "Hell. I just made it sound like I was into your mom."

Wincing, I said, "No, I get what you're saying. I'm also working hard at not thinking about my mom messaging you and pretending to be me. If I think about it, I'll have to burn things down and scrub myself with bleach."

He shook his head. "I should thank her. I've uncovered a whole new segment of mommy issues to deal with."

I wasn't sure how I maintained an easy smile after that comment but I did. I managed to keep a calm, open expression while I sent Troy on his way with a loose hug and no promise of seeing him again.

But I was going to have some words with my mother.

CHAPTER
SEVEN

Dating App Guy 8: Good morning.

Magnolia: Hi! Happy Monday!

Dating App Guy 8: How was your weekend?

Magnolia: Fine. I'm glad it's a new week. Looking for a fresh start on many things.

Dating App Guy 8: Same. Yeah, I'm in the exact same boat with you.

Magnolia: Awesome.

Dating App Guy 8: Let me be blunt. I just got out of a long relationship and I'm fucked up in the head right now but I'm 6'3, 210, and my dick is a solid 9 inches.

Magnolia: I'm sorry about your breakup.

Dating App Guy 8: Thank you.

Dating App Guy 8: You want to help me fuck away the memories of my ex? No strings, no expectations, no emotional baggage?

Magnolia: I understand what you're going through, I truly do, but I don't see how this could be free of emotional baggage.

Magnolia: And I don't really want expectation-less sex.

Magnolia: I'm into strings and expectations and emotions. I want all of those things.

Dating App Guy 8: I can stay hard for a full 30 minutes. No lie.

Magnolia: How old are you?

Dating App Guy 8: I turned 38 last month.

Magnolia: 30 minutes at 38? Now that's a résumé builder.

Dating App Guy 8: Damn straight.

Magnolia: Not a little to the left?

Dating App Guy 8: I can say I honestly laughed out loud just now.

Magnolia: You're welcome.

Dating App Guy 8: I appreciate it. I needed that laugh.

Dating App Guy 8: I also need to get over my ex so...what do you say?

Magnolia: Look, you seem like the most normal person on here...if that's even possible...but I'm not in the market for a fuck buddy or friend with bennies.

Dating App Guy 8: I get it. I can't talk about anything more serious than that but you're beautiful and seem cool.

Magnolia: Am I cool because I didn't block you? You went to the dick size within 3 or 4 messages and that's block-worthy behavior in my book.

Dating App Guy 8: And yet you did not block me.

Magnolia: No. I didn't.

Dating App Guy 8: Why not?

Magnolia: Not sure. Maybe because you led with being fucked up and closed with the measurements. You could've skipped the personal horror story.

Dating App Guy 8: I guess so, yeah, but I only need to fuck

away my issues because of my ex. This is too time-consuming to be my normal mode of operation.

Magnolia: This being the online match-up part? Or the sex as bloodletting?

Dating App Guy 8: Goddamn, stop making me like you.

Magnolia: What?

Dating App Guy 8: Don't say sarcastic, insightful things. It makes me want to talk to you.

Magnolia: And that's bad?

Dating App Guy 8: Yes. Talking isn't part of my offer.

Magnolia: Maybe you need to talk. I'm pretty sure you could've found someone else for the hate fucking.

Dating App Guy 8: Why can't you let me self-medicate in peace?

Magnolia: (glancing around) dude, you messaged me.

Dating App Guy 8: You got me there.

Magnolia: What happened?

Dating App Guy 8: I don't want to talk about it.

Magnolia: Okay. You don't have to.

Magnolia: You don't have to tell me anything. But I don't want to have anonymous sex. If that's what you're trying to find, I don't think I'm the right person for you.

Magnolia: I don't think anonymous sex is right for you either but don't let me stop you from the self-medication.

Dating App Guy 8: You're a little rude.

Dating App Guy 8: I think I like it.

Magnolia: Okay.

Dating App Guy 8: I know this sounds like bullshit since you just asked me to explain myself and then told me to piss off when I wouldn't but I have a meeting in 10 minutes and I have to prep for it unless I want my career to go the way of my last relationship.

Magnolia: No worries. I need to get some work done too.

Dating App Guy 8: Would it be okay if I messaged you later tonight?

Magnolia: Sure.

Magnolia: Protip: keep talking about your dick. It's good to be proud of something.

Dating App Guy 8: What did I say about making me like you?

Magnolia: I believe it is not advised.

Dating App Guy 8: It's not.

Dating App Guy 8: Keep doing it.

CHAPTER
EIGHT

MY DATE HAD A FOOD BABY.

"I could be four, maybe five months pregnant."

I glanced at the nonexistent bump with a shrug, then turned my attention back to my phone. Mr. Nine Inches had been messaging me for two weeks now. This morning he mentioned his niece's upcoming *Moana*-themed birthday party. It was cute, and I did smile and sigh when he said she'd strong-armed him into dressing up as Maui.

But believe me, I knew what he was doing. Bring up the kid, talk about princess movies, prove you're a big cock with a heart of gold.

It was like he was writing the Playbook for Irresistible Men.

Magnolia: Sounds like a good time.
Mr. Nine: It will be. My sister goes all out on these things.
Mr. Nine: Before you congratulate me on being a fully acceptable uncle, can we talk about something less…PG?

Mr. Nine: I mean, we haven't talked about my cock in at least 4 hours.

Magnolia: Your cock requires a lot of attention, my dude. Super high-maintenance.

Mr. Nine: It would like to fill more than your attention.

Magnolia: That one was not your best work.

Mr. Nine: Don't worry. I'm a constant learner. Always improving.

Magnolia: Good for you!

Mr. Nine: I've never been so aware of sarcasm as I am right now.

Mr. Nine: We still haven't exchanged more than handles.

Magnolia: Are we talking about your dick again? AGAIN?

Mr. Nine: I meant screen names.

Mr. Nine: Perv.

Magnolia: Right. I'm the one preoccupied with your dick. Sure. Okay.

Mr. Nine: I'm just wondering whether that's an indication you're not into this.

HE WAS right about the handles. We hadn't shared more than the goofy little identifiers associated with our online profiles. I was MizMaggie19 and he was RRRooster441. And I was into this. I wanted to continue talking to him despite the mismatch in our objectives.

Magnolia: Don't think that.

Mr. Nine: All right then, lady. You've had your time to think. What's the verdict?

Magnolia: No verdict yet.

Mr. Nine: Hung jury?

Magnolia: Oh my god STOP.

Magnolia: You're not helping your case.

Magnolia: You know, I'm not sure I believe your case. Anyone who talks this much about his dick is (cough, cough) compensating for something.

WAS it wrong that I wanted to fact-check his cock claims? No. It couldn't be. He kept putting it out there, and there was nothing wrong with gathering more information before making decisions.

Maybe it wasn't entirely right but I wasn't ready to call it wrong.

Although I didn't actually want a dick pic. Those things were worse than opening the camera app and finding it in selfie mode. Even the most beautiful people in the world looked like triple-chinned potatoes at that angle.

The truth about dick pics was that they served the dick and not the recipient. The guy was proud of his goods—and why shouldn't he be? It did all sorts of magical things and that finicky, fragile length of skin blessed him with an awful lot of power in the world as we knew it. Of course, he'd want to show it off.

"Solidly second trimester with a large gyro bowl."

I slipped my phone into my back pocket and turned my attention to Andy Asani. She was an architect at one of the top boutique firms in the area and we often found ourselves working on the same properties. After I recovered from some self-inflicted weirdness with one of her partners once upon a time, we started meeting up for lunch every few weeks. It'd been three years now and we kept finding new reasons to eat together.

The best thing about Andy was that she was unflinchingly honest. She'd tell you if the jeans weren't right for your ass, if the lipstick was a crime against your skin, if you were making drama where none was necessary, if you were dying on the wrong hill. She was direct and sometimes that was tough, but it was the good kind of tough.

She was staring at her profile in a full-length mirror, running her hand over her perfectly flat belly. "Would you stop it? You're the size of a popsicle stick," I snapped, my tone loaded with faux exasperation. "Really, Andrea. You're a string bean."

Her eyes crinkled as she laughed. "A string bean?"

"Yes." I shoved a section of the hangers to the side on the rack in front of me. "A really fucking skinny string bean with no ass. You could be actually pregnant and eat a large gyro bowl, and still look like Audrey Hepburn with big, kinky hair. You're going to be slender and glowing and beautiful when you're pregnant. Like Kate Middleton or Amal Clooney. Please. I eat a bag of peanuts and I look like I'm full term with twins."

"No, you don't," she said, laughing. "And my name isn't Andrea."

I pulled a dress off the rack and held it out to her. "When I'm giving you a talking-to, you're Andrea. Be careful or I'll invent a middle name for you while I'm at it." I wagged the dress. "Go try this on."

She shook her head, sending her long, dark curls swaying over her shoulders. "I can't squeeze myself into that right now. Why did we eat lunch before dress shopping?"

"We think with our stomachs." I tipped my chin toward the other side of the shop. "Let's look at flowy sundresses."

"Perfect." She plucked the dress from my hands and returned it to the rack. "Flowy is good. That's going to be my summer style this year. Loose and flowy."

"Says the new wifey with baby fever," I said under my breath. After a years-long engagement, Andy finally walked down the aisle last month.

She shot me a pointed glare. "We're not talking about that right now. I am not interested in getting pregnant for at least two or three years. Maybe longer."

She made it too easy to poke at her on this topic. Even when I knew she was dead serious about waiting. Even when I shared her sentiments about wanting a baby but also waiting a couple years to meet that baby. Then again, Andy and I were in different boats when it came to starting families.

For starters, I had to meet a man I tolerated for more than a single evening.

"Baby fever," I repeated, smirking.

"So, Magnolia, are you seeing anyone special? Let's talk about *you*."

My back pocket vibrated. I glanced to the side before responding. "You don't want to know."

She handed me a pink and green sundress. "You called me a skinny string bean. If you're going to call out my ass or lack thereof, you can entertain me with your adventures in dating."

"Adventures." I snorted, pushed a black dress toward her. She didn't believe in wearing color. "That's an interesting way to look at it."

"Any second dates? Or promising leads?"

I snorted again. "No second dates."

We exchanged several more dresses. "But some promising leads?"

Another vibration from my back pocket. Was it wrong that I wanted it to be Mr. Nine Inches? Maybe it was. Maybe the past few months had ground my expectations down to the point that I was optimistic about a guy who seemed kind and genuine, even if he only wanted to bury his dick in someone as a means of exorcism.

"Let's try these on." I nudged Andy toward the dressing rooms. "Enough of this city has witnessed and live-tweeted my shitty dates. I don't need the shopgirls tuning in too."

We dropped onto the bench in the dressing room but made no move to change into the items hanging from the rail in front of us.

"Do you ever have days," I started, staring at the garments, "when you don't want to be a girl boss?"

"What do you mean?"

"I don't know. It's complicated," I admitted. "I love my work. I love being my own boss. I love relying on myself and not answering to anyone else. I love it. I really do. But...but there are days when I want to give it all away and be a bad feminist. Sometimes I wonder what my life would be like if I wasn't a goal digger. If I was married to a man who wanted me to be a stay-at-home wife—"

"You would never go for that. Never in a million years."

"I know, I know." As she started to protest, I continued, "But what if it wasn't him telling me what to do? What if it was him offering it to me? Or us arriving at the conclusion together like a good progressive couple should. Would I still want to conquer the world one roof garden at a time? To prove myself every damn day?"

"Yes. Maybe you'd worry less about proving yourself but you'd want all those roof gardens. And you wouldn't stop there. You've been renovating your aunt's house in your spare time and that's on top of working a ton of projects in the past year. And you read books and go to tons of ball games too. You don't know how to do nothing."

That wasn't the complete truth, but I wasn't going to educate Andy on my history of slovenly ways today. The drive to prove myself came from wasting so much time when I was younger. From flunking out of college—twice. Getting fired from no fewer than five waitressing jobs because I forgot to show up. Struggling to find anything that interested me for *years*.

"I love what I do, but there are days when I wish I didn't have to do it," I admitted. "It's crazy but I wonder what my life would be like if I didn't have to do everything by myself all the time." I glanced at her. "Do you ever feel like that? Like you'd take the throwback housewife gig if it was offered to you?"

Andy regarded me for a moment, her eyes narrowed. "It's worth noting that it's two o'clock on a Tuesday and we drank wine with lunch. We have the cake, we're eating it, and we have the ice cream and sprinkles too."

I gnawed on my lip before glancing at Andy. "I know and I know I wouldn't trade my life for anything. There are just days when I want to turn off my phone and let a man take care of me."

"Now that's something I understand," she said, shaking her head as a smile tugged at her lips. "I understand that and I crave it too. Believe me, I turn off my phone and let Patrick take care of me every single weekend. Most weeknights too."

"Your clients don't call you in the evenings? Or contractors?"

"They do. Doesn't mean they can't wait for me to call them back in the morning," she said, chuckling. "Honestly, yeah. There are days when I fantasize about setting aside all my work and worries and spending my time on posting cute food pics on Instagram."

"What stops you?" I wanted to know because there were moments when the only thing holding me back was a fear of running out of money to feed my dog.

"A few things. First, Patrick and I share a brain at work so I can't abandon him. He'd have a mental breakdown and no one needs that. Second, restoring and renovating houses is my favorite thing. I like it more than anything, even posting food pics. If I didn't have this career, I wouldn't know what else to do with myself. And third, I know that I can lean on Patrick. If I wanted to pull back or change my focus or spend some time tinkering with something new, I know he'd rearrange the firm to make that happen."

Everything inside me lurched. I wanted a partner who'd rearrange the world for me. That was what I wanted. That was it. That was my thing. Right there.

I couldn't put it in my dating profiles, but goddamn, that was what I wanted.

Andy peered at me, her arms folded over her chest. "What's the deal? What's going on with you? Spill your dirty stories, Santillian."

I leaned back against the wall and crossed my legs. "Dating is draining my soul. That, and the house across the street from me is being renovated after hours. I hear nail guns in my dreams."

"You're too damn nice," she muttered. "I would've introduced myself to those fools and made sure the city inspector tagged along." She rolled her hand at me, urging me to continue. "What else is going on with you? It's not just nail guns."

"There's a guy, but he only wants a fuck buddy situation. He's getting over a breakup."

"Explain to me why you're even entertaining this," Andy said, her eyebrow arched high. The woman could form right angles with her brows when she worked at it.

I started to respond but then hesitated. Why *was* I entertaining this? It wasn't the dick. It couldn't be the dick. There was more to life than dick just as there was more to life than coffee and baseball and dogs.

Somewhat.

"I like his vibe," I said eventually. "He's different from other guys I've met online. He's not like the rest of the assholes out there. I mean, he's not an asshole at all. He tried to be one for a hot minute but couldn't keep up the act."

"Well, that is to be applauded," Andy replied. "You said there was a breakup?"

I nodded, murmuring in agreement. "A bad one. He's admittedly fucked up."

"And you want to fix him."

"I don't want to fix him," I whisper-yelled.

"You want to fix all the boys," Andy replied.

"In the past, I've tried to fix a boy or two, yes," I conceded. "But I don't want to fix this boy."

"You want to fix his broken heart," she sang, "with your vagina."

I sniffed, playing hard at the indignation. "I have no desire to do that nor has he given me the impression he wants me to do any fixing."

Andy laughed. "No, honey. He wants you for the fucking."

"That's accurate, yes. Like any good man would, he's suggested he's quite talented at it. The fucking."

"Oh, is he now?" she cooed.

I decided to confess everything. "He says he's working with nine inches and he can work with it for at least half an hour."

She bobbed her head. "You have my attention."

"I don't want to get involved in a dead-end situation," I said. "But...I don't know."

"There's nothing wrong with wanting to get laid. Especially when high-quality equipment is involved." She shrugged. "If you want someone to give you permission to get laid, enjoy it, and not worry about fixing him—I'm giving it to you. It's okay to have a dead-end relationship even when you're trying to find The One. Sometimes, dead-ends turn into cul-de-sacs and everyone loves a cul-de-sac. They're reliable real estate."

"That's some reliable wisdom." I jerked my chin toward the dresses hanging from the rail. "Should we even bother trying on clothes?"

She shook her head. "I want to see this guy's profile. Let's stalk him before you get him naked."

"I'm getting him naked now," I muttered. "Okay. That progressed rapidly."

"Don't play coy and virginal with me," she chided.

I pulled my phone from my back pocket and swiped it to life. My messenger app flashed with several unread messages from RRRooster441. "Looks like he's in a talkative mood today."

"Hm," she murmured, glancing down at the screen.

Mr. Nine: Are you…MizMaggie, are you holding out for proof?

Mr. Nine: My god. You are. You want to know if the juice is worth the squeeze.

Mr. Nine: OK. Not gonna hold that against you since I made it all about the D.

Mr. Nine: Fuck. I admire it.

Mr. Nine: Here you go.

Mr. Nine: (IMAGE ATTACHED)

WE LEANED CLOSER and simultaneously gasped when a photo filled the screen. As far as dick pics went, it was beautifully done. Clothed, trapped behind trousers, but undeniably hard. Circumcised too. No harsh lighting or awkward grip on the base. No ugly feet or ball hair to take away from the heart of the matter.

"I do enjoy when I can identify a man's belief system before he gets his pants off," I said.

"Yeah, you need to get that," she said, pinching her fingers on the screen to zoom in. "That's a good one. It's halfway to his knee."

"Mhmm." Nodding, I toggled back to his message.

Mr. Nine: See? No exaggeration.

Magnolia: Thanks for keeping it classy.

Mr. Nine: That's how I roll, lady.

Magnolia: I like how you roll.

Mr. Nine: Yeah?

Magnolia: Yeah…maybe we could get coffee or something.

Mr. Nine: Come on. Come on!

Magnolia: What? Isn't that what you want?

Mr. Nine: Coffee? No, lady. I don't want coffee.

Magnolia: Oh. Okay.

Magnolia: Listen, I'm not down for a hookup. Sorry, no. I want to have a clothed conversation out in public, preferably with food and drink as a means of distraction and self-defense.

Mr. Nine: Oh my god. You thought I was asking to skip the coffee and go straight to sex.

Mr. Nine: Facepalm.

Mr. Nine: No. I meant I'm good for more than a beverage. Let me buy you a meal. Food on a real plate and a beverage or two. Real knives to stab me with, should it come to that.

Mr. Nine: It won't come to that, I swear.

Mr. Nine: I'm good for a lot more than a dinner and drinks but let's start with the real plates.

"Do it," Andy ordered. "Say yes and tell him you're free on Thursday."

"Why Thursday?"

"Thursday because it gives you two days to prepare and him two days of anticipation, and if it goes well, you can make weekend plans. Friday is too much pressure, Wednesday is tomorrow and that's just too quick, and any other option is too distant. You'll lose momentum if you wait until next week."

"Goddamn," I muttered. "You are gifted."

She shook her head. "Exceedingly strategic." She glanced at my phone. "Thursday. Book it."

Magnolia: How does Thursday sound?
Mr. Nine: Like I'll be seeing you.
Magnolia: Yeah. You will.
Magnolia: For coffee.
Magnolia: Or something like that.
Mr. Nine: Oh, really?
Mr. Nine: You're back on that bullshit?
Magnolia: That's noble of you.
Mr. Nine: I'm walking into a meeting but you can believe we're not finished with this topic.

"OH, LOOK," Andy cooed. "He gets fired up when you're bratty."

"I'm not bratty," I murmured. "I simply believe coffee is the safer route than a full dinner date setup."

She dropped her chin onto her fist, asking, "Because you don't like having sex on a full stomach? I mean, I get it, but just order a salad."

"Right," I said, nodding. "Because food babies and fuck buddies don't mix."

CHAPTER
NINE

Mr. Nine: What do you like?

Magnolia: …in terms of what? Are we talking about autumn strolls through pumpkin patches or some light choking during sex?

Mr. Nine: Yes.

Magnolia: That's not an answer.

Mr. Nine: I was asking about food because I still object to this coffee shop plan of yours.

Mr. Nine: But I'll entertain any discussion of your interests.

Magnolia: I rather enjoy pumpkin patches.

Mr. Nine: And light choking?

Magnolia: Let's focus on the pumpkin patches.

Mr. Nine: Hayrides, fresh apple cider, hot cinnamon and sugar donuts?

Magnolia: Add in the World Series and some football and you have my love language right there.

Mr. Nine: Noted.

———

Mr. Nine: Coffee or tea?

Magnolia: Coffee. You?

Mr. Nine: Same.

Mr. Nine: Sandwich or salad?

Magnolia: Sandwich. Always. I'm willing to bet you're also a sandwicher.

Mr. Nine: Excuse me while I eliminate Sweet Green and Cava from my list of lunch ideas.

Magnolia: Are you saying you'd take a salad over a sandwich? Really?

Mr. Nine: It depends on the salads and sandwiches.

Mr. Nine: I had a sandwich at a little shop on Nantucket about 5 years ago. I haven't stopped thinking about it since.

Magnolia: That's not the first time I've heard that about sandwiches on Nantucket.

Mr. Nine: I also had a salad last month that brought true joy to my life.

Magnolia: It seems to me that any mildly good thing could bring you joy right now.

Mr. Nine: Let's test that theory over sandwiches. Since we both enjoy them.

Mr. Nine: There's a place near my office with amazing turkey sandwiches.

Magnolia: That's wonderful for you.

Mr. Nine: It's from an actual turkey. They smoke it in the shop. That makes all the difference. I hate when it's slimy deli slices.

Magnolia: I think I know that place because my brother shares your devotion to smoked turkey and he goes out of his way to stop there whenever he's in the city.

Mr. Nine: It's a good spot, right?

Magnolia: Yeah. They make their own flavorings for coffee and seltzer. I'm a fan of their raspberry even though I'm ride-or-die for black cherry.

Mr. Nine: So, your brother. He lives out of town?

Magnolia: Linden lives on the southeast coast, near my parents in New Bedford.

Mr. Nine: Just the one sibling?

Magnolia: No, another brother. Ash.

Mr. Nine: Who is the oldest?

Magnolia: Ash was Baby A, I was Baby B, and Linden was Baby C.

Magnolia: We're triplets.

Mr. Nine: Wow. That's not something you hear every day.

Magnolia: About as often as a dude introduces himself with a baseball card of his dick stats.

Mr. Nine: Got your attention.

Magnolia: And look at all the good it's done me.

Mr. Nine: I've offered to do you all kinds of good.

Magnolia: Yep. That is true.

————

Mr. Nine: Tell me about landscape architecture.

Magnolia: That's a broad request.

Mr. Nine: What's a typical day look like? Are you out there digging up yards and planting trees?

Magnolia: No.

Magnolia: Okay, yeah, that was how it used to be but now I spend most of my time developing proposals and designs, managing subcontractors, and evaluating progress rather than doing any digging myself.

Magnolia: I've carved out a niche in the roof garden business. That's the bulk of my residential and commercial work.

Mr. Nine: I was way off the mark.

Magnolia: Not too far, no. When I was starting out, I couldn't afford to pay subcontractors so I did all the work. It made for obscenely long days.

Mr. Nine: When does your day start now?

Magnolia: It mostly depends on when and where I have meetings but it's been too fucking early the past few weeks. The house across the street is under construction but they've been working the wildest hours.

Mr. Nine: That's annoying.

Mr. Nine: You're welcome to take refuge in my bed.

Magnolia: Oh, truly?

Mr. Nine: Of course. My building is shockingly quiet. The benefit of new construction, I guess.

Magnolia: My best friends are preservation architects. Their entire lives are spent restoring old homes in an effort to minimize new construction.

Mr. Nine: Okay. I'll move.

Magnolia: Easy as that?

Mr. Nine: I told you last night…a salad brought me joy. If living in an old building meant you'd hang out with me, I'd call the movers right now.

Magnolia: Maybe hold off on that for a bit. Okay?

———

Mr. Nine: Are you going to tell me your name at any point?

Magnolia: Okay. Wow. You want to use me to forget your ex AND you want to know my name?

Magnolia: Needy much?

Mr. Nine: You are so mean to me.

Mr. Nine: Please don't stop.

Mr. Nine: My name is Rob. In case you were wondering.

Magnolia: I thought you were all about no strings, no baggage, no attachments.

Mr. Nine: You rejected my no strings, no baggage, no attachments deal.

Magnolia: Ah. Right.

Mr. Nine: So…are you going to tell me your name?

Magnolia: Where am I meeting you for lunch?

Mr. Nine: If I answer that, will you tell me your name?

Magnolia: If you don't tell me, I can't meet you so…my name is irrelevant to these proceedings.

Mr. Nine: Yeah. Yeah, I misplayed that hand.

Mr. Nine: Wow. I'm going to take a minute and reevaluate everything I thought I knew about myself and my negotiating skills.

Magnolia: It's Magnolia.

Magnolia: Yes, like the flower.

Mr. Nine: One of the oldest flowers in the world too. Your lineage is 95 million years old.

Magnolia: …how did you know that?

Mr. Nine: Google.

Magnolia: Did Google mention how magnolias appeared before bees?

Mr. Nine: It did and that's fascinating.

Mr. Nine: It makes sense.

Magnolia: How do you figure?

Mr. Nine: You strike me as the type of woman who'd survive in a world that wasn't ready for you.

Mr. Nine: You'd wait for evolution to catch the fuck up to you.

Magnolia: Believe me, I've waited.

Mr. Nine: Meet me at Flour Bakery tomorrow. 1 p.m.

Mr. Nine: No more waiting, Magnolia.

CHAPTER
TEN

My date was less than twelve hours away. Twelve. Hours. Right now, I hated Andy Asani and her *tell him you're free Thursday* bullshit because that provided me two full nights of overthinking.

My freak-out aside, I was looking forward to meeting Mr. Nine Inches—*Rob*—in person. A little excited, a little nervous. But I was fine. Cool as could be and ready for a low-key lunch date with a man who couldn't stop talking about his massive cock and its varied talents.

Okay, all right, I couldn't sleep or turn off my damn mind. Or the tile saw across the street.

My evening had started out just fine. I grabbed dinner and went to the Celtics game with my brothers. They paid for the meal and beers at the Garden on account of their performances during the Great Troy Debacle. After the game, I made my way home and took my Boston Terrier Gronk for a long walk before experimenting with five different face masks and tearing apart my closet in search of the Right Outfit. But it was all good. I was good. So good.

But then they turned on the tile saw.

The people across the street, the ones working on the run-down old Cape, didn't understand the social construct of "bedtime." If they did, they were giving it the finger. There was no other explanation for their *no sleep till Brooklyn* approach to this renovation.

The house stood quiet and vacant throughout the day, only coming alive sometime after I took Gronk out to handle his late-night business. The hammers, nail guns, and power tools were annoying but the tile saw was a different animal altogether. It was too shrill to fade into the blackness of sleep, and the sound seemed to rattle my teeth and scratch at my cerebellum every time I closed my eyes.

And my dog hated it. From his position on the corner of my bed, he was on guard, his little body vibrating with low, furious growls. He let out a few quick barks, warning shots intended to subdue his noisy opponents, and then he looked back at me for approval.

"Strong effort but I don't think they heard you."

Gronk kept on with his snarling and panting while I sat back against my pillows and dragged a hand through my hair. The hair I was waking up an hour early to properly blow dry tomorrow. But tomorrow was already today and my look-hot-to-meet-Mr.-Nine plans were slipping through my fingers like sand.

It seemed like I was turning this date with Mr. Nine into a huge ordeal. I wasn't. I'd already reconciled the fact he wasn't interested in anything beyond the ins and outs, and in doing so, I'd freed myself from much of the usual apprehension with which I regarded dating. He wasn't a potential husband, so I didn't need to polish up my potential wife routine. For once, I could save the self-doubt in favor of being completely, unapologetically myself...with beautifully blown-out hair and flawless skin. And I was eager to meet him. He was fun and self-deprecating in messages and I wanted to believe it would be the same in person.

I wanted to like him and I wanted him to like me too. Was that wrong? No. It couldn't be. If I was going to have mostly meaningless sex, I wanted some mutual admiration between the involved parties.

As the saw chewed through another piece of stone, I grabbed my phone off the side table and scrolled through my messages. Part of me wanted to delegate the noise issue to someone else. My brothers would drive up here and have a few words with my neighbors if I asked them, but I wasn't in the habit of unloading my issues on Ash or Linden. They went hard at the brawny, bossy big brother routine, and as much as I enjoyed bearing that cross, I called upon them only when I needed that brawn to unearth boulders in the backyard.

For a moment, I thought about texting Mr. Nine to complain about my night. I didn't do it and not because I didn't want to bother him with my whining. No, I was concerned he'd offer a distraction and some help falling asleep, and I was concerned I'd accept.

I was concerned he'd aim those sweet, sweet words at me again and I'd melt like sugar on his silver tongue. I'd walk back every one of my vows to have real, face-to-face conversations with this man before trying out his hardware. I was inclined to believe I'd enjoy it too, but that would fade when it was over and I'd regret yet another one of my decisions involving men.

And my hair was unwashed, my legs were prickly, and my dog would anxiety-pee all over the place if a guy showed up at two in the morning. No matter how great Mr. Nine seemed, he wasn't hanging with all that.

The tile saw screamed again, tightening my shoulders. I fucking hated that sound. I intentionally avoided my properties while stonework was underway. I'd take the jackhammer to the tile saw any day of the week.

I tossed off the blankets, jumped out of bed, and gestured for Gronk to settle down. "I'll be right back," I told him, stepping into my around-the-house-and-sometimes-outside moccasins. "Be good. No barks."

He huffed about that and then turned in a circle for a solid minute before flopping down with a grunt.

I pulled a long cardigan over my shoulders, dropped my phone in the pocket of my sleep shorts, and headed for the front door. It was a mild night, living all the way up to the old adage about spring coming in like a lion and slipping out like a lamb. I didn't stop to think about what I'd say, instead marching through my yard, across the street, and up to the old Cape's open front door.

Utility lights hung from the exposed studs and beams. Construction materials cluttered the floor. The offending tile saw was stationed near the kitchen. Or, the space that used to be the kitchen. This house was skin and bones, and barely that. Walls, windows, wiring—all gone.

There was a man operating the saw, his profile shielded by a hooded sweatshirt, but I ignored him in favor of yanking the saw's power cord from its hookup at the generator.

"What the fuck?" he yelled, whirling toward me.

"I could ask you the same thing," I replied, giving him *what the hell is wrong with you* hands. "It's two in the morning, bro. Why the fuck are you cutting tile right now? Do you have any idea how loud it is?"

"I'm half deaf because it's so fucking loud." He shoved his hood back and gestured toward his ears but then shook his head once, his eyes flaring wide. There was no heat there, all horror. That was what I got for leaving the house in jammies. "Yeah, it's, um, I mean, yes. I know it's loud."

"First of all, you should be wearing earplugs or noise-canceling headphones," I said, waving at him. He crossed his arms over his chest and turned his glare toward the ceiling. "And where the hell are your safety goggles? My dude, if a chip of stone flies off that wheel and into your eye, being half deaf will be a quarter of your problems."

"And second of all?" he prompted, still staring at the ceiling.

"Second of all, it's bad form to do loud repairs at night. Not only does it violate local building codes, but it also makes your neighbors very unhappy." My corner of the world was landscape architecture, but I worked shoulder to shoulder with interior designers, general contractors, specialized tradespeople, and preservation architects. I knew the basics—and then some—when it came to building houses. "Save drywalling, painting, plumbing, and finishes for late-night work."

"Great, thank you," he said. Still staring at the damn ceiling. "I'll get right on it. Can I assume that's all the advice you have for me? Or do you plan to continue shouting at me?"

I peered at him, confused. If it wasn't the middle of the night and I wasn't annoyed as hell, I would've handled this with more finesse. Unfortunately, I was all out of finesse. "Is something wrong with you?"

He ran a hand down his face as he shook his head. "Nope. Nothing. Nothing at all."

"You're a terrible liar," I said. Not an ounce of finesse.

"Undoubtedly," he mumbled to the ceiling. "But—uh—if that's all—"

"It's not," I interrupted. "The blade on your saw is wrong for the stone you're working with and, most importantly, where the hell are you putting this tile? Please tell me you're not laying it straight on the subfloor. You need cement board between the subfloor and the tile. It's bad enough you're keeping me up but you're not even doing a decent job at this renovation."

"This is what I get. Penance. This is how it's gonna be for me. All kinds of penance," he whispered at the ceiling. "Can we start over? Don't answer that. We're starting over." He shot me a quick glance. "Hi. I'm Bennett. Bennett Brock. Call me Ben."

"Hi, Ben. I'm Magnolia."

"It's nice to meet you, Magnolia." He waved his hand toward me. "Since we've started over and now we're having a neighborly conversation, it's only right for me to tell you that your shirt is—um—malfunctioning."

"My what?"

Glancing down, I found that my baggy tank top was fulfilling a small fraction of its duty to clothe my upper body. My left boob was escaping out the arm hole and my right nipple was peeking out over the top. It was tit city up in here and Ben was seeing it all.

"Oh, this is fuckin' bananas," I muttered, tucking the girls away and clasping my cardigan shut. "I'm sorry about that. I didn't come over here to flash you."

"But you did come over to give me a lesson in home

renovation?" He met my gaze but looked away quickly. The boy was probably traumatized by my peep show. I didn't blame him.

"Listen," I said, gesturing toward him. "You can't be running a tile saw at two in the morning. It's obscene. Knock that shit off before someone calls the city and you're fined for violating the terms of your building permits." I pivoted toward the front door, careful to keep my sweater shut. "Where are your permits? They should be displayed."

Ben scratched the back of his neck. "Um, which permits would those be?"

"Are you kidding me right now?" I shouted. "Dude, you have to get your show under control."

Ben's gaze swept over the building materials as he nodded. "Since you seem knowledgeable," he started, "can I ask where you'd suggest I begin with that?"

"Not in the middle of the night, no," I replied. "I have a place to be tomorrow and I don't want to be a bedhead-zombie-disaster for that. Okay?"

"Right, sure," he murmured, his gaze still on anything but me.

I should've turned around and gone home then. I didn't. I stayed there, in the middle of this skin-and-bones house, and stared at Ben. When I blinked a few times, I was able to see a man rather than a physical manifestation of my annoyances.

He was all the things. Every last one of them. Tall, broad, scruffy. Thick, wavy, dark hair. A curious scar wrinkling his cheek and a scowly smirk on his lips. His hands were huge and his eyes like midnight. His thighs were wrapped in well-worn denim and they looked strong enough to crack rocks.

And I'd shown him about seventy-five percent of my breasts while yelling about the basics of building craft.

Oh my god. This is my real life.

"Yeah, so, okay," I mumbled.

At the same time, he said, "Here's the deal. Nights are the only time I have. I'm working days right now. Twelve to twelve, most weekdays."

"That explains part of this madness," I murmured. "Got it."

"Yeah," he replied, nodding. "I'm off Saturday, Sunday, and Monday. Maybe you could come over this weekend and tell me what I don't know."

I snorted out a laugh. "As long as you promise to stop using power tools in the middle of the night, sure."

Ben's gaze slid over me, slowly at first, as if he didn't know what he'd find if he looked at me for more than a second. But he didn't glance away this time. "It's a deal. How about Saturday?"

Before I could reply, a wide, ugly yawn hit me. It was all gurgly throat noises and watery eyes, and a grossly unhinged jaw. Ben watched the whole thing, staring at me with an eyebrow arched and that scowly smirk frozen in place.

"Sorry about that," I murmured, pressing my fist to my mouth to keep another yawn at bay. It was par for the tit-city course but I was trying to reclaim some dignity here. "Yeah. Saturday. Awesome. I'll see you then." I pointed at him. "Stay away from the tools, Bennett Brock. Understood?"

"Yes, ma'am," he said, that smirk transforming into a smile. "Understood. I won't touch anything until I see you on Saturday."

With a nod, I headed back toward my house. Exhaustion

hit me hard as I locked the door and made my way into the bedroom. Gronk was pacing the edge of my bed. "It's all good," I told him. "You can chill now."

He responded by flopping on his back, paws up.

"Graceful as always," I murmured as I kicked off my mocs. "I'll introduce you to the guy behind all the noise this weekend. He's a special one." His big hands flashed in my mind. What a treasure. "Real special."

Gronk rolled over to face me, cocked his head, and let out a soft whine.

"Don't worry about the noisy neighbor boy," I said, patting the bed beside me. Gronk army-crawled there and nestled his head against my palm. "You'll always be my main man."

CHAPTER
ELEVEN

My date was running late. Eleven minutes, to be exact.

But it wasn't a date. Not like my other dates. This was a meeting between two people considering a physical relationship, but that sounded too much like a call girl interview so I slotted this event into the date category for the sake of simplicity.

Regardless of the date/not-a-date quagmire, I was working hard at staying calm about Mr. Nine's tardiness. Working hard didn't mean I was succeeding. Every few minutes, I checked my phone and twisted in my seat to glance at the bakery's front door. I thought about switching seats to give me a better view of the door but I knew Mr. Nine Inches would walk in while I was rearranging myself and I didn't need to increase the awkward quotient.

We all knew he'd show up while I was in that strange half-standing, half-sitting position, my ass out and my hands filled with nonsense. He'd be there, staring at me in horror as he realized the full extent of my hot mess, and I'd have to turtle up under the table.

I threw good sense to the wind and did it anyway.

I was strategic about this move, relocating my phone and bag before the seat swivel. It was fast, and a glance at the door told me I'd avoided meeting Mr. Nine ass first. The women seated beside me, the ones in puffer vests with matching aqua-lidded MacBooks, watched as if I was busy fishing bits of tortilla chips out of my bra and eating them.

Not that I hadn't done that, but their judgy faces were wholly unnecessary this afternoon.

Tossing my hair over my shoulder, I studied the entrance again. At this vantage point, I'd be able to spy Mr. Nine on the street. That plan suffered from one fatal flaw in that I didn't know what he looked like. His profile had a few photos, but they were of the baseball-cap-and-sunglasses and snowboarding-helmet-and-sunglasses varieties.

Basically, I knew he was a human man with a big cock who favored sunglasses. The other details remained to be seen.

I checked my phone again and found a text from Andy.

Andy: Are you having sex with him after lunch? How does that work? What's the protocol there? Do you go back to work after? Or are you done for the day at that point?

Magnolia: Irrelevant. This is a getting to know you lunch, not a getting naked lunch.

Andy: Did you shave your legs?

Magnolia: It's spring. I shave my legs any day I plan on wearing a dress without leggings.

Andy: So, yes.

Magnolia: Yes.

Andy: So, you've entertained the idea of fucking him today.

Magnolia: Entertained? Sure. I've also entertained getting my nipples pierced and a tramp stamp of a rubber plant.

Andy: Wait, a rubber plant?

Magnolia: It's a type of succulent.

Andy: Only slightly less odd, but okay.

Magnolia: You're one to talk. You have a tattoo of Harry Potter motorboating your boobs.

Andy: That's...that's not accurate.

Magnolia: It's just a lunch date. Even if I did shave my legs and blow out my hair.

Andy: Let me know if you need me to bring you a change of clothes tomorrow morning and/or save you from any unpleasant exits this afternoon.

Magnolia: I won't but thank you for the offer.

"Magnolia?"

I flattened my phone against my chest and jerked my head up. "Here. I mean, yes, I'm Magnolia. Hi," I said, blinking up at the man beside my table. He was a dark-suited dream and my words were flying away like butter-flies in the breeze. The ass-out seat swivel would've been much smoother than this. "Mr. Ni—uh, no—Rob. We're calling you Rob. Right? You're Rob? If not, how about you lie and pretend you're Rob? That would be easier for all involved."

"I don't have to lie." Nodding, he pressed his lips together to swallow a laugh. They were lip-balm-model lips. He knew a thing or two about moisturizing. "I'm not sure who you were messaging or what you were talking about, but you were making the cutest faces and moving your lips like you were saying the words as you typed them. It was the best thing I've seen all day."

I stared up at him, not sure how to respond to that. How long had he been watching me? Also, was it weird that he was watching or weird that I didn't notice? Eventually, I said, "I was talking to Andy."

"Andy?" he repeated, his eyebrow arching up. "Well, he's lucky to get so much of your attention."

"She," I replied. "She. She's one of those A-N-D-Y Andys because fuck the patriarchy and their arcane gendered spelling conventions, but we work together. Sort of. Sometimes. And we're friends. I mean, we worked together first and then we became friends later. We weren't close at the start. There was a weird situation that was entirely my fault and I still stew in the horror of it all but she was just texting to ask whether I sha—" I stopped myself there and it was quite the accomplishment considering the quantity of babble sliding out of my mouth. "Not important."

To Rob's credit, he grinned at me like I was adorably amusing rather than adorably insane. "I'm sorry I'm late," he said, still standing. That suit though. It was midnight blue with a barely there pinstripe and sweeter than anything in the bakery case. Cut and draped just right across his thick thighs and beefy shoulders. *Just right.* "I was in the weeds all morning and then I was on the conference call from hell. Damn thing wouldn't end."

"Seems like you have your hands full," I said. "Is this a bad time? Do you want to reschedule?"

Rob ran a hand through his dark auburn hair, grinning. "Not a chance." He pointed to the empty seat. "May I? Or would you rather I stand for this?"

"Oh my god, no—I mean yes. Sit down. Please. Sit," I barked.

With a surprised laugh, he tucked himself into the chair. He was tall but normal-tall, not crouch-down-in-the-shower-tall. He had freckles and laugh lines, and those little creases between his eyebrows that suggested he was in his late thirties and spent a fair amount of time thinking. Or worrying—or both.

"Thanks," Rob said, running a hand down his madras plaid tie.

There was no rational reason for it but I loved that gesture. *Loved* it. A man meant business when he did that. Or that was how I preferred to interpret it.

"Have you ordered?" Rob blinked at the empty table. I shook my head. Damn, those hazel eyes of his were pretty. Golden and green like a gemstone. "No, obviously not. I haven't eaten since six this morning and I'm ready to gnaw on my suit coat. What would you like?"

He shifted toward the counter and, oh my marshmallows, the way his white dress shirt stretched over his torso was delicious. As I took in the beauty of his chest—and another perfect tie-smoothing move—two things dawned on me. One, I'd started off crazypants and he'd rolled with it like a pro. And two, what the hell did he see in me?

No, really. I was down with loving myself but Mr. Nine and I were leagues apart. He was here with his tie smoothing and lips worth biting and I needed a mop to clean up my word vomit.

"I like a sandwich here," he said, running his fingers along his stubbled jaw.

That subtle rasp was like an ASMR video. It was all I could do to hold back a sigh. "The smoked turkey."

Rob turned back toward me, his brows drawn together. That was where those lines came from. That expression. The inkling of a smile pulled at his lips and he was watching me like he couldn't look away. Or I had food stuck between my teeth. I noticed those things after I dragged my gaze away from his engraved belt buckle. *RRR*. Either it was his initials or the sound women made when they got his belt off. Both seemed equally likely.

"Yeah," he said. "Did I tell you that or are you a sandwich whisperer?"

"Sandwich whisperer," I replied, bobbing my head. "For sure. That's so much better than remembering that you mentioned the smoked turkey sandwich when you insisted on this place."

He tapped his pointer finger on the table twice as he nodded. "That's right," he said. "That was when you were insisting on a lunch date even though I wanted a dinner date with wait service, cloth napkins, and plenty of liquor."

"Something like that, yeah."

He cast a glance around the bakery. "And why was that, Magnolia? Do you have something against dinner or is the issue dinner with me?"

My phone continued buzzing—either Andy or any number of tiny crises in need of my attention—but I tossed it into my bag. "I have a busy schedule. I have to be scrupulous with my time. Sorry."

Rob folded his arms on the table and leaned toward me. The tips of his fingers brushed against my wrist. "You're a little rude."

"It can't be much of a problem because you are still here," I mused. I didn't own that confident air but it was easier to fake it knowing there was no future here.

"Only because I don't know what you'd like for lunch," he replied. "Tell me now or I'll order one of everything."

Helpless to stifle a laugh, I eyed him. There was a touch of silver at his temples and the shadow of a long-abandoned nose piercing on his right side. Who was this guy and what did he want with me? Was it just about sex for him? I couldn't be the only available vagina.

"The mortadella," I said.

"You got it, lady," Rob said as he pushed to his feet. "I'm getting one of every cookie too. There's gotta be at least nineteen of them. I don't share cookies. You should know that about me. Do you want some? Never mind, I'll get a few extras for you."

He didn't wait for a response, instead stalking to the counter and giving me a killer view of his backside. *Good god*. As if his list of wonderful wasn't extensive enough, his ass was art. Watching him reach into his back pocket for his wallet was almost as swoony as the tie smoothing. I needed that move in GIF form.

When he shifted away from the counter, part of me resented the shopgirl's efficiency. I wouldn't have complained about a couple more minutes to study the lean lines of his body and undeniable confidence from a distance.

"Sandwiches are on the way." Rob set a bakery box and two drinks on the table before settling into his seat. He gestured to the clear plastic cups, saying, "Raspberry seltzer. You prefer black cherry but you like the house-made raspberry here. Do I have that right or did I turn it around?"

I've dated a bunch of guys over the past twenty-ish years. Some for several years, some more seriously than others. I've said "I love you" to more than one man. But never once in that time had a man ever recalled my seltzer ranking system.

Hell, most of them couldn't remember my birthday without Facebook's help.

"Yes, that's correct," I said, my words stiff. "Thank you."

"You're welcome." He laced his fingers around his drink. "I keep wanting to call you MizMaggie," he said, referring to my handle on the dating app. "I'm still getting used to thinking of you as Magnolia." He held out his hand. "It's nice to finally meet you. I'm Rob Russo."

"Magnolia Santillian." I accepted his hand but had to work at keeping my expression neutral when our palms met. There was nothing outwardly amazing about his touch but it warmed me straight down to my toes. I glanced at my reflection in the window to see if my cheeks were as flushed as they felt.

He nodded as if this information unlocked the world's great mysteries. "Do you prefer Magnolia or Maggie?"

"I answer to a lot of names," I said, jerking a shoulder up.

"Like what? Tell me," he ordered, his chin tipping up as he spoke.

Shit. Just...shit. This man was forceful. It wasn't scary forceful or aggressive forceful but pleasantly assertive while still decent forceful, and it occurred to me that I liked his version of forceful. More specifically, I liked it on Rob.

And...I liked Rob.

"There's Magnolia, of course," I started, ticking off the name on my finger, "and my family calls me Magnolia or Mag or Maggie. Then there's Roof Garden Girl and Gigi, which is an obscure derivative of Roof Garden Girl. RGG, drop the R. I hated Gigi at first but I dig it now. Everyone calls me Gigi when I'm at work. Most of my friends use it."

"You're right. That is a lot of names," he replied. "I asked you which one you prefer. You haven't answered me yet."

"Oh, it doesn't matter," I said with a wave. Where the hell were those sandwiches? I needed something to do with my hands—and my mouth—but more importantly, Rob needed to stop staring at me. "I come when I'm called."

He propped his chin on his steepled fingers and his gaze fixed on my lips. I'd never known a hot stare until now. Hot like a sunburn.

"I bet you do." His knee brushed mine under the table and then it nudged, edging my legs apart. I wasn't sure whether he intended that or it was a happy accident. "Close your mouth, rude lady. You're giving me ideas that have no place at lunch."

My cheeks were pink and my heart was pounding but I managed an indifferent shrug. "I'm sure you can save them for another time."

"I tried to save them for dinner but you weren't having it." He studied me, his eyes narrowed and his lips pursed. After a pause, he asked, "When can I see you again?"

"You're seeing plenty of me right now," I said.

"And as I've been telling you for weeks, I'd like to see more of you," Rob said.

I shook my head while I sampled my drink. Perfect as always, none of that fake raspberry flavoring bullshit. "And as I've been telling you for weeks, I need to know you before any of that can happen. You don't need to tell me about your first grade teacher, but I don't know what you do or where you live and I'm not even sure I like you."

"You like me," he argued, his knee pressing against my inner thigh. "You like me enough to insult me. That has to count for something."

"Less than you'd think," I replied with a grin.

Rob leaned back when the shopgirl arrived with our

sandwiches, but kept his gaze steady on me. I wasn't accustomed to this kind of attention. I was familiar with men who eye-fondled every pair of tits to cross their line of sight and men who couldn't focus on a conversation for more than five minutes without checking out or reaching for their phone. Since I was conditioned to accept that behavior, I was expecting it now.

And that conditioning left me wondering what this man wanted with me.

When the sandwiches were delivered and the shopgirl was out of earshot, he announced, "Investment banker."

I shook my head, not sure how to place those words in our conversation. "What?"

"I'm an investment banker," he said, gesturing toward me with his drink. "I should've mentioned it sooner. Unless you hate bankers, in which case I do something entirely different."

"I have no issue with bankers," I said, laughing. "I'm a landscape architect but I don't give a fuck if you hate architects. That would be a personal problem and you'd need to deal with it on your own."

Seltzer sprayed out of Rob's mouth as he laughed. After wiping a paper napkin over his mouth and down his tie, he said, "It hurts so good when you're mean to me."

I took a bite as I turned his words over. "You can count on me for the realism."

He gazed at me, his strange amber and emerald eyes glowing and his lips edging up into a smile. "You're a fucking gorgeous dose of reality, Magnolia." Nothing else mattered after that. He could've told me he lived in a van down by the river and I'd still be floating on his words. "I live in the South End. It's a decent place and I like the vibe but what I pay for garage parking is more than I paid for the car and I don't love that. Tell me what else you need from me so I can see you again."

"You can see me again," I started, "but I'm not sure about the arrangement you want. I need a few more lunches where you offer to lie about other things in case I hate them. I'm looking for you to explain your cookie bingeing tendencies because I require more info on that. I need to know you before any—anything else can happen."

He chewed his sandwich as he considered this. "I need to think about your terms. I'm all right and I'm keeping it together," he said, waving a hand at his chest, "but I'm a fucking mess. The thought of letting another person know me again gives me hives. Even someone as real and gorgeous and interesting as you."

Real and gorgeous and interesting and oh my god. It required actual effort to keep myself seated in this chair and not throw myself at him. Somehow, I managed an indifferent shrug. "Another personal problem."

Rob's shoulders shook as he laughed, stretching his shirt in glorious ways. I wanted to meet the tailor who managed to encase all this thick goodness in cotton. "I'll try," he said, reluctance heavy in his words. "But only if you stay rude."

We stared at each other for a long beat as we sized up the stakes. We'd been burned too many times to trust fire. We were fucked up in the feels. And here we were, negotiating the terms of a treaty to nowhere. My head was flashing every warning sign but my heart was lurching up into my throat, starved for more.

I knew better but I couldn't do better.

"Since I have plenty of material to work with, that won't be a problem." I jerked a shoulder up, inviting him to contradict me. He only grinned back at me, and I was a goner. "I live in Beverly, in an old stone cottage with ample parking. That's one of the reasons I love it. My aunt and her partner retired to New Mexico, and they left it in my hands. But when I say 'old,' I mean old. I've been ripping up orange shag carpet and scraping avocado green wallpaper for the past year. It has an elaborate garden in the backyard, though, and that's my favorite part of the property. Even if it is overrun with weeds and vines and a dozen other problems."

"Do you need any help with that?" Rob asked.

I quirked a brow up. "Did you miss the part about me being a landscape architect? I can handle one jungle-y backyard, thank you."

"I didn't miss that part," Rob said, his lips twitching with a smile. "I was offering free labor. I'm in the mood to rip up some vines."

"Only if you do it shirtless." My cheeks flamed red when I realized what I'd said. My gaze flitted between his arms and his chest because there was no way in hell I was looking him in the eye right now.

Rob dipped his chin down, chuckling. He ran his hand over the length of his tie once again and I barely kept myself from purring. "Happily," he replied. "If that gets me an afternoon in your garden, I'll wear—or not wear—anything you'd like."

I looked at my plate and focused on rearranging the sandwich's layers. It was all I could do to wipe the fiery blush from my face and get control of my word vomit.

When I glanced up, a group of men streamed through the door. Clad in tight navy t-shirts with *Engine 10* printed on the back, they turned every head in the bakery. I watched them over Rob's shoulder for a moment, as fascinated by this gaggle of guys as everyone else.

I started to say something to Rob about coming to the garden this weekend but stopped myself when I sensed someone staring at me. It took a minute to find the source of the stare among all those navy t-shirts, and by the time I did, he was headed this way.

"Hello, Miss Magnolia," he said, propping his hands on his lean hips. "Didn't think I'd see you twice in twelve hours."

"What?" Rob glanced between me and this unwelcome guest.

"Ben," I gritted out, tilting my neck to glare up at my noisy neighbor.

"Who the fuck is Ben?" Rob asked.

Ben glanced to my date. "Who the fuck is this guy?"

CHAPTER
TWELVE

MY DATE WAS FURIOUS.

Not gonna lie…it was pretty hot.

I mean, I didn't like guys with anger problems. I didn't need any toxic masculinity in my life, thank you kindly. But this didn't feel like an anger problem to me. It felt like my noisy neighbor boy interrupting an otherwise lovely date and making things peculiar with the suggestion I *saw* him late last night.

Yeah, I *saw* him. Technically, he saw a lot more of me than I did of him but that was beside the point. We weren't *together* last night. He was disturbing the peace and I was the concerned citizen who'd shut up him and his tile saw.

And promised to help him with his remodeling efforts over the weekend.

Jesus Lord, I strolled into some real special situations, didn't I?

"Magnolia," Rob said, a sharp edge in his voice that raised goose bumps on my arms. The best goose bumps. Interesting goose bumps. I could get on board with goose bumps like these. Maybe not right now, in the middle of

Flour, but at some point in the potentially naked future. "You know this guy?"

"I'm wondering the same thing," Ben added with a flippant wave toward Rob. I swiveled my gaze toward him and damn, that t-shirt worked. The hoodie he wore last night, it hid all the goods. "Who's the suit?"

"All right, listen," I started, holding both hands up. "I'm having lunch with Rob. He's a—a friend of mine."

"I'd say we're past the point of friends," Rob argued, his brow creasing. This boy. He couldn't talk about anything more than no-strings sex but went all prickly porcupine at the suggestion of mere friendship. So damn prickly. "After everything we've shared and everything you've—ahem —seen."

Still holding my hands up, I shot him a withering glare. "Don't you worry, sweetheart. One of the many wonderful things about me is that I don't forget." He started to argue but I shook my head, saying, "Hush now. I'm talking."

"Can't wait to hear this." Ben crossed his arms—my god, how did anyone get forearms that ropey?—over his chest and rocked back on his heels. For real though, those forearms were straight out of Gaston from *Beauty and the Beast.*

"And as for this one," I said, tipping my head toward Ben. "This is the guy who's flipping the house across the street from me." I caught Rob's steely glare. "I told you about that. Remember?"

"I think so," he murmured, busy sizing Ben up.

If I wasn't truly annoyed about this interruption and my brain's inability to process while Ben's bare forearms and Rob's chest were in the picture, I would've enjoyed this moment. I would've sat back, thrilled that two men were metaphorically fighting over who got to piss the circle around me.

Moments like these didn't happen to me. I was the chubby friend, the weird friend, the friend with the hot (or so I was told) brothers. I was always the *friend*. Never the one everyone wanted.

"What I didn't tell you is that he's been working through the night and waking the dead with his tile saw," I continued.

Rob's glare softened as he blinked at me. "You should've told me about that. I would've—"

"Nope," I interrupted. "I had it under control."

Rob blinked at me again. "I can't decide if that's infuriating or fucking awesome."

"We're going with awesome," I said, glancing back to Ben.

"I'd say infuriating," Ben murmured.

"You would," I replied. "You've been going hard for the past month but you're doing a shit job of it." I pointed at Ben while catching Rob's eye. "I went across the street in the middle of the night—"

"Infuriating," Rob muttered.

"And politely asked him to suspend the home improvement games for a bit," I continued, ignoring Rob as he tossed his hands up and shook his head.

Ben pivoted to face Rob. "Dude. She unplugged my saw and then yelled at me about how to work on a house for ten minutes," Ben said. "There was nothing polite about it. It was actually very indecent."

"That's how I roll, buddy," I replied. This time, he got the withering glare. "And if you want me to help you with your projects, you'll—"

Rob's chair screeched against the floor as he pushed to his feet. "You're helping him?"

If there was anyone in this bakery who wasn't engrossed in our conversation, they were in it now. Goddamn, I did not want to be the subject of another live-tweeted date.

"Yes," I replied, as calm and even as possible. Even if I wanted to tell him to shut the fuck up and sit the hell down. "It drives me crazy when virgin flippers do shoddy work and then sell houses that are basically duct-taped together."

"I'm no virgin," Ben announced, tipping his chin up at me.

There was a challenge in that gesture. Something that whispered, *Try me.*

And those fucking forearms. They demanded attention, a challenge to anyone who spotted them. *Just try and get your hand around me*, they taunted.

Rob down stared at me, his eyebrows crawling up his forehead and his hands on his lean waist. "Magnolia, I don't —" He stopped himself, shot a sour glimpse at Ben, and then looked back to me.

Holy shit. I was the jam in a Rob-and-Ben sandwich. Not that I wanted a sandwich. Open-faced, sure. Not a panini.

"Yo, Brock," a voice boomed from the other side of the bakery. "Time to roll."

Ben glanced over his shoulder at the crew of firefighters waiting for him. "I'll see you Saturday," he said. Then, facing Rob, he said, "Seems like I'll be seeing you around too."

"Bet on it," Rob replied, smoothing his tie as he settled into his seat.

Ben laughed to himself, nodding, and then hit me with a quick smile. "Saturday."

"Permits," I called as he walked away. Once Ben and the

other firefighters filed out of the bakery, I glanced at Rob. "Sorry about that. It was this whole weird thing last night where I went over there and realized he was committing every renovation sin known to building craft and I had to jump in."

I casually omitted all references to my free-boob situation. Just didn't seem relevant.

Rob sat back and clasped his hands in his lap. He smiled at me, a curious, almost amused smile that made me wonder for the second time this afternoon whether I had poppy seeds in my teeth.

"What?" I asked.

"Nothing." He shook his head. "I wanted—I just needed to get over my ex. She really fucked me up and I'm...I don't know what I am."

"What happened?" I asked. "What did she do that traumatized you so much?"

Rob shook his head again. For the first time, I saw inside his weariness, into the bleak blankness where his relationships once lived. I understood his desperation to fill that space at any cost. "I don't want to get into it. Nothing atrocious. Just people who had different expectations and different definitions of loyalty," he said. "But I thought I'd find a hot woman who looked nothing like my ex"—I was inwardly squeeing at that—"and fuck away the memories. Instead, I met you."

End the squeeing.

"Oh, well, I guess I'm sorry about...something," I said, stumbling over each word. "Maybe I should—uh, just—maybe I'll go now."

"No, no, not—no." His entire existence seemed to cringe.

"I said that wrong. I meant that I had a very narrow objective."

"Mmhmm."

He tucked a finger under his collar, dragged the fabric away from his neck. I couldn't explain it but I wanted—I wanted to lick him there. "I didn't expect to, you know, feel anything."

"Mmhmm," I repeated.

"I thought my ex had reached in and torn out my heart with a soldering iron and I was incapable of doing anything but slowly bleeding to death."

Again, "Mmhmm."

He looked up at me, his brow wrinkled and his lips pulled up in a slight grin. "But I wanted to beat the shit out of that guy just now."

"And that's a good thing? I wouldn't call that progress, Rob."

He laughed. "It's something. It's a lot more than I've managed in months." He brought his fingers to his temples, his smile faltering. "But you should know I don't share. I can't. Not after what she—no, we're not poisoning this air with that story."

"I'm helping Ben with construction because I don't want him to accidentally take down the power grid in my neighborhood," I said. "Not for any"—those forearms flashed in my mind before I chased them away with an impatient eyeroll—"other reason."

Rob pressed both palms to his eyes and let out a groan. The noise was deep, sexy. "Yeah, it's not you I'm worried about, Magnolia. It's the way that guy looked at you."

He pulled his hands away from his eyes and pushed to his feet. A pang of sadness quivered through my belly when

I realized he was leaving. Despite our odd history, I had a soft spot for Rob and all his personal drama. I didn't want to nurse him back to health, but I enjoyed the guy.

Instead of leaving, Rob rounded the table and beckoned toward me. "Stand up," he ordered.

I stood but asked, "Excuse me?" That was how I rolled—I followed directions while arguing about them.

"Just—just come here," Rob said, gripping my elbow. He tugged me closer and slipped a hand up my spine, into my hair. He gazed down at me, his focus locked on my lips. "I don't know whether I should resent you for making me feel again or love you for it." Before I could respond, he continued. "Don't say anything. I already know."

Then he kissed me.

Lips, tongues, hands, heat, sighs—all at once. Everything beyond us dissolved. The bakery, this city, the convoluted premise behind our lunch date. None of it existed when I pressed my hands to his back and urged him closer.

I was certain he hadn't gone looking for it but somewhere between yanking me into his arms and claiming my mouth, he stumbled upon my bleak blankness.

CHAPTER
THIRTEEN

My date was a disaster.

Ben knew nothing about home improvement. Nothing worth knowing. Still, he wielded his tools with a swagger that suggested otherwise.

"Stop, stop," I yelled, waving my hands to get his attention. He was cutting plywood to replace parts of the subfloor in the living room, but even from ten feet away I knew he was doing it wrong.

Ben switched off the saw and pushed his safety goggles to his forehead. "What now?"

I walked over to him, studying the long, narrow strips of plywood on the bench. "What...what are you doing?"

He gave me *isn't it obvious* hands. "Cutting the flooring, just like you told me to."

I stared at the boards for a long moment. "But why? Given the dimensions of that room, you should only need to cut a few pieces. The rest can be nailed down as is."

Ben glanced between me and the saw bench, his lips

pressed together in a scowl. "If you say so," he murmured. "I just thought it would look better if they were all the same size. Fancier, you know?"

I brought my gloved fist to my lips to hold back a laugh. It was better than crying—which was how I wanted to react after taking a hard look at Ben's work—but I didn't want to be cruel.

"Right, so, this isn't the floor-floor," I said, dropping both hands on the boards. "This is the subfloor. We put this floor down, the subfloor, to keep the actual flooring surface level and steady. In other words, we're going to put something on top of this. Something fancy."

Ben blinked at me for a second before ripping his goggles off his head and chucking them across the room. "I fucking hate this shit," he yelled. "Fucking *hate* it."

Before meeting Ben this morning, I'd decided I wasn't going to mention anything about our run-in at the bakery. I didn't want to harvest any of those sentiments again and I didn't want to defend myself or Rob. Also, I wasn't sure I wanted to return to the alternative universe where he was sorta-kinda-maybe flirting with me. Without my boob flapping in the wind, I didn't understand the motivation for it at all. And even if he was flirting with me, I didn't have the brain space to juggle two men. If history served as any proof, I barely possessed the skill to juggle a single man.

Instead, I'd slipped into my favorite on-the-job jeans and t-shirt, laced up my boots, and stepped into boss mode. No time was wasted on pleasantries. I rattled off a list of basic tasks for Ben while I set to righting some of the more alarming issues at this property. I didn't ask after his intentions for this remodel or why I'd seen several people here previously, but it was only him on the job now. Nope, I went straight for the electrical panel and then checked the water shut-off, and left Ben to organize the materials and cut some plywood to size.

But now, as I watched him pacing the length of the room with his hands fisted on his hips, it seemed as though I'd made a mistake. There was work to be done, yes, but why was he alone? Why was he doing this? I was especially curious about that given he didn't know screwdriver basics. I'd spent five minutes on righty tighty, lefty loosey.

"Why don't we sit down for a minute?" I gestured toward a large ice chest, the one I'd left near the front door this morning. "I have some drinks and sandwiches. In case you're wondering, I didn't make them. My mother did. I told her I was working on a project today and she dropped by with all this food because she thinks I survive on takeout alone. If you knew her, you'd see that's an issue for her."

Ben stopped pacing but kept his fists on his hips. His sleeves were pushed up past his elbows, exposing his corded forearms. There was a tattoo peeking out from under his shirt, near his elbow. I couldn't make out the design.

God, those forearms. I needed a fan.

"What the hell are you talking about?"

"Food. I have food. Let's take a break and eat," I said. "Maybe outside? The snow is gone, it's not raining like the end of days, and I saw a sunbeam or two poking through the clouds on my way over here. In other words, a perfect spring day in New England."

Ben didn't say anything but edged me aside when I tried to collect the ice chest. He hefted it up and followed me into the backyard. The house sat on a deep lot with long-abandoned gardens and overgrown trees. We settled on the edge of the brick patio, in a sun-warmed spot.

I dug into the ice chest, setting the foil-wrapped sandwiches, fruit, and drinks between us. Ben popped the top on a black cherry seltzer and guzzled it down. "God dammit, this is awful. It's like drinking fizzy, fruity hairspray. No, I take that back. It's not even fruity. It's like fruit-inspired." He held out his arm, peered at the can. "Cherry. Huh. It tastes like it was *near* a single cherry once for five minutes."

"You're disparaging my favorite beverage," I said.

"Maybe you should reevaluate your beverage choices. This is the worst thing I've ever put in my mouth." Then, he demolished a ham and Swiss sandwich in three bites. "That was good," Ben announced with a sigh. "Got another?"

I waved my arm over the spread between us. "I have a dozen more."

"That's what I'm talkin' about," he said, holding each package up to read my mother's precise printing on the foil.

I waited until Ben was halfway through his second sandwich to say anything. He seemed famished, and I needed the time to figure out how I wanted this conversation to go. That was the smartest way forward: knowing where I wanted to go and getting us there.

The only trouble with me and smart ways forward was that I always, always, *always* fucked it up. But I was working hard at avoiding all manner of fuck up today.

Today, this month, forever.

"Let's talk about this place," I said, pointing toward the house and gardens with my seltzer. "Not that you've asked for my opinion on the landscaping but I'd build some rock features in here to break up the flat space and restore habitats for pollinators and other local species. Something to add a bit of depth and regrow the moss and lichen populations. They don't survive well in suburban lawns. I'd also prioritize drought-tolerant plantings. Hosta, sedum, chokeberry. Inkberry, maybe some American holly. If you added forsythia along the side of the property, you'd create a natural privacy fence from the street. Those are just a few ideas but they are more efficient but also require far less maintenance than your current setup. That might be something to consider if you don't want to spend your weekends working in your yard."

"Haven't asked my opinion on the landscaping," he murmured. "Sweetheart, I don't think I've asked your opinion on a damn thing but that hasn't stopped you yet."

I regarded him. "Shall I take my opinions—and my sandwiches—and go?"

"Don't even think about moving that fine ass of yours," he replied. "Sit right there and mouth off about all the things I'm doing wrong."

"It's not mouthing off when it's accurate."

"And that fizzy water, the kind that had a nightmare about cherries, is disgusting." He arched a brow. "We'll survive this disagreement."

"All right. Fine. How did you decide on this property? What are you looking to do with it?"

He stared at me as he tipped back another sip. "What am I looking to do with it?" he repeated, the words tinted with bitterness. "Get rid of it and get some of my money back. That's all I want. I'm not looking for a side hustle here."

"Then…why did you buy it?" I asked.

His gaze skated down my body and back up again. He winced, looked away. Staring into the yard, he asked, "What's going on with you and the suit?"

"We're talking about the house," I said.

"He seemed like a douchebag," Ben continued, glancing back at me. "Why would you be interested in a douchebag?"

It was fascinating how Ben seemed to toggle through attitudes when it pleased him. Impatient and angry when faced with remodeling issues. Arrogant and brash when faced with Rob. Friendly and decent when faced with my breasts.

"Not that it's any of your business but he's not a douchebag," I said. "And just so you know, defaulting to the argument that he's a douche because he wears a suit to work is as unimaginative as you can get. If you have a point worth making, I'll listen. Otherwise, save it for someone who appreciates low-hanging insults."

Ignoring me, Ben continued, "You should get outta that situation real fast."

"Thanks for the tip," I murmured.

"I'll give you more than the tip, honey," he replied. "A whole fuckin' lot more. And you'll enjoy it more than anything that douchebag has for you."

My lips parted as a furious blush climbed up my neck and over my face. "I can help you here or you can say that shit," I countered. "But not both."

"I never asked for your help."

"That's funny," I replied. "It's really funny because you invited me into this hot mess when you decided to run the tile saw in the middle of the motherfucking night, dude." Ben shrugged that off as he balled the foil in his palm. "You can have my help or you can have the city and county inspectors knocking on your door." I turned an exaggerated glare toward the house. "Oh, wait. You don't have a door right now because you thought it was a brilliant idea to rip the doorframe off. I guess the inspectors will have to climb in through the damn window when they come to shut you down."

He shrugged. "Whatever."

"You know what's even more funny? You'd rather say rude things and make unwelcome advances than have my help. If you're the kind of person who enjoys making women uncomfortable, then, yeah, I'll be going now." He pitched the foil ball across the yard. "Fucking hilarious, Ben. I knew you were a lot of talk but I didn't realize it was this kind."

Without looking in my direction, he said, "I'm not trying to make you uncomfortable. I'm sorry. I shouldn't have said what I did." He glanced to the side, swore under his breath. "Not *all* of it."

I stood, crossed the yard to retrieve the foil, and stalked back to the patio. "Then what are you trying to do?"

"I—" He stopped himself, let his shoulders drop. "I don't know. I can't deal with anything right now and everything about this house makes me crazy and I don't know what your regular voice sounds like because you're always fucking yelling at me."

"Like I said"—I gestured toward him with more graciousness than I felt—"you can say that shit or I can go."

"I'd tell you to get the fuck out but I'm sure you're a skilled multitasker."

"While that's true," I conceded, "we're focused on fixing up this house so I don't have to listen to tile saws all night."

"That might be your objective but I'm focused on hunting down that douchebag from your lunch date and telling him to keep his spiffy-ass suits away from you. Come on, now. You'd break him over your knee, wouldn't you? You can tell me the truth."

"We are not talking about Rob or his suits right now," I

said, trying—failing—to stifle a shocked laugh. I hadn't thought about Rob over my knee. Didn't want to think about it. "And you have no reason to quote-unquote hunt him down. He's a nice guy and I like him and that should be all you need to know about the situation."

Ben pretended to gag. "First the fizzy water and now this. Why the hell are you hanging out with him, honey?"

I shifted to face him fully. "Why did you buy this house if you hate remodeling?"

He bit into another sandwich. I wasn't counting but it seemed like his third. "Is this one of those situations where I have to answer your question before you'll answer mine?"

"No," I cried, laughing. "This is one of those situations where we're not talking about Rob because my relationship with him is none of your business."

"Oh, but me buying this house is your business?" he countered.

I grabbed my work gloves off the grass and smacked his shoulder with them. "Yes! I'm here working on this damn house. I deserve to know why you're doing this."

Ben shrugged but didn't respond, turning his attention back to the sandwich in hand. After several quiet minutes, he said, "My fucking grandmother."

I almost choked on a chunk of apple. "Excuse me?"

He didn't look at me when he said, "My fucking grandmother. I bought this little place because I thought I could fix it up and she'd like it better than the shitbox retirement community she was living in. I had a bunch of guys from the firehouse who were helping me out at first and things were going good."

They must've been the ones who'd handled the plumbing

because it was the only element of this project that wasn't a disaster.

"But she died," Ben continued. "My grandmother fucking died and now I have this money pit of a house on my hands and I hate everything about it."

His words were an ice bath and I felt tears prickling my eyes. *Oh, hell.* Here I was, yelling at this poor guy about subfloors and tile and permits, and he was grieving a fresh loss.

"Oh my god. Ben," I said, touching my hand to his forearm. "I'm so sorr—"

"Don't say it," he snapped, wagging a finger at me. "Don't tell me you're sorry. I don't want to hear it." He looked over his shoulder, staring off toward the gardens as he knuckled a tear from his eye. "Your turn. What's the deal with the suit who may or may not be a douchebag?"

"He's not a douchebag," I said softly. "Rob is—" I stopped myself, not certain how I wanted to describe my relationship with Rob. "He's a nice guy who is going through a rough patch right now."

Ben glanced toward me but kept his gaze low, not meeting my eyes. "Does that mean you're friends? That's it? That's all that's going on?"

"It means we're hanging out." I shrugged. "I like it. He's funny and interesting and—"

"And he's got a lotta cash," Ben interrupted.

"That's not part of my mental calculus," I replied. "Nor has it ever come up in conversation."

"Still don't like him," Ben said under his breath.

"That's good," I replied. "You're not the one hanging out with him."

"Not for nothing but we basically had a three-way lunch

date," Ben replied. "We should do that again. It was entertaining."

"You know," I said, pointing at him with my apple core, "you make that sound like a threat."

Ben gathered up the empty cans and tinfoil, still avoiding my stare. "Nah. I don't make threats. Just promises."

CHAPTER
FOURTEEN

MY DATE WAS EDGY.

He'd read the wine list cover to cover, set it aside. Straightened his tie, the tablecloth, his water goblet. Then he reread the wine list, scowling and shaking his head like the pages insulted his origin and ethnicity. When he was finished with that exercise, he glanced around the restaurant. This wasn't the type of place I frequented so I didn't know what he was looking for.

If anything, I was busy dying by degrees because we were at a new swanky-fancy restaurant in the Back Bay and I was wearing a jersey knit dress. Probably hadn't spent more than ten dollars on it. It still qualified as a simple black dress thing but that wasn't the point. I hadn't realized we were going somewhere swanky-fancy, but I was delighted I'd changed out of my knee-high yellow rainboots beforehand.

"Would you like to share a bottle of red?" Rob asked, his pointer finger pressed against the wine menu. "Do you...do you like red?"

As far as conversation went, this was a major improvement. Since meeting him at this restaurant, he'd only managed to ask how I was doing, how my day went, and now, if I wanted to go halfsies on some Bordeaux. That, and all the scowling, straightening, and side-eye glances he'd been shooting my way.

"Is everything all right, Rob?" I folded my hands in my lap. I hadn't seen him since that afternoon at the bakery café and he'd been traveling for work the past week so his texts had been few and far between. When he'd arrived back in Boston last night, he'd insisted we meet for dinner. I'd agreed right away because I'd wanted to see him too. "You're not yourself tonight."

He started to respond, his lips parted and his brows knit as if he was about to impart something profound. But then he snapped his mouth shut and pressed both palms to his eyes.

"I'm having a hard time with the fact you're hanging out with the firefighter," he said from behind his hands. "It's really fucking with me right now."

I rolled my eyes and took a swig from my water glass. This would've been the perfect moment for wine to appear. I had to deal with Ben complaining about Rob over the weekend and now I was dealing with Rob complaining about Ben. In all my fantasies about being the object of dual affection, I'd never once accounted for the time and energy I'd put into project managing that affection.

And it wasn't even dual affection, not really. Ben was an epic flirt and nothing more. He talked a big game and he had swagger for days, but much like his home improvement prowess, I didn't think there was anything behind any of it. He was grieving and his periodic displays of possessiveness were likely a strange product of that. He wanted to hold on to anything he could. It broke my heart.

Rob was a different story. He liked challenges, I was sure of it, and he interpreted my refusal to let him blindly fuck away his ex as just that. He wanted me because he couldn't have me —not the way he wanted. He liked it when I called him on his games and pushed back on his bullshit, and I'd be lying if I said I didn't like it too. There was something about Rob that clicked with me. Andy insisted it was my need to fix him but if there was anyone in need of fixing in this runoff, it was Ben.

"Why is that?" I asked. "Why is it an issue for me to help my neighbor with a project at his house when A, I'm good at that work and I enjoy it and B, it's not about you?"

Rob folded his forearms on the table with a sigh. It was a ragged, broken noise that suggested this conversation—this specific topic—was causing him a measure of agony. "You're going to make me talk about my baggage and my shit. Aren't you?"

Men. They had the nerve to insist women were the fairer sex. The ones who couldn't see through the haze of their hormones. The wildly emotional ones. The ones who couldn't be trusted with parking, credit cards, front-line combat, nuclear codes.

Fucking men.

Not that it was worth my worry in the first place but I wasn't fretting over my t-shirt dress anymore.

I motioned to the table, the restaurant. "Is there something else you'd rather do tonight? Because I don't need any of this. I don't need to name-check the cool new place on my Instagram or with my friends. But I do need my dinner date to put up or shut up when it comes to the issues he flags on the regular. So, Rob"—I peered at him—"what's it going to be?"

He tilted his head. It was only a few degrees but it shifted his entire countenance from sulky to seriously sexy. "Since you asked, there is something else I'd rather do," he said, his gaze fixed on my lips. "I'd do it right here if we had the place to ourselves."

Okay. Yes. That was seriously sexy but it wasn't working on me. I wasn't the kind of lady who could switch from totally annoyed to totally turned on with one well-placed head tilt.

"Since we don't have the place to ourselves and I'm waiting on this water to turn into wine—a Pinot Grigio, if you please—why don't you explain why you're being salty about something that requires no salt whatsoever?"

The waiter chose this moment to stop at our table and babble on about the backstory of each dish and its ingredients. The carrots were cruelty-free, the bacon knew its grandmother, the chef had trekked all the way to the Malabar coast to handpick the peppercorns. It was a whole big thing. Through it all, Rob and I studied each other in another round of *Look at all of our issues and the curious ways in which they manifest themselves*. There was Rob with his inability to reveal the inner parts of himself without tremendous cost and there was me with my inability to abide any amount of secrets or shadows because I expected the worst was headed my way.

We ordered two bottles—red and white—and I could almost hear my mother asking, "What? You're planning to drink that entire thing by yourself? You better not plan on walking the dog too. Not unless you want your picture on the front page of the newspaper because you've been kidnapped and killed."

I swallowed a hysterical giggle at that, waving away Rob's curious expression. "It's nothing," I said. "Ignore me."

He shook his head. "Can't."

"All right." I gestured toward him. "Where were we?"

"You said something about salt. I have no salt?"

"You have a ton of salt," I replied, holding my arms out wide. "So much salt."

"No," he answered. "Not that much."

"You're saltier than the Great Salt Lake," I replied. "And the Death Valley Salt Flats."

"Combined? Or separately?"

I leaned forward, flattened my hands on the table. "Both."

"Are we talking that cool pink salt or lame-ass table salt?" he asked.

"Oh, as lame as it comes," I replied. "No one is grinding your salt into artisanal flakes or sprinkling you over chocolate or caramel."

"That's disappointing," he murmured.

"It really is," I replied. "You're a slab of salt, my friend. If I licked you, I'd need to chase it with an entire bottle of tequila."

He motioned to his torso. "All yours."

I waved him off and shifted my gaze to the tables around us. "I don't lick guys who can't manage their shit," I said. I didn't say, *Not anymore.* Thought about it. Kept that tidbit under my hat. "Or guys who think they can legislate how I spend my time or who I spend it with."

The waiter returned with our wine and went to great efforts to present each bottle, uncork them, pour a sample sip, wait for our approval—who the hell sent back wine?—

and then top off our glasses. He tied cute little cloth napkin kerchiefs around the bottles and set each in a silver canister. It was a lot of damn effort for wine. I understood there were varying levels to this stuff but I was perfectly satisfied with my screw caps and pink Corksicle tumbler.

Rob held up his glass, waiting for me to follow suit. When I joined him, he said, "My ex cheated on me while I was away on business. Not just once. She cheated on me for two years. With my best friend. The guy I grew up with. I was going to propose to her, and I was going to ask him to stand up as my best man."

Staring at him, I blinked several times. Then I looked away, swinging my gaze from side to side in search of the space to absorb this information without him watching. That was some real shit, and from the two people you were supposed to trust the most.

After a wild-eyed pause too long to be anything but uncomfortable, I asked, "And we're drinking to that?"

He looked at our glasses, still held aloft, and his tight expression broke into a quick laugh. "No. *Fuck* no," he said. "I just...I hate saying that shit out loud. I hate that it happened. I hate that it happened to me. Sometimes, I hate that I found out because ignorance never fucked me up like this. Then I hate that I'm still fucked up over it and I can't leave town without..."

Rob set his glass down and glanced away.

"Without thinking the person you left at home is going to fuck you over again," I said. *Goddamn.* I hadn't known I was walking right into the snake pit on this one but here I was, stomping all over Rob's king cobras. "Even if it's irrational, you can't help thinking it." He nodded, still blindly staring across the restaurant. "If it helps, I'm fucked up too."

"You're not fucked up," he replied, hitting me with a half-smile. It was sad and sweet, and left me aching for him. "You're perfect."

My belly swooped. Circumstances aside, I couldn't resist a half-smiled "You're perfect." Nope. I wasn't too proud to admit it either.

"Not too sure about that," I said. "I can't leave my dog with a man I'm dating. Not even for five minutes. I'll call him to follow me if I leave the room because I can't deal with the possibility my dog will get hurt. It's been...hmm, what is it now, three years? Yeah, three years this summer and I can't leave my dog alone with a guy. Not without a full-blown panic attack."

Rob's gaze scraped over me as if he was trying to find my soft spots by looks alone. "Someone did something to your *dog*?"

I pinched my fingers around the stem of the wineglass and twirled the base against the tablecloth. "My ex stole my dog. Some other stuff too but my dog was the most important thing he stole. A bunch of my friends had to raid his place to get Gronk back."

"I love that you named him Gronk. Such a big name for a little dog," Rob said, that half-smile still in place. "Does he have that Gronkowski spirit?"

"Oh, yeah," I replied, grinning at the thought of the former New England Patriots tight end. "Feisty as fuck. Except he doesn't know he's a small dog. He thinks he's just as big and tough as his namesake."

"That's amazing," Rob murmured. "But I hate that ex of yours. I want to fucking kill him."

"I hate that ex of yours. The ex-friend too. I'm not the murderous type but I hope some Black Swallow-wort takes over their yards. It's one of the most invasive vines in the region. Impossible to kill."

We studied each other, the moment stretching long and taut as we assessed the texture and shape of each other's war wounds. They were numerous, several as raw and pulsing as the day we'd earned them. And yet here we were, lining up for another battle as if we'd fortified ourselves enough to stay safe and whole this time.

"I feel like an asshole saying this but it's not you, it's me," Rob said. "I'm not trying to imply that you'd do anything like they did or that I don't trust you. This is all about me and I can't change it."

I could finally hear those words without feeling the urge to make excuses or apologize. I'd done it before. It wasn't me, but I was still sorry about the version of myself available for consumption. It wasn't me, but let me list all the reasons I could've been better.

This time, I offered no apology because I was as close to whole as any broken girl could be. Pieces of myself were gone, lost to previous relationships. Tough, leathery scar tissue filled the gaps and holes where my naïveté once lived.

"I know," I said. "And I know this isn't what you want to hear but are you sure you're ready to get over her with a meaningless fling?"

"It seemed like a good plan at the time," he said, his brow crinkling. A beat passed between us before a warm glow spread over him as if he'd stepped out from behind a shadow. "But this isn't meaningless, Magnolia. Nowhere near meaningless. Hasn't been since you demanded a dick pic, love."

Another belly swoop. This guy. He didn't stop with them.

Even when he should. Because, come on. He was twenty thousand leagues under the sea with his trust issues.

"Then maybe you should make a new plan," I said with a shrug.

"Let's drink to that," Rob said with a laugh. He lifted his glass. "To new plans. The meaningful kind."

I reached for my glass, paused before raising it. "Does this meaningful plan imply you're no longer looking to fuck away memories of your ex?"

"I'd still like to do that," he conceded.

I pressed my fingers against the goblet's narrow stem. "Are the terms the same?"

"I don't know yet." He reached across the table, clinked his glass against mine. "I can't make any promises."

"I don't want promises."

"Then what do you want?" he asked.

I brought the glass to my lips, smiling as I drank. "I don't know yet."

CHAPTER
FIFTEEN

My date was scarfing donuts like it was almost hibernation season.

"You eat these," I started, gesturing to the Blackbird Donuts box between us, "and you don't gain a pound. Do you?"

Andy licked a dollop of blackberry jam from her thumb, a casualty of an overzealous bite into her third donut of the morning. She spared me a sheepish glance before returning to her pastry.

"I'd hate you but that seems pointless," I muttered.

"Completely pointless," she replied. "Who would you complain to about the men chasing after you if you didn't keep me around?"

"I never said anything about getting rid of you," I replied, glancing into the box. "I'm capable of hating you while keeping you as my friend."

I'd already had a vanilla old-fashioned with Blackbird's special vanilla bean glaze but now I was thinking about that Boston Crème Bismarck. I freaking loved Boston Crème and

I would've chosen it if this bakery didn't make such incredible vanilla cake donuts. I would've gotten two but I also wanted to be able to function this afternoon and not fall into a carbs-and-sugar coma.

Andy nodded, saying, "Women are complicated."

"Only the human ones," I replied. "You, my friend, are not human. You're some kind of fairy or sprite. Tinker Bell, but goth."

She put her donut down, wiped her hands on a paper napkin, and held up her pointer finger. "I'll be right back."

I figured she was going for another dozen. Instead, she headed for the counter filled with cutlery, straws, and coffee complements. She grabbed a few things before giving the display case a meaningful glance. She was thinking about another dozen. I knew it. When she returned to the table, she produced a plastic knife and cut the Bismarck down the middle.

"Eat that and explain this issue with your boys again," she ordered, wagging the knife at me.

"I mean, there's not an issue per se," I said, picking up my half of the Boston Crème. Damn, I loved me some Boston Crème. Cake, donut, scented candle, you name it, I wanted it. There was nothing better in the whole world than chocolate, cake, and pudding in one bite. "There's just these two guys and they're both...I don't know. They're both *around* right now."

"Do you want them around?" She wiped her fingers clean and reached for her iced tea. "Based on everything you've said recently, it seems as though you find them amusing. Right?"

"Amusing is one way to put it," I said with a laugh. "First there's Rob, and I really like being with him. I'm not sure what it is but he's—he's funny and smart and easy to be with and I like all of those things. I like them so much. When we first started chatting, it was as if we'd known each other forever. I never have to explain my humor to him and there were never awkward *oh shit what did I say* moments. He has some issues from his ex-girlfriend and they're rather significant, but—but he looks at me like he wants to listen to everything I say."

Andy nodded, setting her tea down. "It sounds as though you really like this dude."

"I do. He has some shit to work through but so do I. When you're in your thirties and single, everyone is fighting the ghosts of exes past."

"You're not wrong," Andy said, her gaze dropping to the seven donuts remaining in the box. "Then what's the story with Ben? Why is he in the picture if Rob is the model of fucked-up perfection?"

"He's in the picture because he owns the house across the street from me," I replied.

"He's the fixer-upper?"

"Him and the house he bought, yeah," I replied. "Andy, you'd freakin' die if you saw the way he was reno'ing that place. Electrical and water both on during demo. No permits to speak of. He was laying tile on subfloor. No mortar board in sight."

"My god," she whispered, lifting her hand to her mouth.

"I know, right?"

"Yeah, that's tragic," Andy replied. "But this Ben, the bad flipper, does he look at you like he wants to listen to everything you say?"

"N—" I started to respond but stopped myself. I didn't

know how Ben looked at me, not really. "I don't think so. I'm not sure."

Andy crossed her arms. "What do you mean, you don't know?"

"I mean, I am not sure about him," I replied, enunciating every word. "Every time I see him, I have to yell at him about something. First it was the tile saw at two in the morning, then it was him crashing my lunch date with Rob, and then it was him fucking up everything he touched at his house."

She poked at the remaining donuts. "Sounds like a lot of work. Sounds like every guy you've ever dated before. One in particular."

I reached into the box. Me and sugar, we were going down today. "I see how you're drawing that comparison but Ben is just bad at home improvement and I have no patience for that shit. He's not a couch-dwelling, dog-stealing, no-motivation, self-centered man-baby."

"Well, I'm pleased we're not dealing with another man-baby," Andy replied. "But he still sounds like a lot of work."

"You're right," I conceded. "And I'm not one hundred percent certain he's not hanging around and dropping suggestive comments simply because he likes playing the game."

"Ugh, no," Andy wailed. "Not a game-player. We're not twenty-two anymore, thank you."

"Believe me, I know. That's one of the reasons I'm not sure about Ben," I confessed. "I'm not sure what he really wants. I'm not sure what would happen if I stopped going to him, you know?"

"I don't. Explain," Andy said, cutting a s'mores donut in half.

"The first time I met him was when I went across the street in the middle of the night, a supermajority of my boobs out, to complain about his tile saw. Then I went back and literally fixed his issues and listened to his problems. Aside from running into him when I was with Rob at Flour, I've always made the gestures."

"Does he text you?" she asked.

"Not really," I replied. "I assume that has something to do with fighting fires but I've only received"—I held up my finger as I scrolled through my phone—"three texts from him. One telling me he was on his way to the house the weekend we met there, one thanking me for helping him at the house, one asking if I wanted to show him how to hang drywall."

"A drywall date," Andy deadpanned. "Adorable."

"But the thing is, when I'm with him, he seems...I don't know. He's always an asshole but he's not a jerk if that makes sense."

"Makes sense. I know assholes who aren't jerks. Several." She reached for her tea and gestured at me with the cup. "You have to do something with these guys."

"I am aware of that," I said.

"Just sleep with both of them," she suggested. "Separately or together. Whatever."

I nearly choked on my iced coffee. "They were in the same room together once and wanted to tear each other apart. It had nothing to do with me and everything to do with exceeding the allowable amount of testosterone in a small space. They would've reacted the same way around any set of ovaries. Their heads would explode if I even suggested group naked time. No cuddle puddles for these boys."

Andy tapped her fingers against her lips for a moment. "It's interesting how *you* didn't object to my recommendations."

Good grief.

"I don't want a threesome," I whispered, swinging my gaze to the donut eaters around us. "And believe me, neither do Rob and Ben."

"Then you're test-driving both models," Andy supplied. "Right? That's where we're going with this?"

"Girl, where is your husband?" I asked, glancing around the bakery as if Patrick Walsh was hiding in the shadows. True story though, Patrick was known to keep a close eye on Andy when she was out shopping. He'd appeared in stranger places at stranger times, especially around the holidays.

"Why? You want his opinion?" Andy asked. "I have an idea which side he'd choose."

That was all we needed. Patrick's take on my feast-or-famine dating life.

"No, I don't need anything of the sort," I said, busying myself with my napkin. "I'm not sure I'm test-driving anyone."

"Oh, don't lie to me. Don't even try."

I met her gaze but glanced away quickly. Of course, I'd thought about it. About them. About reconciling the idea of seeing two men at the same time. About having sex with two men, not at the same time but damn near close enough. About unraveling the emotions long enough to make that plan plausible because I couldn't imagine my head and my heart allowing such an experiment without concerted effort.

"I'm not lying," I said quietly. "I'm not sure I can do it. With both of them." After a moment, I added, "Separately."

Andy lifted a shoulder. "You don't have to. You only have to do what you want."

From behind me, I heard, "Funny running into you here."

Swiveling in my seat, I expected to find Patrick. Like I said, he had a knack for showing up. But it wasn't Patrick.

Oh. Oh shit.

It was Rob.

CHAPTER
SIXTEEN

MY DATE WAS ENJOYING THIS TOO MUCH.

Far too much. Andy—the chick who didn't usually smile in the course of normal interactions—was fighting off a grin as wide as the Mississippi River and trying to hide it behind another donut.

"Oh. Hi," I said. He dropped his hand onto the back of my chair and gifted me with a warm smile before glancing to Andy. "Uh, Rob, this is my friend Andy. Andy, this is Rob."

At the same time, they replied, "I've heard a lot about you."

"Oh my god," I whispered.

"Sit a minute, won't you?" Andy asked Rob. "I eat donuts once, maybe twice a year so I'm not likely to share these with you. I hope that's not an impediment to you hanging with us."

Rob glanced inside the bakery box and back at Andy. "Once or twice a year? I'd heard you were a bit severe but that type of deprivation is insane."

"Severe?" Andy repeated, leveling me with an arched eyebrow. "You said I'm severe?"

"Severe is good," I replied. "It's great. We all want to be severe."

Andy studied Rob for a moment. "It's not insanity," she replied. "I don't favor sweets. On occasion, I'll get donuts or ice cream or chocolate on the brain. When I do, I put that craving to bed."

Glancing back at the half-empty box, Rob said, "Apparently."

"What brings you here today?" she asked.

"Rob has a sweet tooth," I replied. "The first time we had lunch together, he ordered two dozen cookies for himself."

"It wasn't two dozen," he argued. "Eighteen. Maybe nineteen. Twenty, tops. Nowhere near two dozen."

"That is still more than the average daily cookie consumption of adult humans," Andy said. "You're in elven territory there."

"Excuse me? What?" he asked, glancing between me and Andy.

"She's talking about witches and wizards and hobbits," I said. "Don't worry about it."

"What if I want to worry about it?" Rob asked, nudging my arm with his elbow.

I took that nudge and did him one better by leaning in, pressing the length of my arm against his. Goddamn, his eyes were fascinating. The ratio of amber to emerald seemed to vary according to the day, the light, the lunar phase. And he smelled incredible. I couldn't pin it to anything particular but I knew he smelled fresh. Rising above the heavenly scent of fresh donuts and coffee was noteworthy but doing it in a subtle, natural way was remarkable.

"Go ahead," Andy said. "Ignore me."

Still focused on Rob, I replied, "Don't worry. We will."

The t-shirt he wore was proof the angels and saints loved me. In fact, they wanted me squeezing my legs together in a bakery because his bare forearms gave me a tiny orgasm. A little squeak of an orgasm, just enough to part my lips and send a rush of heat over my body.

He reached for my iced coffee, his arm ghosting over the side of my breast as he moved. Without asking for permission, he pursed his lips around my straw and drank. The way he gazed at me as his throat bobbed, it was intimate. Almost overwhelming.

Tiny orgasm number two, thank you very much.

He set the cup down, murmuring, "Thanks." The backs of his knuckles ran over my arm and that was it. That was all it took for a third pulse to sizzle through me.

"You're welcome," I replied. "Although I don't recall offering it to you."

The corner of his lips lifted. "You didn't."

"You should ask." Then, I added, "Nicely."

"I ask when it's important." Still gazing at me, he jerked a shoulder up. "The rest of the time, I take what I want."

"That's horseshit," I replied.

Another shoulder jerk. "Maybe it is." He drew his fingertips over my wrist, my pulse, my palm. Curled his fingers around mine. "What are you going to do about it?"

I had a response to that. A wicked good response too. But the world tilted and my train of thought rolled away when I heard the unmistakable rasp of Ben's voice wafting toward me from the other side of the bakery. I was positive it was him. There was a rough quality to his words. I didn't have to set eyes on him to know it was him. I felt it like a cannonball of sweat rolling down my back.

Sweet mother, that sounded ridiculous. Really ridiculous. And I didn't have time for sweaty cannonballs, not when Rob was patiently waiting for a clapback to his grabby hands.

"Well, I'll have you know, I, um," I stammered. "Wouldn't you like to know what I'd do."

"Mmhmm." Rob grinned at me. "I would."

I didn't want to glance away from Rob and I didn't want to burst this bubble. But I had to know whether the major league perspiration was from Ben or—or I'd daydreamed his voice while Rob stroked my wrist.

I was praying it was the former because why the hell would my subconscious complicate matters? Wasn't my entire existence an object lesson in complicated? Why couldn't it be easy for once in my damn life? Meet a nice guy, go on normal dates, have satisfying sex, get married, live happily ever after. Not that I was on the road toward any of that today but I was enjoying some flirting and tiny orgasms.

What was wrong with that? Nothing. And why did everything have to be so difficult? *No.* Difficult was determining whether I was imagining men's voices without anyone catching anyone's attention while I did it.

I knew I wasn't shifting in slow motion but that was how I was seeing this moment. Like every second was a full heartbeat and every breath was a choice as I turned in the direction from which I'd heard his voice.

As Rob and Andy faded into my peripheral vision, I told myself I wasn't making any choices. I wasn't choosing anything—or anyone. I was merely locating the source of a sound. If I was right, if it was Ben, that didn't mean anything. It meant something but it didn't mean my inner compass was swinging toward him. I wasn't in any position to make that choice.

Innuendos and length-and-girth competitions weren't offers. They were the games played by boys who had over-sized opinions of themselves and little more to offer than their Swiss cheese promises. They weren't offering happy-ever-afters. It wasn't clear what—if anything—Ben offered, but Rob was only available for a short-term distraction. Nothing more than tiny orgasms in donut shops. And maybe that was the truth behind my daydream. Rob didn't check the right boxes. There was no future for us, not beyond sex without strings.

Even if Rob happened upon me in this donut shop, I had to keep searching. Keep hunting.

I turned in my seat, *slowly slowly slowly* but only in my mind, and found Ben on the other side of the shop. There he was, a goddamn manifestation of my biological clock with his tousled-slash-bedhead hair and drowsy eyes. If I hadn't known the thin line on his cheek was a scar, I would've guessed it was a crease from his pillow. I would've traced it with my index finger as I curled into his sleepy warmth.

Biological clocks like whoa.

But Ben wasn't looking at me. He wasn't hearing the clanging of any clocks.

No, his dark olive skin glowed like a Coppertone commercial and his biceps tested the limits of that t-shirt and his hand was low on a beautiful blonde's back. Her fingers were curled around his thick forearm and her long lashes—had to be extensions, that was no Cover Girl mascara—fluttered as she smiled at him. His lips grazed her cheek and he whispered something that had her laughing and nodding.

And there I was, staring at them. I rolled my eyes at all the manifestation bullshit I'd bought into a second ago but that didn't stop me from staring. Ben wasn't checking my boxes either.

As if he felt the weight of my gaze on his shoulders, Ben shifted toward me. He blinked twice, shaking his head. Without glancing away from me, he spoke to his companion. He held up a finger as if he was asking for a minute but then I saw his lips form a definite "No." There were other words but I couldn't make them out and then—then he was moving toward me.

Andy shook her cup, the tumble of ice cubes shaking my attention away from Ben. "I need more tea," she announced. "Do me a favor and don't get your pheromones on my donuts."

"Don't you dare leave," I hissed. I was mentally calculating the seconds until Ben reached our table and this morning went from coincidental to crazy. "Sit your skinny ass down and eat another donut."

"Did my invitation get lost in the mail again?" Ben asked as he dragged a chair over. He greeted Rob with a sharp stare—and an unimpressed frown at our joined hands—before turning his attention to Andy. He held out his hand. "Hi. Ben Brock. Nice to meet you."

"Hm." Andy, ever the ice queen, took a moment to wipe her fingers on a paper napkin and rake her gaze over the firefighter before accepting his hand. "Andy Asani. It's bold of you to invite yourself to sit down."

Ben pulled a bashful, *aw shucks, ma'am* smile. "In my line of work, most people are happy about me barging in."

"Hm." She treated him to another pursed-lip study. "In my line of work, most people are happy when I tear walls down but I don't make a habit of demolishing things in social situations."

"I think the lady is trying to say"—Rob gestured toward Andy—"that some manners wouldn't kill you, Brock."

Ignoring Rob, Ben turned toward Andy. "My bad, my bad. I just saw my neighbor"—he spared me a smile that could burn up the entire city—"and had to come. I take it you know the feeling, Russo."

Rob growled and...and yeah, that was the password to activating my nipples. I freed my hand and folded my arms on the edge of the table, aiming for easy, but Ben answered the gesture with a smirk.

Was there anything this guy didn't notice? No. Probably not. If I had to bet, I'd say he had an extra eye under all that wavy dark hair and that was his fatal flaw. The eye and the lack of basic handyman skills.

"Aren't you with someone?" I asked, craning my neck to find the blonde waiting in line. She was gazing at the menu board, her fingers pressed to her lips.

"Sara? Am I *with* her?" he asked, his eyebrows quirking like I'd asked whether he'd walked in with a flock of sheep. "No. No, dude, no. She's my buddy's sister. He lives in Georgia and she just moved to town. I met her at his wedding a few months ago and told her to get in touch when she got settled. I said I'd show her a few spots around town. Completely neutral territory. She's a little too"—he grimaced at the table before finding the words—"high-test. Right? Like, good people but she says some strange shit. You, my neighbor, you're all kinds of all right."

"As fascinating as this is," Rob started, "it sounds like you should probably get back to Sara. I don't think your buddy would appreciate you ditching his sister."

Ben shifted to face Rob. They glared at each other for an unpleasantly long period of time. It was like the extreme pauses during elimination ceremonies on reality television. That kind of long and unpleasant. I could've left the table, ordered another box of donuts, returned to the table, and eaten most of those donuts in the time they spent glaring at each other.

The stare-off broke only when another voice sounded over my shoulder. "There you are."

At once, Rob and Ben twisted to scowl at the man standing beside me. "Who the fuck is this?" Ben asked.

"Who the fuck are you?" he replied.

"What the fuck is going on?" Rob added.

"He's not with me," I yelled over the testosterone.

At once, Rob and Ben quipped, "What?"

Patrick pointed at Andy. "Mine." He pointed at me. "Not mine." He shuffled past Ben to join Andy on the bench against the wall. "I've been looking for you for half an hour. The Find My iPhone app is not very accurate around here."

"Say that again without sounding like a creeper," Andy said.

"Can't," Patrick replied. "Won't."

"Should," Andy said.

"Wife," Patrick responded.

"Creeper," Andy challenged. She laughed as he placed both hands on her face and moved in for a quick kiss. "Husbands can be creepers."

"Not true," he whispered. "I looked it up."

I choked back a laugh and busied myself with swiping a dollop of chocolate ganache off the remaining half of that Boston Crème.

Ben glanced to Rob, his hands held open. "Let's call that a small victory, yeah?"

"Yeah, it was beginning to feel like presidential primary season in here for a minute," Rob replied.

"I know, right?" Ben bobbed his head in agreement. "I can deal with you but add another motherfucker to the mix and I'm outta my depth."

"For a second I was thinking, holy shit, how many are there?" Rob remarked. "There's a difference between a 5K and an Ironman, you follow me?"

"Oh, I follow you," Ben said. He extended his fist across the table and bumped knuckles with Rob.

This time, I laughed out loud. There was a snort in there too, and it wasn't cute. Honestly, I didn't understand why these men were fighting—and forging a strange friendship —over me.

"Gigi, what's the deal here?" Patrick asked, wagging his finger between the unlikely duo of men in my life.

"This is Rob. That's Ben." I shrugged. "They're, I mean, they're here. With me. They showed up. I didn't invite them. But they're with me and it's…it's complicated."

"Can we decide right now to make it a lot less fuckin' complicated?" Ben asked.

"Yeah," Rob agreed, pressing his knee against my thigh. I was sure he interpreted my gasp as a response to him but it was his knee and Ben's hand covering my kneecap at the same time. That was always the way of it. Rob, then Ben, then me losing my shit. "Go find Sara and get the hell out of here. No more complications."

Ben shot him an unimpressed glare. "Not what I meant, cocksucker, and I think you know that."

I held my palms out as if holding them both in their

corners. "Listen, listen. I cannot handle the two of you at once."

"Thank god for that," Ben murmured. "I don't want to be anywhere near his dick."

It was my turn to shoot the unimpressed glares. I didn't care whether his fingers were tormenting that tender backside of my knee. He was getting the glare. "I definitely wasn't referring to that but thank you, Ben. That was super helpful."

"I don't think she'll have any complaints about my dick," Rob said, tipping his chin up. "She already knows what's under the hood."

Ben swiveled toward me, his eyebrows arched up. "I see I have some catching up to do." His stare dropped to my chest, pawing over my breasts. There was no mistaking the familiarity behind his gaze. "But answer me this: Am I the only one lagging behind? Or am I ahead where it matters?"

Never again was I walking across the street in the middle of the night while wearing a baggy tank top. Or asking a guy for dick pics.

Or anything loosely resembling either of those offenses.

Rob pressed his knee into my thigh. "Magnolia, what the fuck is he talking about right now?"

"Andy, I don't understand what's happening here," Patrick said. "What is this about?"

She handed him a chocolate cake donut, saying, "Just eat this and watch. I'll explain later."

I brought my fingers to my temples and rubbed. "Ben. Rob. It would be cool if you'd both shut up. Just stop talking and don't say anything. That would be perfect."

Ben drilled his index finger against the tabletop. "No, that's not how this is going to work."

I laughed again but this time it was stiff, a little annoyed. I batted his hand off my leg. He put it right back. I knocked him off again and this time, he heard the message. "You're not going to dictate the terms of my social life," I said to him. "That's not one of your options. Try again."

"Date us both," Rob said, sitting back in his chair. He crossed his arms over his chest. The move sent his knee sliding higher up my thigh. "We can't keep getting into pissing contests. If you're not willing to cut one of us loose today, then I propose you date us both for a bit."

"Rob, no," I argued. How could he handle that? It drove him crazy knowing I was *helping* Ben with his house. I couldn't imagine how he'd react knowing we were seeing each other. And I didn't want to do that to him after he'd discovered his ex was the worst woman on the planet. "That's not fair—"

"It's fair. It is. No secrets, no lies, no hiding. I'm not ready to walk away, Magnolia," Rob replied.

"But, Rob…" My words trailed off. I didn't know what to say. Why was he volunteering for this? Why was he still here? He wanted to forget his ex but instead of finding someone who could help him with that, he was signing up for these shenanigans. I didn't understand it.

"It's not going to be easy," he replied.

"No," I agreed, the word booming out. "You're damn right it's not easy."

"You could get the fuck outta here and make it easy," Ben said under his breath.

Rob kept his gaze on me as he pointed at Ben. "I'm going to rip this antagonistic bastard apart if we don't establish some rules of engagement real fast."

"I want to rip both of you apart and I've been here for ten minutes," Patrick said.

"Shush, sweetheart. We're just watching," Andy whispered.

I gestured toward Ben. Part of me still wondered whether he was all innuendo and no action. Whether it was a game to him. That I wasn't taking any of his shit or falling for his charms —aside from his forearms—and that was why he wanted me. That he savored this distraction from the grief rising around him. His silence during this portion of the discussion was giving me pause. "What do you think about this?"

Ben raked his fingers through his hair and blew out a breath. "I can live with it," he said. "I'd rather you send him on his way right now—"

"I'd rather you go find Sara," Rob interrupted. "What the fuck's wrong with you? Bringing a woman out for breakfast and then leaving her at the door? That's fucking rude."

If I didn't understand Rob, Ben was a brand-new level of incomprehensible. He wanted an escape from dealing with the loss of his grandmother but I couldn't help thinking he'd find himself at the limits of that escape soon.

"Sara is fine," Ben replied. "Don't you worry after her."

All at once, we shifted to put eyes on Sara. She stood at the counter; her back to us while she spoke to the clerk and pointed at pastries in the display case.

Patrick cleared his throat. "Shall we invite her over here?"

"Oh my god," I whispered to myself.

"Patrick, sweetie," Andy started, "we can manage many things but adding another person to this mix might test our capacity." She tipped her head toward Ben. "Are you sure this is where you're supposed to be, young man?"

"Yes, ma'am." Ben bobbed his head. "And no disrespect, but I don't think you can call me 'young man' when I'm thirty-eight."

Patrick pointed at him. "She'll call you the Abominable Snowman if she damn well wants to."

Ben considered this, nodded. "All right, man. All right. And, look. I might be an asshole but I'm not about to do wrong by my buddy's sister."

"I'm glad we've established the facts," Rob murmured.

"Are you required to be a dick all the time?" Ben asked him. "Like, is it part of your fraternity's honor code or something?"

"Now that you mention—" Rob stopped himself when he noticed me staring, eyes wide and lips parted, over his shoulder. He shifted, glancing in that direction. Under his breath, he murmured, "Oh. Wonderful."

Sara marched up to our table, her arms wrapped around two large bakery boxes. "Hi," she chirped, wiggling one hand from under the bakery box in an attempt at a wave. "This seemed like a fine idea when I was walking over here but now I realize I don't know eighty percent of you and I don't have a meaningful connection to the twenty percent. I blame the donuts." She glanced down at the boxes. "I bought one of each but now that seems excessive. I don't know what to do with twenty-eight donuts."

The men started to speak at once, but Andy silenced them with a quietly lethal "Stop." She studied Sara for a moment before asking, "Do you like farmers' markets?"

"In theory, yes," she replied. "In practice, I end up with an obscure collection of items I don't know how to cook and then I order takeout. Again." She shrugged. "I've had a spaghetti squash on my countertop for six weeks. It confounds me."

Andy waved off this argument. "We can fix that. Give me your number."

Rob tapped his fist against his chin before saying, "I'm no expert but I think it's time to let the squash go. Before it decomposes."

Patrick pointed at him. "That is solid advice."

Sara replied with a curt headshake. "I don't mind decomposition in flora or fauna." She glanced to the side, humming a bit. "Or humans."

"High-test," Ben said through a cough.

"Yeah, give me your number," Andy insisted. Her thumbs flew over her phone's touchscreen as Sara rattled off the digits. "Since we have you here, can you clear something up for us?"

"Does it pertain to human or plant decomposition?" she asked.

Andy barreled forward, undaunted by the straight-up ickiness of Sara's response. "Neither." Pointing to Ben, she continued. "Did this gentleman behave appropriately in your company?"

Sara's gaze swung between Andy and Ben. "Excuse me?"

"Did he invite you out and then ditch you?" Patrick asked.

Frowning, Sara studied Ben for a beat. "Oh, no. No. He asked if I wanted to meet his neighbor. I'm not sure which one of you that is but I wasn't sure about compounding the layers of newness here. I think that's why I bought all these donuts. Coping mechanism." She crouched down, close to Ben. "Here. Take the top box. I'm going to bring the other one to work."

Ben collected the box, saying, "You heard the lady."

"Yeah, so," Sara started, glancing around the table, "I should go."

"Get rid of that spaghetti squash," Rob said.

As Sara darted away, Andy called, "I'll text you about the farmers' market."

"What's the big deal about farmers' markets?" Ben asked.

Patrick pried open the new box. "Don't ask."

"Yes, ask," Andy argued. "Don't listen to him. I have thoughts on the best markets in and around the city."

As Andy launched into her dissertation on the region's agricultural output and corresponding farm-to-table retail model, I curled in on myself. It was easier that way, quieter. And I needed to step back from this reality to hear my thoughts. How else could I kick around the notion of dating both Rob and Ben?

It didn't seem real and I couldn't determine whether I wanted it to be real. Whether I wanted Rob to backtrack or soft-pedal his suggestion. It was less risky than to imagine myself as the woman in a relationship with two men.

But it wasn't the men making this risky. It was the illusion of abundance. I'd spent the entire winter wandering through the Death Valley of Dating and I knew *that* was my reality. This—Rob and Ben and all of it—was a mirage. An optical illusion. A set of atmospheric conditions refracting my greatest wants and needs through heated air.

I knew this was an illusion, but that didn't stop me.

"If we do this," I started, glancing at Ben and Rob, "we're going to be civil. This animosity was cute for a hot second and now I'm over it."

"I can be civil," Rob replied.

"I'll tattoo 'civil' anywhere you want it," Ben added.

"If we do this," I continued, "we're going to stop running into each other like this."

Rob folded his arms on the table, laughing. "I live in the new building around the corner," he said, pointing toward the street. "And I've told you I like this place."

"Best donuts in Boston, a million years running," Ben said. "Where the fuck else would I take the new chick in town?"

I wagged my iced coffee cup at them. "Whatever. I don't care how it happened, we're going to make sure it doesn't happen again. No more group dates."

Andy raised her hand. "Does that include me? Because I'd love to just observe this social experiment."

"Same," Patrick added.

I rolled my eyes, setting aside her question for a time when I didn't have Ben and Rob staring me down. "No gaming the system. Don't look for loopholes. Be legit or be gone." Ben started to speak but I stopped him, adding, "Unless it's civil, don't say it."

"Motherfucker," he murmured. "I'm gonna bite my fuckin' tongue off before noon."

Rob smiled at me and said, "My tongue is just fine."

He didn't check the boxes. He didn't want any emotional attachment or intimacy. But hell, he knew how to heat me up with the barest of touches, glances, words. "Thank you for that update."

Ben closed his eyes, pressed his fist to his mouth. "Time limit," he gritted out. "We need a fucking time limit on this experiment."

"Yes, please," Rob added.

I looked around the bakery, hoping to find an answer tucked in between the dough and yeast and sugar. I found none, only a gentle reminder in the form of chalkboard signs heralding the impending launch of the seasonal special strawberry-rhubarb glazed donut that summer was almost here. The strawberry season was obscenely short. Most of the local growers I knew managed only a two- or three-week harvest.

I could manage more than that. *Right? Yeah.* I needed more than that and…and I had this on lock.

"The summer," I said. "I'll give you two the summer."

I wasn't certain of many things but I knew this wasn't what my mother had in mind.

CHAPTER
SEVENTEEN

My dates—dates, plural, as there were now two of them —wasted no time. I'd barely shooed them out of the donut shop before the texts started hitting like rockets during The Blitz. I held my phone's screen up for Patrick and Andy's review but the two of them were too busy critiquing the flavor profiles of the remaining donuts to notice.

"Are you seeing this?" I prompted, my arm still suspended over the table.

"I love when you get all fired up about things," Andy mused. "It's almost as entertaining as when everyone BCCs me on emails to Patrick because they erroneously believe I don't know he's a tyrant. Better yet, they think I'm going to intervene on their behalf."

"It's more entertaining when I'm sitting there with you while those emails come in," Patrick said as he studied a raspberry-lime donut. "I love watching you smirk at your screen."

"And you get to watch me smirk at my screen because

you've parked yourself at my desk and forgotten you have a desk of your own."

Patrick arched his brows up, shrugging as he bit into the donut. "And?"

"And you have all day, every day to love on each other whereas I've tripped into a universe where I'm somehow seeing two guys," I said, reaching for a paper napkin. I balled it up and reached for another. "Two of them. Two separate men. At once. How did I get two? Really, all I need is one. Just one."

"You had the opportunity to eliminate one of them," Patrick said.

"This isn't the proper spot for an elimination ceremony," I replied. "Additionally, my life is not a reality dating show."

"You don't want to eliminate either of them," Andy said. "I remember when Rob first matched with you on that app. You were hooked on him. Then you yelled at the cute firefighter that one night and you were hooked on him too. You don't want to eliminate either."

"I beg your pardon," Patrick said, shifting on the bench seat to face her. "Which cute firefighter?"

"I'm married." Andy wiggled her snowball-sized ring at him. "Not dead. There is a difference." Patrick grumbled something under his breath and went back to his donut. "And you, my dear," she said, pointing her iced tea at me. "You deserve this, Gigi. You've kissed all the frogs. Some toads too. Now you get your choice of, you know, non-amphibious creatures."

She was right about the frogs. And the toads. I'd given too many days to men who cared little for me. I'd settled for nothing and convinced myself it was everything. I'd smiled through the warning signs and turned a blind eye to unacceptable behavior. I'd excused the inexcusable—lies, cheating, even stealing—and told myself it was as good as I was going to get.

I'd made bad choices, and I'd allowed myself to stay in bad situations. It took a kidnapped dog and one hell of a talking-to from one of my very best friends—and then a relapse with another no-good man and another Come to Jesus talking-to—but I knew how to spot douchebags and fuckboys and assholes now. And I knew I deserved more than that.

It was a strange thing, being okay with myself. I was still getting used to it. Most days, I wasn't used to the fit and feel while others forgot I was wearing it at all.

"While you're thinking deep thoughts, I'm going to eat the last donut," Andy said.

"Are you going to share it with me?" Patrick asked. "I'd like you to share it with me."

Andy met his gaze and bit into the donut. "Only because you're cute," she said, handing the pastry to him.

Rather than watching them eyefuck each other over the food, I turned to my phone.

Ben: There's a cool place in Revere Beach. Hasn't been hit by hurricanes or hipsters. Good beer, good food. I think you'd dig it. Let's go. Tonight.
Rob: I just called Talulla and asked them to hold a table for two at eight. I've heard the peach upside-down cake is crazy good. Does that time work for you?
Ben: Or I can pick up food and swing by your place. I'm good for a chill night on the deck if you are.

Rob: If you're not up for dinner out, we can do takeout. What's your preference?

Ben: Your choice, babe.

Rob: I'm down for anything you want.

IN THE SPIRIT of full transparency and a strong desire to avoid jealous man tantrums, I started a group message with Rob and Ben.

Magnolia: Hey guys. I'm going to the game at Fenway with my brothers tonight. Some other time. Okay?

Ben: Enjoy it. Talk soon.

OF COURSE, he responded first. Such a competitive little shit.

Rob: If it goes into extra innings and you want to crash in the city, you're always welcome at my place.

Ben: FLAG ON THE PLAY

Ben: PASS INTERFERENCE

Ben: Get your ass back to the line of scrimmage, boy.

Rob: Settle down. The pass is good. No interference.

Magnolia: You guys. For real. Chill.

Rob: As I'm sure you can see, I'm completely chill.

Ben: You wouldn't know chill if you were literally frozen.

Magnolia: If you two weren't amusing, you'd be annoying as fuck.

I SLIPPED my phone into my bag as a smile pulled at my lips. Andy was right. I was hooked on these two.

CHAPTER
EIGHTEEN

Ben: I'm going to mow your lawn.

Magnolia: Is that some kind of innuendo?

Ben: No. I'm mowing your lawn.

Magnolia: With…a lawn mower?

Ben: Yeah.

Magnolia: I'm sorry but do you know how to operate a lawn mower?

Ben: Of fucking course.

Magnolia: I want to believe that so much.

Ben: It's going to be awesome. Just you wait.

Magnolia: Or maybe you find a different project?

Ben: It's no sweat.

Magnolia: Mmhmm. Okay. But it's not actually a lawn so it doesn't require mowing.

Ben: What the fuck is it?

Magnolia: Evergreen moss with patches of low-growing turf grass.

Ben: Why?

Magnolia: There are several reasons.

Ben: Such as...?

Magnolia: Lawns waste upwards of 3 trillion gallons of water each year plus hundreds of millions of gallons of gas for mowing and pesticides. Those pesticides then destroy aquatic ecosystems with toxic rainwater runoff.

Magnolia: Lawns also drive out pollinators and native animal and plant species.

Ben: Okay. I won't mow your moss.

Magnolia: Thank you.

Magnolia: And thank you for offering.

Ben: Let's not give me too much credit.

———

Rob: Sox game tonight. At Fenway.

Magnolia: Yes, sir.

Rob: Got a date?

Magnolia: lol, always...because I share a set of season tickets with my brothers.

Rob: Ah. All right. Enjoy.

Rob: ...but if you want to stay overnight in the city, hit me up.

Magnolia: Do you have room for Linden too? He's about your height but probably has 30-40 pounds on you.

Rob: I will get Linden a very comfortable suite at the Taj.

Magnolia: I think we're good but I'll keep you posted.

———

Ben: I brought your recycling bins in from the curb.

Ben: After they were emptied.

Magnolia: Thank you—and good clarification.

Ben: It's the least I can do without fucking up your moss.

Magnolia: I appreciate it.

Ben: Your dog, though. He didn't like me hanging around your yard.

Magnolia: For what it's worth, he barks at my brothers that way too when they visit. Anyone outside the house is the enemy.

Ben: Smart boy.

———

Ben: Explain to me again why we can't work on one room at a time.

Magnolia: Because you ripped the walls and floors and windows out and we have to fix those things first.

Magnolia: You can't spend your time on finding cool shower fixtures until you have walls. You need walls.

Ben: You're saying I should stop buying stuff.

Magnolia: Among other things, yes.

Ben: Can you tell me what else you're saying because I don't know how to read between the home renovation lines.

Magnolia: You need to figure out what you're doing with this place. Once you determine whether you're renovating the entire place to sell or renovating it for you to live in or selling it as-is right now, other questions will answer themselves.

Ben: I'm not ready to sell it. I don't know. I just can't be finished with it yet.

Magnolia: I get that.

Ben: No. It doesn't make sense.

Ben: But I should sell it. I don't want a house in Beverly, of all places.

Magnolia: HEY

Ben: Sorry.

Ben: But I don't want a house. I don't want the responsibility.

Magnolia: And you don't want to sell it.

Ben: Not yet.

Magnolia: In that case, you shouldn't buy any more shower fixtures.

Magnolia: Any fixtures. At all.

Ben: I just don't know when I'll snap out of this. I need to get on with my life.

Magnolia: I think you have to take it as it comes and do your best. It's not the sort of thing you can rush.

Ben: I'm trying.

Magnolia: I know, sweetie.

Magnolia: Do you want to talk about it? You can tell me about your grandmother.

Ben: No.

Magnolia: Okay.

———

Rob: Here's how fucked up my day has been.

Rob: I had a call at midnight with Osaka and then a 4 a.m. call with Brussels and sometimes I hate that I'm good at my job because my job is exhausting.

Magnolia: That is more fucked up than my day.

Rob: What's going on with you?

Magnolia: Nothing important. Just issues with subcontractors and materials and timelines and budgets and also weather.

Rob: Yeah, so, nothing much.

Magnolia: Nope.

Rob: Have you eaten lunch?

Magnolia: Lunch? What is this lunch you speak of?

Rob: Where are you?

Magnolia: Back Bay. Why?

Rob: I'm sending lunch over to you.

Magnolia: You don't have to do that.

Rob: I want to.

Rob: Mortadella and raspberry seltzer, right?

Magnolia: Only if you're having cookies with a side of smoked turkey.

Rob: Give me an address.

Magnolia: Are you delivering this lunch yourself?

Rob: That depends. Do you want to see me?

Magnolia: I wouldn't send you and your cookies away.

Rob: That's the nicest thing you've ever said to me.

Magnolia: It's the first time you've offered to hand-carry lunch to me.

Rob: We can make a habit of this.

Magnolia: Let's see how this one goes before making any rituals.

Rob: Come on! You know how it will go. We'll eat cookies and I'll invite my cock into the conversation and your day will be better for it.

Rob: Also, I want to watch you boss people around.

Magnolia: Is that so?

Rob: Yeah. I need to add some texture and dimension to my fantasies.

Magnolia: Since it's for a good cause…the brownstone at the end of Fairfield between Beacon and Marlborough Streets.

CHAPTER
NINETEEN

My date was a renovation disaster.

I didn't know where to find the patience to keep up with Ben's missteps. When he fouled up the mitered angles on the molding I tasked him with cutting, I stopped to contemplate whether he was doing it on purpose. He had to be doing it on purpose. How else could someone fuck up on the regular like this?

But he wasn't doing it on purpose. I watched him as I measured and re-measured the dining room, one eye on the wall, the other on Ben. He was trying to get it right. He studied each board until I had to wonder if it was talking to him, positioned the miter box then checked the angle I'd written on the back of the board, and then positioned the box again. By all accounts, he should've had it right.

He just *didn't*. He didn't have it at all.

When I saw him switch the saw on, I dropped my hold on the tape. It recoiled into the device as I crossed the room. "Wait, wait, wait," I shouted, waving my hands to capture his attention.

He glanced up at me through his safety goggles—one of my victories on this project—with a confused scowl. "I haven't even done anything," he said. "How is it already wrong?"

In the week since deciding I was going to do this wild thing and date both Rob and Ben at the same time—separately—Ben never failed to compete the hardest. He was the first one to text in the morning and the last at night. He was working for it. The gold star, the prize. The validation—the distraction—of winning.

Ben did all those things but Rob...Rob was subtle. He asked after my work, my dog, my family. He made small but significant gestures that proved he was paying attention. It was a strange form of courtship but I liked those things. I appreciated those things.

I knew it buttered Rob's buns that Ben got "extra" time with me because I was physically incapable of letting this house fall into shambles. For reasons I didn't understand but nonetheless appreciated, Ben didn't compete while we were working on the house. He wasn't angling for a gold star here, that much was certain. He was his regular brash, ballsy self when he pulled on the gloves and goggles. No jockeying, no sweet words for the sake of earning another point on the leaderboard.

It helped that I didn't see this as Ben-and-Magnolia time because I was squarely in Gigi territory while I worked. I wasn't a girl here, I was the job boss. I wasn't anyone's to woo.

"It's still wrong, buddy." I reached across him to turn off the saw's spinning wheel. "Trust me, it's possible."

Ben pushed the goggles to the crown of his head with a

grunt. His hands found his hips and his body shifted into Very Annoyed, a pose in three parts.

One: hands on the hips. This often included his sleeves rolled up to his elbows, but there were no sleeves today. Nope. No sleeves. Ben was wearing a tank that fit like a sunburn and it was bare, bronzed skin for days. I repeat: *no sleeves.*

Two: scowl face. It didn't stop at the tilt of his lips. This expression involved narrowed eyes, a pinched forehead, and a ticking jaw underneath a day or two of stubble. The scar running the length of his cheek seemed to deepen, darken with the scowl.

Three: wide stance. He stood there, his feet planted shoulder-width apart and his entire body tense as if he was daring a tornado to rock him from this spot. Today, this stance accentuated the narrow line of his waist and the way his jeans seemed to hang there like a parabola. The button sitting at the vertex forced my attention low, *low.*

It was funny that, in the Cartesian coordinate system, the focus sat above the vertex in a positively opened parabola. In the Ben Brock system of screwing up basic tasks while wearing fuckhot jeans, the vertex and the focus were almost the same thing. And that had me thinking about focal length. If the vertex and focus were the same thing in this weird world where I was dating two men—and remodeling a house with one of them—what was the focal length? Fair question, right? I already knew Rob's, ahem, length. I could at least calculate Ben's.

If this parabola's vertex was at the origin, and if it opened in the positive y direction, then it was only a matter of solving $y = x^2\ /\ 4f$.

Trigonometry. Always useful.

"You're staring at my crotch again," he said.

I waved him away but kept my gaze on his waist. *Again.* As if I did it often. "I'm solving for *f.*"

"Yeah, me too."

He pulled his gloves off and tossed the goggles to the workbench. He advanced on me but I was only peripherally aware of it as that shiny vertex, the one stamped with the jeans' brand, moved closer. I lost sight of that point when he stepped into my space, his midnight eyes still Very Annoyed.

Ben's hands found my hips and he forced me backward until my ass hit the wall. "I have had," he started, his fingertips driving into my soft tissue like he was trying to snatch something from beneath the surface, "I've had enough, Magnolia."

I dragged my gaze up, over his neck, his chin, that scowl, that scar. And I met his eyes. He was still Very Annoyed but there was more. Something I needed time to catalog without him holding me, without his chest rising and falling as breath moved through him.

"As have I. Wasting good building materials is ridiculous," I said. "I'm firmly against filling up landfills because someone isn't following directions."

His eyes fluttered shut and he bowed his head a bit, as if the weight of my words was dragging him down. But then he edged up, his scruffy cheek passing over my jaw. "Do you know how much it costs me to fuck up in front of you? How much I fucking hate that I'm getting this wrong? That I'm surrounded by proof that I can't do anything right?" he whispered. His hold on my hips tightened. It didn't hurt. That was the benefit of having plenty of padding there. "I keep telling myself that I'll get it right and then—then I'll earn it."

"Earn what?"

"But I don't," he continued, ignoring my question. "I don't get it right. Do you have any idea how much I want to do this thing, even though it's too fucking late? How much I want to follow your orders and meet your expectations? And then how much I love it when you don't put up with my shit?"

"Oh, you enjoy that?" I pursed my lips in exaggerated annoyance. "I was unaware."

"There are so many things you don't know," Ben whispered, his scruff rasping over my cheek. "I'm not saying that like some kind of mansplainer asshole. My grandmother didn't raise me to be like that." He squeezed his eyes shut, blew out a breath. "But you don't know what it does to me when you come in here yelling orders with that little t-shirt and those jeans and the tool belt straight outta the 'Girls Who Hammer' edition of *Playboy*."

"The March '92 edition?" I quipped. "Or the August of 2011?"

He pressed his teeth to my jaw, growling. "Both."

"Mmhmm" was my only response. What was there to say? I'd already used my allotted sassy tokens for this conversation and I was notoriously bad when it came to handling deliciously hot, tense interactions like a normal human lady. Instead, I went for obscure humor (I mean, I'd been talking trig) and awkward comments or—even better! —straight-up silence.

Again, it was no surprise I was single.

"Magnolia?" he asked, pressing his body against mine. He felt glorious. The sweetest rock and hard place in the world.

I ran my hands up his back, settling on his shoulders. My

fingers slipped under his shirt, introducing myself to his skin. "Yeah, Ben?"

"I'm going to kiss you," he said. "If that's not what you want, tell me now."

He kept one hand on my hip but released the other as he stroked my waist, my flank, my shoulder. When he reached my face, he dragged his knuckles down the line of my jaw before tucking stray hairs over my ear.

"Tell me now," he repeated.

I met his gaze, blinked. I didn't say no. I wasn't going to.

Ben kissed me like the sand was almost out of the hourglass and this moment was slipping away. Fierce, unrelenting, frantic. His tongue swept over mine in a command, an order levied just as sharp and exacting as any of mine. And I surrendered to him. I wanted it.

"I've needed this for so long," he murmured against my cheek. He pressed a kiss to the corner of my lips. It was sweet. Chaste, even. It was nothing like the heat pulsing between us but it was right. "Goddamn, it's been so long."

"Not that long," I replied. "We met a few weeks ago."

"Yeah and you came in here with your tits out, honey," he said, his hold on my hip shifting to my backside. "I almost followed you across the street that night."

"Almost, huh?"

"I stood there, staring out the door, wondering how a little thing like you could walk in and rock my entire world." Ben nodded, dragging his rough scruff against my skin. Up my neck, my jaw, behind my ear. Right into tingle territory. "I watched from the front door. After you yelled at me for forty minutes."

"No more than five minutes."

"I watched you go home, turn off the lights. Thought

about you getting into bed in that loose shirt. Jesus. Held on to the doorframe so hard I yanked the damn thing off."

"Is that what happened?"

"It is," he replied with a laugh. "I'm going to kiss you again. The molding will wait. We're doing this now. Okay? Answer me this time. I want the words."

"Okay," I said.

I didn't have to solve for f this morning. Not when the focal length was pressed right up against my belly.

CHAPTER
TWENTY

MY DATE WAS GOING TO TOWN ON A WAFFLE CONE.

When I noticed this, two thoughts crossed my mind.

First, demolishing a double scoop of gelato should be an Olympic sport, and second, that tongue had skills.

"Not liking the pistachio?" Rob asked when he took a breath.

His lips were shiny. It reminded me of...*mmm*. Like I needed that reminder. Every time I was with Rob, my body felt like a harp string pulled too tight.

Just waiting to be plucked.

I hadn't been plucked in ages. And I did mean ages. I barely remembered how a good plucking went but I knew shiny lips usually meant we were off to a good start.

I glanced down at the small dish in my hands. I hadn't touched it. I tended to do that when Rob was around. Forget about everything save for the quiver of anticipation conveniently located right between my legs, at least for a few minutes. "Oh, no. It's fine. I like pistachio. Love pistachio. It's great. Like, if I had to rank the nuts, I'd put pistachio right up—"

Rob swirled his tongue around the inner edge of the waffle cone while he stared at me, and yeah, yeah this was what it meant for panties to fall right off. For a chick with hips like mine, that was some kind of magic.

"Stop that," I said through a groan. I reached for him, wrapping my fingers around his forearm. "You have no idea what you're doing right now."

I glanced around Hanover Street, expecting to find someone staring at this obscene display of tongue prowess. Perhaps a mother covering her child's eyes or a police officer writing up a ticket for public indecency. The only thing I found was pistachio gelato melting onto my hand.

"No idea?" he repeated with a grin. "That's what you think?"

My eyes widened. This man. Mercy, this man. "Then you're doing this on purpose?"

He speared his tongue into the gelato, scooping up a creamy bit. It was filthy. We'd spent the past two hours together, wandering around the North End and talking about everything and nothing until we decided on dessert.

But now I understood. The jig was up.

To Rob, this was the audition. Not the time we spent talking about our families—my brothers, his sister—our work, our long paths from kids not knowing what to do with ourselves and doddling in and out of college and crummy jobs to mostly successful adults, our enjoyment of campy disaster movies like *Volcano* and *Deep Impact* and *2012*, our hope the world wasn't driving itself off a cliff and our corresponding inability to watch as we careened toward the edge.

All of that? The warm-up. The gelato was the performance.

He reached for my gelato, freeing it from my hands and setting it on the bench beside him. Then he reached for my hand—the one with melted pistachio dotting the fleshy space between my thumb and forefinger—and brought it to his mouth. Licked. Sucked. *Suuuuuucked*.

"What—what are you doing?" I stammered. He swept his tongue over my skin, and the fabric formerly known as my panties was gone. Just gone with the wind. "We're on the street. This is a street, Rob. With people. There are people around and you're—you're—what are you even doing?"

"Just a preview, love," he murmured as his teeth scraped over my hand.

I hadn't considered going back to Rob's place when he invited me out for a walk tonight but that was the trouble with these boys. They kept turning simple, innocent moments into situations where my underwear, my inhibitions, and my intentions flew out the window.

Not that I'd taken off my underwear for either of the men in my life right now but I'd thought about it. Oh, yes. I'd thought. Thinking. Lots of thinking. That was exactly it.

But I could barely think of anything aside from the way he teased my hand. Whoa, that was weird. Right? Never had a man sucked on my hand.

"We're not in the right place for a preview, Rob," I said, a gasp slipping through my words.

He laughed, shaking his head as his teeth pressed against my skin again. Damn, that was good. I couldn't explain why but it was *good*. "That's hardly a problem," he replied. "Grab my phone. Back left pocket."

I didn't move. I couldn't move. Not with his lips on my hand and the promise of something *more* lingering in the air.

Rob pressed the remains of the waffle cone to my free hand after a minute. "Hold this," he ordered.

Once I had my fingers around his cone—fuck, this was *such* strange foreplay—he pulled his mobile from his pocket. I watched while he keyed in the code right in front of me. He didn't angle the phone away or make any attempt to conceal the numbers. Then he shot me a *see what I did there?* smile. He wanted me to know. This man, the one who melted down at the notion of anything more serious than working off some nasty breakup energy, was offering access to his digital life.

What was happening right now?

"Since we're not in the proper place for this, I'm gonna call my car service," he said. "All right?"

"You have a car service?" I asked, focusing on all the right things. "Not Uber or Lyft but a legit on-demand driver?"

Rob jerked a shoulder up but offered no other response. He wasn't flashy when it came to money. I liked that about him. More than that, I liked the maturity and sense of self backing it up. Just as he'd known who he was when he first approached me with his performance statistics, he made no attempt to argue his worth. He knew it and he let it speak for itself. That was enough.

"That's convenient," I murmured.

"It is," he replied. "I don't use it too often but when I have somewhere I'd like to be or someone I'd like to be with, they get me there in a hurry. I appreciate that."

Nodding, I asked, "If you call this car service, what happens then?"

"Whatever you want." He shifted, moving his lips from

my hand to the crook of my neck. Yeah, like I needed this to get more intimate. "No expectations. We can go back to my place and avoid the news if you want. Watch a movie or just sit outside with some wine. I'm embarrassed to say there's a real shortage of living things on my terrace." When I frowned up at him in confusion, he continued. "I thought it was better to tell you about it now than conceal the fact."

"Thankfully, I know someone who can fix that," I said, laughing.

Did I want to go home with Rob? To this point, I hadn't been in a confined space with either of the men on my dance card. I wasn't counting the time spent at Ben's renovation house. That was mostly work and the occasional moment pressed against the wall while he kissed me, and it wasn't as though we had any soft surfaces around for it to go much further. Maybe I was splitting hairs or drawing wobbly lines but that was the beautiful part of making the rules. If I was content with my decisions, that was the only thing that mattered.

And I was content with Rob in confined spaces.

"Okay," I said. "Let's go to your place."

———

ROB LIVED in a new building in the South End, all concrete and exposed ductwork and huge, yawning windows. The furniture was reliably manly—a leather sectional, a big-ass television, no curtains. Somehow this wide-open space felt cozy. It probably had something to do with the vintage rug on the floor, the books packed into a set of shelves, the pile of throw pillows discarded under the coffee table.

A wall of floor-to-ceiling glass doors offered a panoramic

view of the city, just like the long, skinny photos sold at Quincy Market. But better because the real thing was always better. Those edgeless doors also showed off a terrace with a serious lack of green.

"You weren't joking about the shortage of living things out there," I said, tipping my chin toward the terrace. It was gray. Just...gray. Whoever designed the masculine-but-comfortable interior flaked out on the exterior.

"What's your recommendation?" Rob asked. He was on the other side of the room, plugging in his phone.

"If you want my recommendation, you need to call my office and make an appointment," I said, mostly joking. "My assistant will walk you through my consultation fees. I'll warn you right now, they're high."

"Worth every penny," he replied.

"This really is sad," I said, sweeping my gaze to each end of the terrace. It was at least thirty feet long, probably ten feet deep. Completely barren. A concrete wasteland. "You have the right exposure for some big containers filled with perennials. Grassy, maybe flowering. Lavender if you can handle the bees. Just something to keep the local pollinators busy. Maybe a Japanese maple or a flowering cherry. Then again, you have space for both. This isn't the right setup for rainwater catchment but we can work out a smart irrigation system, no problem."

His hands landed on my hips. I liked the feel of him there. Strong, capable, certain. I liked him. I didn't need his hands or his tongue to confirm it.

I smiled up at him. "But only if you want more than sad, empty concrete."

"I moved in not too long ago." He blinked away the teasing fun of this moment, replacing it with a solemn frown. It lasted no longer than an eyeblink but I saw every cold, bloodless memory of his exes blow through him. Inside that eyeblink, I felt the sinking devastation of finding yourself a fool. They'd lived together. They were going to be engaged, married. And now I was here and his terrace was a wasteland because none of that existed anymore. He blinked again, forced a laugh, gestured to the living space. "I'm not home enough to take care of anything."

I pointed at his white dress shirt. The man knew how to wear a shirt, I'd give him that. Especially when the collar was open and his cuffs were rolled to his elbows. *Mmmmmm.* My god. Rolled-up sleeves got me every time. Almost as good as the tie smoothing.

"You pay someone to wash and press these shirts," I said, my hand on his chest because I could. "You probably pay someone to clean this place too. You can pay someone to look after a few potted plants."

"Correct on all counts," he said. "I'll call your office tomorrow."

"You do that," I quipped, laughing. "Let's grab some wine and—" I looked around, not knowing how I wanted to direct these activities. "And, um—"

"Let's just start with wine," he said, tipping his head toward the kitchen.

When I nodded, he hooked his arm around my waist and led me across the open room. His kitchen island gleamed with stainless steel and white marble—and a small mountain of mail. "What is this all about?" I asked.

Rob was busy squatting in front of the wine fridge, two bottles tucked between his chest and arm as he inspected the label on another. "I just don't get to it. Everything I need is online so I'm not missing anything."

"I find that extremely difficult to believe." I shook my head and started sorting. If the guy could tell me the exact specifications of his anatomy and suck my hand in the North End, I could organize his mail. It was fine.

Magazines in one pile, catalogs in another. Assorted junk in the empty fruit bowl. Bills off to the side. Anything that looked vaguely personal went on the opposite side. Rob watched while I did this, a smirk on his lips as he popped the wine, set glasses on the counter, filled them. Never stopped with the smirk.

"Anything good in there?" he asked, sliding a balloon-bodied glass toward me.

"It doesn't matter if it's good," I replied. "You have to go through this stuff. What if there's a birthday card in here from your grandmother or a reminder postcard from your dentist?"

"That would be miraculous since my grandmother's been dead for twelve years."

"But don't forget about the dentist."

Near the bottom of the pile, I found a thick white envelope. It nearly crossed the line from paper into fabric. Rob's name was scrawled across the center in elegant calligraphy. I flipped the envelope over, glancing at the return address as if it would mean something to me. It did not.

"Looks important," I said, handing it to Rob.

Brows furrowed, he tore into the envelope. He stared at the flat card for a long moment as he pulled a deep breath in through his nose and then pushed it out in a whole-body sigh.

"I'm guessing that's not your dentist," I said.

He shook his head, dropped the card and envelope. He

flattened his hands on the countertop as he stared up at the ceiling.

I lifted the card and skimmed the ornate lettering.

PLEASE JOIN US TO CELEBRATE THE ENGAGEMENT OF MISTER EDWARD HUNZERT AND MISS MIRANDA LASALLES

I DIDN'T RECOGNIZE the names, but I didn't need those details to understand the situation. The bride was Rob's ex. He didn't need to tell me; the reaction told me everything I needed to know. And the groom, that was Rob's former best friend.

I continued reading, grabbing key details as I went. Ritz-Carlton. Next month. Black tie optional. Registered at Bloomingdale's.

Goddamn Bloomie's.

"We're going," I announced, still staring at the card. It was thicker than most paper plates. I could eat a sandwich off this invitation and then use the envelope as a napkin.

"We're fucking *what*?" he snapped, his gaze meeting mine for the first time since opening the envelope.

"We're going," I repeated. "You, me, black tie optional. We are going because A, fuck *her*. B, fuck *him*. And C, they can go fuck themselves."

Rob stared at me from the other side of the island for a long, long moment. The kind of moment that made me wonder whether I'd made a terribly wrong turn. I had a habit of doing that. Making the worst choice and convincing myself to go full steam ahead even though my belly shimmered with bubbles of doubt. You name the bad decision, I'd made it. But this didn't feel like one of those times.

This felt absolutely right.

Rob rounded the island and stepped into my space, crowding me until my back hit the hard marble edge. His hands went to my face, his fingers in my hair. He held me like that, his forehead pressed to mine and his gaze all over me. Then he kissed me. It started soft, brushing sweet, gentle kisses on my lips. But then it turned wild, starved. Biting, bruising, crushing. But good. All those things, good. So good.

He boosted me up onto the counter, stepped between my legs, locked my ankles around his waist, thrust against my center, groaned when his length rocked into my heat.

"You," he said against my lips, dragging his finger from my ear along the line of my jaw, down my neck, over the jut of my breastbone. "You are dangerous."

"Why's that?" I ran my fingers through his auburn hair while my thoughts pinged between wondering whether I could rip his shirt open and send the buttons flying like I'd always wanted, and whether I was in danger of knocking over the wine if I shifted back an inch.

"You keep making me do things I don't think I want," he said. "First it was dating you. Then it was sharing you with the firefighter. Now it's showing up at that engagement party. I didn't want any of this. Not a single thing. But here I am, eating ice cream and talking myself out of hating the other guy and—and seriously thinking about seeing Eddie and Miranda at their fucking engagement party. Because of you. Because you want it and I can't help but do everything you want. I don't know why, Magnolia. Why am I doing this? Tell me, please, love. Tell me how you're putting me back together because I need to know."

I reached for his buttons. I was going to undo them one by one. No dramatic shows for me. Just step by step, sliding into the space he never wanted me—or anyone else—to occupy. Part of it felt wrong, as if I was forcing him to follow a path he didn't choose and would eventually resent.

But the other part...it was right. This was right. Rob and I, we were right. At least right now.

"I asked nicely," I replied. "I asked, and that was all it took." I reached for his belt buckle, unfastened. Drew his zipper down as his eyes went hazy. "You're welcome."

His fingers closed around my wrist, halting the zipper's descent. "If I"—he stopped himself, growled, swore under his breath—"if I want to wait, does that change everything?"

I brought my lips to his collarbone, kissed only enough to shake a shiver out of him. "Nothing at all," I replied. "And if you're not into this anymore—"

"Oh, I am fucking *into* this," he interrupted. "I am losing my mind with how much I'm into this. Into you." He leaned back a bit, separating me from the slope of his shoulder where he smelled like an herb garden. "But I was wrong. In the beginning, I was wrong about everything and I think—I know—I want to do this right, Magnolia. I want—"

"There was nothing wrong about the dick pic you sent me. That was all right." No, it wasn't possible for me to participate in a conversation without making it A. weird, B. sarcastic, C. filthy, or D. some ludicrous combination of weird, sarcastic, and filthy. Not possible.

His forehead crinkled, the corners of his eyes creased, and his lips parted. He didn't say anything. Instead, he studied me as if seeing me for the first time. I matched his gaze, and as the seconds slipped into minutes, it occurred to me this was the first time.

Somewhere between lunch at Flour and that engagement party invitation, we'd shed a layer or two of armor. My hair wasn't blown out and he wasn't hung up on that plan to get over his ex by getting under someone new and anonymous. And we weren't hiding our war wounds, weren't shining them up as if to say, "Look, I'm healed! I'm all right now!" because we didn't need to pretend anymore.

"Are you going to tell me what you're thinking or am I going to have to create my own explanation? I'll tell you this, my explanations are wacky. I fall off the cliffs of crazy real fast."

Rob laughed under his breath. "I'm just wondering if you're going to bring up that pic when we—" He ran his hand over his mouth, blinked, glanced away with wide eyes. "Sorry. Lost my train of thought for a second. I was just thinking how lucky I was that you didn't block me on the app."

That wasn't it. He'd meant to say something about us, about a future for us. I knew it. But I didn't intend to push him. Whatever he'd started to say would keep. If I was meant to hear it, the day would come when he'd tell me. Hopefully, when that day arrived, my belly wouldn't slosh as if it couldn't decide between butterflies and full-out seasickness at the mere suggestion of the future.

"I have to get home to my dog," I said.

Rob took a full step back, then another, leaving me in the lovely position of having my legs open at an obtuse angle and my dress rucked all the way up to my waist. Just lovely.

"Yeah." He bobbed his head. "Of course. You should—"

"Stop. Let me finish." I hopped off the island, twisted my

hand around his open shirttail. "I have to get home to feed Gronk. He needs a good, long walk. There's also a late game tonight. The Sox are in Seattle." I gestured behind us, at the uncorked bottles. "And then there's all this wine. I wouldn't want it going to waste."

"Are you asking me to go home with you?"

I grinned at his freckled chest, the thick line of fuzz running down to his navel. "If that sort of thing interests you, yeah."

"It does," he replied.

"Would it interest you to spend the night with me?"

"Also, yes." He glanced away, barked out a laugh. "Was that all I had to do? Ask you to wait and then"—he snapped his fingers—"I get an invitation to your bed?"

"That might be an oversimplification of things," I replied. "And you should know you'll be sharing the bed with me and Gronk."

"I'm aware of the hierarchy in your life," he said. "No one ranks above that dog."

"Completely true, yes." I tapped my finger against his sternum. "But please don't interpret this as a request to stop talking about your dick. I don't know what I'd do without constant reminders about its specifications and skill set."

Rob skimmed his hands down my back. "I can't tell whether you're being serious or snarky right now."

"That's my charm."

CHAPTER
TWENTY-ONE

My date crossed his arms over his chest and declared, "Bullshit."

"What's bullshit?" I asked, my hands flat on the bar top. "What? Why?"

Riley Walsh shook his head and stared at the televisions suspended over the bar. We hadn't met up for drinks or a game in months but the stars aligned today. The Red Sox were in Tampa and a summer storm had dropped a dark blanket of clouds and fog over the city. Tampa was beating the piss out of the Sox and the bar was mostly empty, two conditions ripe for a review of my adventures in dating.

"You're with two guys—at the same fucking time—and you're trying to tell me they're both decent. I'm calling bullshit on that."

"And I'm asking why you're calling bullshit," I said, more than a little indignant.

Riley went on shaking his head as if he had an eternity of frustration to work out with that one motion. "Because, Gigi, sweetheart, I've known you for nearly five years and you've never once given me a reason to trust the guys you bring around. If anything, you give me reason to send them on a long walk off a short pier."

Few people were allowed to put my track record on trial without finding themselves on the receiving end of a death glare. Riley was one of them, Andy was another.

"They're different," I remarked. "I know I've said that before but it's true this time."

"You told me Peter was different." He held up his index finger, a sure sign I was getting a list out of him. God help me. Always with the lists. "Then we discover Peter has a wife and a kid, and he's awaiting trial for money laundering. Did you ever get paid for that last set of penthouse roof gardens?"

I groaned. "The Feds froze his assets."

"Uh huh. Yeah." He kept shaking his head. "Will they be calling you as a witness?"

"He's going to plead out," I replied. "No trial."

"That's a bright spot in the shitshow." He glanced up at the game and then back at me. "You told me that fuckbag who stole your dog had changed. You said that not too long before he stole your fucking dog, Gigi."

"And I was wrong," I admitted. "I know I've made bad choices, Riley."

He reached for his beer, getting in another head shake. "Really bad choices," he muttered. "I don't know if I can take on two dudes when this goes tits up."

"If," I argued. "*If* this goes tits up."

"Fine, if," he said with one more head shake. "All right, then. Tell me. What makes these two so fucking different? Why won't I be cold-cocking them one of these days?"

"Because they're—they're different, Riley," I argued.

He shifted on his stool, turning to face me. "I want to believe you. I really do. And it's not you I doubt. It's them."

I turned my attention back to the game. I didn't know how to explain that Rob and Ben were nothing like the men of my past. "Different" just didn't sum it up. But Rob and Ben weren't the only differences. I was different too.

I wasn't the same woman who'd dated a client despite a million warning signs.

I wasn't the same woman who went back to her ex after he'd "borrowed" her social security number to open credit cards and rack up tons of debt.

I wasn't the same woman who'd interpreted a collaborative professional relationship as hardcore flirting and attacked Riley's brother Sam with her mouth.

Somewhere along the way, between the dog kidnapping and the federal indictments and the online dating pleasure cruise, I'd changed. I learned—*finally*—that I was better than men who forgot my name and told half-truths and never texted first. I was better than all of it and I could demand better too.

"I like black cherry seltzer," I said.

"You've mentioned this," Riley answered, his eyebrow arched up. He blinked at me before glancing at the game.

"There's a brand I like that's only available in vending machines," I said. "I must've mentioned that to Rob at some point."

"I imagine you're going somewhere with this." He rolled his hand in my direction. "Proceed."

"Rob tracked down the bottling company and the distributor, and he bought a few cases of my favorite black cherry seltzer."

Riley bobbed his head. "Rob sounds like a detail-oriented guy. Cheers to him and his details."

"I'm not trying to sell you on him," I said. And I wasn't. Really. I wanted him to understand that these guys were light years away from the douchewaffles I used to date. It seemed insignificant but vending machine seltzer was my proof. That move took work. That took time. Yeah, maybe he'd delegated it to one of his assistants or underlings but he was the one who marched into my office with an armful of black cherry goodness like a goddamn superhero. If I called up all the men I'd ever dated and asked them my preferred nonalcoholic beverage, I wasn't convinced any of them would even name seltzer. Let alone black cherry and this specific variety. It was tiny, fallible proof.

"Ben bought a renovation house," I continued. "He wanted to move his grandmother into that house. She passed away before he could finish the work."

My last few boyfriends never would've done that. Peter might've bought a building and given his grandmother a condo for free but he never would've lifted a finger to make it just right for her. And the dude before that...well, he didn't give anything to anyone.

"I'm sorry to hear about Ben's grandmother," he replied.

"They're good guys, Riley," I said. "They're good guys but I don't have to prove that to you. I've figured out a lot of things in the past few months. I think I get it now and...and I don't think you have to worry about me anymore. I don't think I'm going to make those same mistakes anymore. I know that's probably hard for you to believe since you've watched me crash and burn so many times but I believe it this time."

Riley propped his arm on the bar and rested his head on

his palm. He stared at me for a long moment, his jaw working as he studied me. "Have your brothers met these guys?"

I dragged my teeth over my lower lip, humming. He wasn't asking after Ash and Linden as an exercise in patriarchal approval. He knew my brothers would find extraordinary levels of amusement in this and they'd stay amused for actual decades. "No. I don't know how to explain this to my family so I haven't."

He tipped his head to the side as he considered this. "I'll allow that excuse, but if you do tell your family, please let me be there so I can watch them pop like piñatas."

"Only if you promise to get me out of there before my father asks whether I'm using protection," I said with a laugh. "Because that would be his only comment and you know it."

"Done." He reached for his beer and asked, "Is your mom still swiping for you?"

"Mmhmm." I nodded, grimacing. "Yeah. She's having a lot of fun so I haven't stopped her yet. I'm not talking to anyone new. I have my hands full with these two."

Wincing, he said, "I'd rather not think about you having your hands full, Gigi."

"Sorry," I replied. I wasn't sorry. I was mostly amused at Riley's newfound inability to talk about sex without growing uncomfortable. The committed life had changed him.

With his glass raised to his mouth, he paused. "Wait a second. Do they know about each other? Or are they none the wiser?"

"They know about each other." I couldn't stop the eyeroll. "They've met. We all kept running into each other at the same places so I laid down the ground rules. Sometimes I send group texts and just tell them I need alone time. I mean, a girl's gotta do laundry and eat an entire box of mac and cheese and watch *The Real Housewives*. I don't need them around for that. But then again, I tell them that and then get nonstop texts checking in on me because they're worried about something ridiculous." Still holding the glass, he smiled at me. It wasn't a regular Riley smile, the kind with a dash of devil. It was surprised, maybe a little...proud? That was strange and confusing. I wasn't certain I wanted his pride. That wasn't our relationship. "What? What is that face?"

"You're running the game," he said. "You...*you're* in charge this time."

"Yeah, I am," I said, as if it was no big deal. "It's not a big deal."

"You're not sitting in my seat, Gigi," he replied softly.

The moment shifted, a weight sliding over us like the heavy, black clouds outside pressing the sky down, down into the city. Riley and I didn't do heavy. If we did, we did it with a thick layer of humor. No big emotional moments, no exposed souls. We made outrageous bets over sports and argued about renovations and sandwiches. This wasn't how we operated and I wanted it to stop.

If it didn't stop right now, I'd have to turn around and face the century of growth I'd crammed into recent months. I wasn't ready to look back at the path behind me. I wasn't ready for the full frontal view of my mistakes and missteps.

"Hey, you're engaged!" I yelled, swatting his arm to break the spell. "You're getting married! We haven't talked about this yet!"

"Has it been that long since I've seen you? That's old news," he said.

"Give me the whole engagement story, not just the cute pics and captions Alex posted on Facebook. She's adorable, by the way."

"She really is," he agreed. "She's at some doctor conference this weekend. She told me I could go along with her but I didn't want to accidentally see surgery photos or walk in on something bloody. But now I kinda wish I'd gone."

"Great," I said flatly. "Glad I'm such good company."

"I didn't mean it like that," he argued.

"I know, I know," I said. "Okay, I want the story. When did you pop the question?"

"Opening day at Fenway," he replied with a nod. "It wasn't the plan but there were some extenuating circumstances that forced my hand." He blinked up at the game. "It was Batman underwear. Batman panties forced my hand. No regrets though. It was time and I'm happy."

"Have you set a date or made any plans or—" My gaze darted to the bar door as it opened, filling the room with the sound of thunder and pouring rain. Through the doorway came a group of soaked men, all busy wiping away the rain and wringing out their clothes and complaining about the downpour. Just as I started to needle Riley for wedding details, one of the men pulled a ball cap from his head. He looked up and our eyes met across the bar.

Ben.

I hadn't realized I'd missed him this week until seeing him now. Despite his soggy condition, a warm grin pulled at his lips. I motioned him over but he was already striding in our direction, his wet shoes squeaking as he walked.

"Are you even listening to me complain about these shenanigans? Her family truly, honestly believes we're going to roll on out to Nevada and get married in some randomly significant chapel despite the fact Alex has no desire to do that. It's a whole thing and I'm beginning to think my sister Shannon had the right idea with eloping." Riley paused, turning to follow my gaze. He spotted Ben and both eyebrows shot up. "What is this shambles?"

"What kind of magic are you, pretty girl?" Ben asked as he approached. "Because I was just thinking about you and here you are."

He stepped between me and Riley, and leaned in to press a kiss on my temple. "Look at you," I murmured, pushing damp hair off his forehead.

"Please do," he replied. "I really was thinking about you. I was gonna call you once I got out of that storm. See if I could take you out tonight. Dinner, movie, whatever you want."

Riley cleared his throat. "Which one is this?"

I dropped my hand onto Ben's hard—but very wet—chest and eased him back. "Ben, this is one of my best friends and occasional business partner Riley Walsh. Riley, this is Ben Brock. He's renovating the house across the street from mine. When he's not running the tile saw at all hours, he's fighting fires."

The men shook hands, regarding each other with a metric ton of skepticism. I loved it.

"Riley was just telling me about his upcoming wedding," I said. "He proposed on opening day. Can't imagine anything better."

That did the trick. Ben's grin returned and he nodded, saying, "Nothing better than opening day."

"Yeah, well, nothing better than finding the right girl," Riley murmured. He reached into his back pocket and pulled a few bills from his wallet. He tossed them on the bar, glanced at me. "I'm heading out now." He turned to face Ben, clapping his palm on the other man's shoulder. "There are a lot of spots in this town to bury a body and I keep a shovel in my car. You feel me, son?"

"Believe it," Ben replied.

Riley shifted off the barstool and gifted Ben with another smack on the back. "Good," Riley replied. He pointed at me. "Text me this week. I need your advice on my North End project. It's shenanigans left and right."

"Andy already told me all about it," I replied. "I think I blocked some time on Wednesday to check it out."

"Lunch?" he asked.

"Of course," I said. "Stay dry out there."

Riley held up his hand in a wave and left us at the bar. Ben reached for my beer, taking a pull before glancing back to me.

"Did I pass?" he asked.

I shrugged. Riley wouldn't have left if he didn't approve. Not that I required his approval but that was how friends worked. He would've stayed, third-wheeling it until the end, if he had any issues with Ben. At the minimum, he didn't disapprove and that was something. "Maybe."

Ben took another sip and then set the empty glass on the bar. "He threatened to kill me," he mused. "I like him."

"Good," I said, laughing. "He's one of my best friends and before you ask, no, our relationship has never been more than friendly. We go to ball games and drink beer and work on old houses together. That's it. That's all it's ever been."

"Small blessings," he murmured. "Can I take you out tonight, pretty magic girl?"

I ran my hand down Ben's arm, wiping away more rainwater. "No, not tonight," I said with a decisive head shake.

"Oh. Okay, then," he said, his shoulders slumping a bit.

"But I can take you home with me and toss those wet clothes in the dryer if you want," I suggested. "Maybe order takeout. Watch another game."

Ben stared at me. A glass shattered on the other side of the bar. A bolt of thunder cracked overhead and the power flickered. A rivulet of rain ran over his forehead, around his nose, down the scar on his cheek. He went on staring.

Then he drove his fingers into my hair and brought his lips a breath from mine. "Yeah," he whispered, pressing a tiny kiss to the corner of my mouth. "Take me home, pretty magic girl."

CHAPTER
TWENTY-TWO

My date was dripping wet. I wasn't much better.

"Um, okay." I watched as rainwater pooled at Ben's feet. The drive from the bar to my house did little to dry his clothes and now my entryway was experiencing flood conditions. Hurricane Ben, making landfall. "You need to take those clothes off."

"Took the words right outta my mouth," Ben said.

I raked my hand through my damp hair. The storm was bearing down hard and even the quick sprint from the driveway to the door had my t-shirt plastered to my skin. I banded my arm over my chest to keep the print of my bra from screaming through the now-sheer fabric.

"You're going to catch your death like that," I said, waving a vague hand at his chest. "And—and wet jeans are super uncomfortable. I've walked around Canobie Lake Park after getting soaked on the log ride enough times to know how unpleasant wet jeans can be. I remember spending most of my eighth grade class trip sitting on a bench, cursing my friends for insisting on hitting the log ride first and wishing my pants were dry." Another vague gesture. "You need to take those off."

Ben motioned up and down his body. "I want to be extremely clear about what you're suggesting before getting naked in your living room because I'm not gonna fuck things up with you over a misunderstanding," he said. "You're asking me to strip, pretty girl? That's what you want? Right here? Right now?"

My dog Gronk, that lazy bones, chose this moment to wander out of my bedroom with a jaw-popping yawn. He eyed me with mild interest, a half-hearted *Oh, you're back? Do you plan on feeding me now?* snort but then he spotted Ben and the bark-a-thon commenced.

"Hey, buddy," Ben called to the pup. "Remember me from across the street? We met a couple of weeks ago. You marked my yard in fifteen or twenty spots and I gave you carrots. I thought we were friends."

Gronk stopped barking for a second, his body vibrating and his little paws tap dancing in place as he regarded Ben.

"Friend," I said to Gronk, my hand pressed to Ben's chest. "Quiet down. You don't need to defend the fortress from this guy."

That didn't stop Gronk. He went on huffing and snorting, shaking with each bark.

"I get it, buddy. You're just protecting your mama," Ben said. He knelt down, holding out his palm to Gronk. The pup stared at Ben, his barks quieting to low snarls. Then Gronk inched closer. "That's right, buddy. Come here, give me a sniff, give me some licks." Gronk lapped at Ben's palm. Then he growled with delight when Ben shifted to scratch his head. "We can be friends, can't we?"

"He doesn't usually like men," I said, an arm still

shielding my bra from view. Leave it to me to wear a cute sailor-striped bra with a white t-shirt on a stormy day. Brilliant. "He's had some bad experiences."

"No, we're gonna be good friends," Ben argued, pushing him onto his back. He scratched the dog's belly and head at the same time and yeah, he was charming Gronk like a dog whisperer with bacon in his pocket. "Me and this guy, we're on the same team."

Ben gifted Gronk a full-body rub and ear scratch before standing up. The dog was lying on his side, his tongue lolling out as he panted. Blissed out.

Gronk wasn't the kind of dog who fell for cheap tricks like belly rubbing and head scratching. No, Gronk made people work for his affections and he rarely granted them to men. After the situation with my ex—the dognapper— Gronk turned his back on anyone with a penis. Not that I blamed him. I did the same thing, mostly.

"Still want me to strip?" Ben asked, his thumb hooked around his belt buckle.

I reached for him, bringing my palm to his chest for a second as if I needed to confirm he was actually wet. Done. Confirmed. But I didn't pull my hand back. No, I went on rubbing all over him like I was marinating meat.

"You need to dry off. You're cold and wet, and that can't be a good way to, you know, watch a game."

"Terrible way to watch a game." A grin pulled at one corner of his mouth as he toed off his shoes. He pointed over my shoulder, toward the back of the house. "You got a bathroom back there? A shower, some towels? I smell like a wet newspaper and that's no treat."

Holy hell. I was the worst hostess. The absolute worst. If my aunt was here, she would've smacked my ass with a dish towel while simultaneously scooting some stuffed mush-rooms under the broiler, mixing a pitcher of Manhattans, and asking whether Ben kept crystals. I didn't know how to stuff mushrooms and I doubted Ben wanted any fungus from me, and Manhattans were out of the question on account of what the fuck were Manhattans? And I wasn't getting into it with him on the topic of crystals.

To start with, I didn't have a Manhattan recipe at the ready. But more importantly, my aunt wasn't here. It was just me and Ben—and a zonked-out dog—and the whole night ahead of us.

"Come on," I said, waving toward Ben. "Let's get you warmed up."

With his free hand—because he couldn't possibly stop drawing my attention to the thumb tugging his waistband indecently low—he grabbed my elbow. Squeezed just a bit. "Yeah. Let's do that."

He followed me down the hall, toward the back of my home, his fingers loose around my elbow. I didn't know what I was going to do when we reached the bathroom. Was I going to watch him undress and then hop in the shower? Was I hopping in there with him?

I didn't devote much energy to answering those ques-tions, instead pushing the door open and flipping on the lights. Before I could tear back the shower curtain, Ben hooked his arm around my waist, pulling me tight against his chest.

"I'm gonna rinse off," he said, his lips on the side of my neck. That spot was dangerous. Just real damn dangerous. I lost my sense and spatial awareness when touched there. "I'm not going to ask you to join me but I won't turn you away if you invite yourself in."

His lips brushed over that sensitive spot and Kenny Loggins's "Danger Zone" started playing in my head. He moved around me and reached into the shower stall. The sound of running water filled the room. I had a flash of the locker room scene from *Top Gun* but instead of Tom Cruise and Val Kilmer, it was Ben.

"I'll order some food. And get you a towel too," I said, stepping back. Distance was the key to keeping myself from jumping in there with him and I wasn't doing that right now. Naked and showering together was one hell of a leap. "I'll go do that now. Just leave your clothes on the sink. I'll toss them in the dryer when I come back."

I stepped back over the threshold, my hand curled around the door. Ben went right on grinning as he unbuckled his jeans. He knew I was thinking about bare skin and hot water. He knew it. That was the thing about Ben. He could read my mind from fifty feet away.

He pulled his t-shirt over his head, dropped it in the sink with a soggy *thunk*. There he was, shirtless.

A line of dark hair ran down the center of his muscled chest, his deep olive skin glowing under the overhead light.

One tattoo circled his bicep. Another ran from the ball of his shoulder down to his elbow. An arrow.

His torso's muscular cuts seemed to point toward his crotch.

His jeans hung low. Explicitly low.

He brought one hand to his waistband, the other to his zipper. "Medium rare. Brown rice. Extra provolone. No anchovies," he said.

"Huh-what?" I mumbled, my gaze glued to the space below his navel. I didn't even try to look up.

"Whatever you're ordering," he replied with a snicker.

"Make mine medium rare. Or brown rice on the side. Or extra provolone if that's what you're feeling. No anchovies."

"Got it." Still staring. Still waiting for that zipper to come down. "Got it," I repeated. "No anchovies on the brown rice burger."

The zipper inched down but—dammit all to hell—his bright blue boxer briefs kept the goods under wraps. "Thanks, Magnolia," he sang. If a shit-eating grin had a tone of voice, it was that one.

Finally, I glanced up to meet Ben's sapphire gaze. "I'll be right back with that towel."

I closed the door but kept my hand on the knob for a minute. Maybe more. I needed every one of those seconds to catch my breath as I imagined Ben climbing into the shower. The water rushing over him, traveling down along his body's grooves. When I heard the curtain scraping along the rod and then back into place, I gripped the knob harder. Thought about turning it, pulling back the curtain, staring at him while he washed. I didn't even have to get in there to enjoy this. The visual impact would do it for me.

It would do just fine.

But I shook my head and turned toward the linen closet. I was getting him that towel and snatching his wet clothes, and I was ordering food—no anchovies—and then I'd get my fill of Ben. When he was clean and dry. And clothed.

Maybe it was silly to center around this point but I'd never had a man in my shower before. Not this one. Not here. The dognapper and I had lived together, as all slow-moving train wreck tragedies should. Peter refused to visit the suburbs because everything about him was a red flag. Rob was the only other man I'd welcomed into this house.

I yanked a towel out of the closet and pressed it to my

face, squealing straight into terry cloth. It was a mix of frustration, hunger, happiness. All those things bubbling up into a cry that needed to go somewhere. It needed to escape me or else I'd burst.

The shower curtain screeched on the rod again and damn, I needed some WD-40 on that thing.

"I heard that," Ben called over the water.

"Heard what?" I yelled at the bathroom door. "I didn't say anything and this place isn't haunted. You're imagining things, Brock."

"Just get in here," he said, a laugh softening the command.

I pushed the door open a few inches, peeked inside. Ben leaned out of the shower stall, his shoulders looking like the broad side of a barn and his ink black hair plastered to his forehead.

"Something you needed?" I wagged the towel at him before dropping it on the closed toilet lid.

He sucked in a breath through his nose, his gaze heating me like a splash of liquid sunshine. "Yeah," he replied, his head bobbing in tiny degrees. "Yeah, pretty girl. I swore I wouldn't ask but I need you to get in here."

"I'm not having sex with you in there."

"Whoa, whoa, whoa. Who said anything about sex in the shower?" He was good enough to play hard at being offended. "Certainly wasn't me."

I traced the neck of my t-shirt. "Then what are you hoping will come from me squeezing in there with you? Because it *is* cozy."

He dropped his gaze, tilted his head toward the floor. "Just want to be close to you," he replied. "Just for a little while. Okay?"

I didn't know how it happened. I didn't know how I went from watching him through a crack in the door to pulling my t-shirt over my head or kicking off my shorts. I didn't know where I found the confidence to walk toward him as I dropped my panties, unhooked my bra and let my breasts bounce free while he drank up every inch of me. I didn't know how I stowed away the ever-present fear of being hurt, being used, being abandoned. And I didn't know how I pulled back that curtain and joined him under the hot water.

I didn't know, and I didn't care because I did it. I took what I wanted, and that didn't require an explanation.

I was leaping.

CHAPTER
TWENTY-THREE

MY DATES LOVED THEIR MIMOSAS.

I mean, *loved* their mimosas. Honestly, I loved them too.

"Okay, okay," Tiel Walsh said, waving her hands over the brunch table as if she could sweep away the hodgepodge of half conversations percolating between us and her sisters-in-law, Andy, Shannon Halsted, and Lauren Walsh. "Start over. From the beginning. Whole story. How did you come to be seeing two men?"

"It's not that uncommon," Shannon said. "People do that. Dating isn't what it used to be and that's probably okay."

"I don't think people date, period," Andy argued. "They hook up and sometimes they hook up with the same few people over and over."

"This is depressing," Tiel murmured. "For many reasons."

"Because you never hooked up with a bunch of dudes before getting married?" Lauren asked. "If it helps, I didn't either. Shannon and Andy did but that's because they have better game than we do."

"I think your game is just fine," I said to Lauren.

"You didn't know me when I was single," she argued, laughing. "My game was nonexistent. My game was Bambi-in-the-forest."

"Oh my god," Shannon grumbled. "You and the fragile fawn thing again. Just because you didn't slut it up in your single days doesn't mean you were innocent. I've heard the things you say to my brother and I've seen more than a few text messages too. Bambi you are not."

"Can we not call it 'slutting'?" Andy asked. "Women are allowed to seek out sexual partners and then have sex and also enjoy sex. None of that makes them slutty. None of that necessitates judgment. It's a normal, healthy part of life and it's not necessary to add value judgments."

"You're right," Shannon said, wagging her empty champagne flute at a passing waiter. "Even using it for fun—like, taking it away from slut-shamers and making it our own and eliminating their ability to wield it in a shame-y way—carries some shitty baggage. Because no one looks at the dude on the other side of all that sex and calls him a man slut."

"Thank you," Andy said. "I'm not trying to be a purist. I don't want to police the way people speak but I hate the way words are weaponized against women sometimes. I hate how fucking everything is weaponized against women when it suits others. I'm a little sensitive to all that noise right now."

"You're allowed to be sensitive," Shannon said. "You're allowed to feel your feelings. You're also allowed to drown them in champagne so long as you don't start telling me about the things you do with coconut oil when you're alone with my brother."

"What about the things that don't involve coconut oil?" Andy asked, her eyebrow arched like a Sephora ad.

"I don't want to hear about those either," Shannon said with an exaggerated shiver.

Lauren shifted to face me. "You must have a favorite. Or a slight preference. With your boys, not coconut oil. Right?"

She was the only sober one at the table by virtue of being extremely pregnant. By my count, she was at least seventeen months along. Had to be. She'd been pregnant forever. Since Nixon was in office, at least.

"How long have you been pregnant?" I asked. There was some slurring involved. It sounded like "How long 've be pregnant?" and ended with a hiccup.

To her credit, she smiled. That was the best thing about Matt Walsh's wife. She made everyone comfortable. She was good to people even when they hadn't earned her goodness.

"Eight-ish months. This kid has a few more weeks to go."

"Okay, good," I murmured, nodding hard enough to slap myself in the face with my ponytail.

"Back to the topic at hand," Andy announced, snapping her fingers. I wasn't certain but I got the impression she'd picked up that move from Patrick. He was a snapper. The snappiest.

Shannon leaned back against the booth with her champagne flute in hand. "Allow me to recap the key points, boss. Two guys. Both fun and pretty. Cool dudes. Big event with one of them coming up. Am I missing anything?"

"I showered with the firefighter last weekend," I confessed. "That was, uh, illustrative."

"Because you got your hands on the goods?" Lauren asked.

I hummed in agreement.

"Fun times," Tiel murmured.

"Yeah, mostly." I held up both hands as if I was weighing something. "My shower isn't big enough for too much fun. It was mostly like, 'Oh, hey, you're naked and I'm naked and we're both slippery so that's exciting but all we can do is stand here and be naked together.'" I dropped my hands, shrugged. "And then we ordered delivery from Beverly House of Pizza and watched the Yankees-Dodgers game and I scared him when I yelled at the television."

"I don't care how small the space is, how do you shower with someone and not have sex?" Tiel asked. "Not positive but I think I got pregnant in the shower."

"Will talks about getting me pregnant during shower sex but I don't think it's panned out that way for us," Shannon said.

"Chances are good that shower sex is to blame for this," Lauren said, patting her belly.

"Like you weren't trying on every damn surface in your apartment, Matt's office, and the entire city," Shannon said to her.

Lauren shrugged. "You never know what will do the trick."

"Topic at hand," Andy repeated.

"You're only saying that because you don't like shower sex," Lauren remarked.

"You're right," Andy replied. "I don't like it. I don't have pretty shiny blonde California girl hair like some people. My hair is complicated. My hair requires a protocol, a routine. And I refuse to have sex while wearing a shower cap."

"That's fair," Tiel said. "I wouldn't be able to say anything remotely dirty while wearing a shower cap."

Shannon rolled her eyes toward the ceiling. "I don't need to hear about the sex lives of my brothers, thank you."

"And my interest in getting pregnant is less than zero," Andy continued, ignoring Shannon. "So, if everyone is getting knocked up in the shower, I'll keep locking the bathroom door behind me."

"I'm with you on that," I replied. "The last thing I need is to get pregnant while figuring out what to do with these guys."

"It would either make the decision very easy or very difficult," Tiel said.

"Difficult," I replied. "It would be difficult. I'm sure of it. And regardless of any of that, I'm not ready for a real live baby child with one of these men."

"Okay, then," Tiel said. "What are you ready for?"

I blinked at her, my lips parted and words were waiting on my tongue. But I didn't say anything. I couldn't form the sounds. Instead, I swallowed it all down with a mouthful of boozy orange juice.

"Magnolia needs two things from us," Andy said, jumping in where I was flailing. "She needs help picking out a fancy dress, and some objective opinions on the dicks she's juggling."

"I am not juggling any dicks," I argued. "I'm merely rubbing them in showers."

"Oh, so there was more than one shower?" Tiel asked.

"And more than one dick?" Lauren asked.

"There was a sleepover," I said, setting my glass down. " Take the champagne away. I'm getting sloppy."

"Moving on," Shannon murmured. "You need a dress. We know how to do that."

"What's the event?" Tiel asked. "Not that I'm very helpful on the fashion front but what are we dressing you for?"

"You *are* very helpful," I argued with a gesture toward her boho summer dress. "Your style is amazing."

"What's really amazing is that you two are friends," Shannon mused. "Of all the unlikely pairings."

"We are all unlikely," Andy said. "That we manage to love each other is the best thing."

"The boys are good. They're really good," Tiel said. "They're great but girlfriends are the best."

"You guys are too nice to me," I said, reaching for my napkin. I felt the prickle of tears behind my eyes and I needed to be ready. Magnolia plus champagne equaled sobby effusiveness. "Seriously, you're too nice to me. I thought you guys were going to hate me forever."

That was the straight truth. When I'd made the super massive epic mistake of kissing Sam, it was because I thought it was the right way to get his attention. I thought I was being bold and forward, taking charge the same way Andy and Shannon and Lauren take charge. They went for what they wanted and nothing held them back and I wanted to be that, even if only once.

I thought I was getting his attention when a short eternity of flirting seemed to float right over his head. But it hadn't floated over his head. He'd ignored my advances because he was in love with Tiel. And it was Tiel who'd walked in when I was jamming my tongue into his mouth.

I went for it but I didn't even know where I was going. I wasn't in love with Sam. I was flirting with him because he was there. He was a constant in my life—a single man who took me seriously as a landscape architect—and I was too fucked up and fucked over to realize he wasn't for me. Oh, god, not at all. I didn't have deep, angsty feelings of lust and longing for him. I thought he was quirky and fascinating, and we had a shared love of solving random architectural problems. He was a fixture in my life at a time when I desperately needed someone to pay attention to me. To validate my competence in my craft, to see me as an alluring woman.

I thought Sam could do all of that for me. I was wrong.

That kiss was a ridiculous intersection of very bad things. It wrecked Sam and Tiel's relationship for months. It killed my professional partnership with Sam. For a time, it killed my professional partnership with the entire Walsh Associates firm. I was *persona non grata* as far as they were concerned.

Except for Riley. The youngest Walsh at the firm knew I'd never intended to destroy relationships or harm anything. Riley was the one who brought them back around and forced them to see I wasn't trying to break up Sam and Tiel. I was just trying to be the girl who went for it. He forced them to see I hadn't done anything wrong, not really. Not intentionally. Not more than humiliating myself.

That was a tough time for me. I was embarrassed by my actions and wounded by the backlash. I struggled to keep my business going. It was difficult to pitch my services to clients when I felt so fucking worthless. This was a small town and that meant I constantly looked over my shoulder at the hopes of avoiding a Walsh or one of their allies. I was anxious all the time. Worried and ashamed and devastated that I'd worked this hard, and I was losing it all because I kissed a boy who didn't want me.

Somewhere along the way, Andy and I became friends. She kept me at arm's length at first, but Andy does that with everyone. Icy cold and distant was her thing. But just as gradually as a sapling grows into a tree so thick you can't get your arms around it or remember a time when it wasn't a deep-rooted anchor in your life, she grew into one of my best friends. And she brought her posse along with her.

When I thought about the steps I took and the mountain I climbed toward being all right with myself, Andy and her friends were the ones clearing the way and holding my hands. I wouldn't have made it here and I wouldn't have two men vying for my affection if not for these women. They were hard on me once upon a time and that was the ugly way of it—women were often hard on each other. Unnecessarily so. But when they came around, they came all the way around. Circled up so tight they pulled me back together and squeezed the darkness right out.

It was absolutely unlikely. It was also the best outcome of a very bad thing.

"We have bigger problems than hating you," Lauren said. "Like the fact my house doesn't have floors yet and we're moving out of the loft at the end of the month and having a baby right after that. Those are real problems. Floors are problems."

Shannon dug inside her bag and retrieved her phone. "Tell me who I'm yelling at and I'll yell."

Andy reached across the table and plucked the phone from Shannon's hand. "We're not doing that, sweetie." She leaned closer to Lauren, wrapping her arm around the woman's shoulder. "You have subfloors. I know they aren't the reclaimed wood Matt promised you but those will go in soon. It will be done and buttoned up, even if I'm putting down the flooring myself."

"And I'll be there unpacking for you," Tiel added. "I know Riley is working on painting a mural for the baby's room."

"And I'll be there with my whip, cracking it as necessary," Shannon said.

"And I'll have the landscaping done later this week," I said. "I'll come over on moving day. I can bring a firefighter and an investment banker with me if you need extra muscle. They both have plenty to spare."

"Oh my god, that would be awesome," Tiel cried. "We can judge them!"

"I love judging men," Shannon mused. "Objectification is an essential element in taking down the patriarchy."

"I'm sure that makes sense to you," Lauren said to her.

"You know what's funny?" Andy asked. "My phone auto-corrects *fuck the patriarchy* to *fuck Patrick*. There's a statement about something in there but I haven't decided what it is yet."

"Aaaaand you're cut off," Lauren said, snatching Andy's champagne flute.

"Scorecards," Shannon continued, ignoring her sisters-in-law. "Ranking criteria." She nodded to herself, humming. "This is outstanding. Let's make this happen."

"It's not like I don't have a plan for finishing your house and getting you moved in," Andy remarked. "But sure, let's invite Gigi's boyfriends over for a meat market. That's far superior to my strategic timelines and critical threshold planning."

"I know you have a plan," Lauren replied. "And I can't even explain how much I appreciate your plan and every-thing you've done to help me and Matt. I'm just...I'm feeling some pressure."

"Are we talking deep, twisting pressure or *my soul is*

telling me to nest pressure?" Shannon asked. "Because there's a difference, and if it's the first one, we need to start timing that shit."

"It's not the first one," Lauren said, laughing. She patted her belly again. "This kid is high and tight. Not ready to go anywhere."

"Let's not eliminate the possibility," Tiel said. "You're talking to two women who went from living their pregnant lives to birthing babies in the span of twenty minutes."

"Yeah, I know. I don't really want to hear that right now," Lauren said. "Can we go back to talking about my house now and how Andy saved the day?"

"Jumping in on projects is my favorite thing," Andy said. "Even if it is because Matt crammed the shit out of his schedule these past months and hasn't had time to sleep, eat, or breathe. He did it so he'd have more flexibility when the baby arrives and I can't fault him for that. Even if he did fall asleep in last Monday's morning meeting."

"The amazing part was how he stayed asleep for two hours after the meeting ended," Shannon added. "Just sitting there in his chair, arms crossed over his chest, dead to the world."

"Wait. What are we talking about?" Tiel asked.

"Lots of things," I replied. "It's all good."

Lauren snatched the champagne flute from her sister-in-law. "You're cut off."

"This event you're going to," Shannon started, "what are the details? I have a few shops in mind but I want to make sure I'm operating with the right idea."

I nodded. "The investment banker, Rob—"

"The one with the big cock," Andy added.

"Yes. That one." I gave her a smirk. "Rob's ex-girlfriend

and his ex-best friend are having an engagement party. They're getting married."

Shannon blew out a breath. "I have an idea why they're his exes."

"Yep." I stared at my plate and the half-eaten French toast there. Why eat when you could talk to the best ladies in town? "He's doing okay but it's a tricky situation. Definitely not ideal. He needs this party to go well."

"And you need a killer dress," Andy said. "Lethal."

"We should call April," Shannon murmured, her empty glass dangling between her fingers. "Lethal is her first language, middle name, and last known address."

"I don't know April," I said. "I feel like that might be a good thing."

"My husband's business partner's girlfriend-slash-common-law-wife," Shannon replied as if that made perfect sense. "I don't think I'm supposed to tell you that she's an assassin. I don't think I'm supposed to know that either."

Lauren gestured for Shannon's glass. "That's enough. You're cut off."

"Can I have my phone back so I can call April?" she asked.

Lauren wagged a finger at Shannon. "No. Eat something, would you? I don't want to hear your husband complaining about us getting you liquored up again. He was not happy the night he picked us up from the pedicure place."

Shannon shook her head. "Nah, he'll just get me pregnant again. He's been thinking about it. I can tell."

"In the shower?" Tiel asked.

"Are these promises or threats?" Andy asked.

Shannon speared a piece of my French toast off my plate and popped it into her mouth. "Yes and both."

"Right, so we're not calling April the assassin," I said, laughing. "The party is black tie and I want his exes to know exactly what they lost when they fucked him over. Like that scene in *Pretty Woman* where Julia Roberts goes back to the boutique that wouldn't serve her."

"'Big mistake,'" Lauren said, quoting the film.

"'Big. Huge,'" Tiel added.

"You like the one with the cock," Shannon said.

I pressed my hand to my chest as I laughed. "For the record, they both have cocks."

"The one with the impressive cock," she clarified. "And don't tell me they're both impressive. I'm sure the firefighter knows how to work the hose."

I nodded, my cheeks heating. He did. He really did. "I do like the one with the impressive cock, yes."

"And you like the firefighter too," Lauren said.

Another nod. "I do."

Shannon held up her hands, letting them fall to her lap. "You could just have two men. Don't make yourself sick trying to choose. Even if I'm excited by the prospect of a meat market and some scoring criteria, that doesn't mean you have to make a decision."

"They're a lot to handle on their own," I admitted. "I couldn't imagine them together. It would end in a mushroom cloud of testosterone."

"No, I wasn't suggesting you have them together," Shannon replied. "Just have two boyfriends. There's nothing wrong with that. Plenty of people do that or something like that. If we're placing value judgments on anything, I'd say that's an improvement over randomly fucking your way through hookup apps. But there's nothing wrong with the random fucking if that works for you."

"I thought about that, about having two boyfriends. It's been on my mind this week," I said. "I thought I'd feel totally conflicted and horrible about things...*progressing*...with both of them. But I didn't feel any of that. I like them both. I like who I am with each of them. I don't want to give up either of them. It hurts me to think about not having one of them in my life."

"Then don't," Tiel offered. "Do your thing, girl. Get it."

"I will but...but I don't want to do it forever," I said. "Or even much longer than the summer. I adore them both and I hate the idea of giving one of them up but this is project management. I do enough of that during that day. They're a lot to juggle."

"Dicks *are* difficult to juggle," Shannon murmured. "Balls are easier."

"I mix up things constantly," I continued. "I forget what I've said to which guy. I forget which person I'm meeting for dinner or whether I've asked one of them about their work thing yet. It's fun but I'm not cut out for long-term polyamory. Honestly, neither are they. They're a little unchained when they remember they're not the only dude in my life."

"That's their problem," Tiel said. "Not yours. They need to handle themselves without putting pressure and baggage on you."

"They do," I said. "Really, they do. Some of the baggage is part of the bargain. Ben can't forget his grandmother died. Rob can't forget the people closest to him betrayed him. I can't forget that I've been burned too many times to trust fire."

"I know all about burns," Tiel replied. "I know how tough it is to tolerate heat."

I stared at her chin-length black hair as she tapped a beat on the edge of the table. Was she making a pointed comment about me and how I forced her into the fire? Or was this another instance of me jumping to the worst conclusion and assuming everything was about me?

"It sounds like a lot of work," Shannon mused.

"Yes," I agreed. "They're not meant for a poly situation either. They didn't actually choose that. None of us did. We just fell into it and now we're tunneling out. The whole thing is messy. It's going to be messy until it ends and it will probably be messy after that point too."

"I think you might know," Lauren said softly. "I think you know and you're bracing yourself against the pain and upheaval of that choice."

Andy pointed at Lauren while looking at me. "She's mad smart when it comes to this stuff. She understands relationships and knows what should happen next. You should listen to her."

"I do understand," Lauren said, laughing. "But only when it comes to everyone else's relationships."

"I'm hoping the choice makes itself," I admitted. "It's probably silly but I'm waiting for a sign. Something that helps me figure out how to go forward without hurting anyone or getting hurt myself."

Lauren, Andy, Shannon, and Tiel were quiet for a moment. They studied the plates in front of them, the empty glasses Lauren had commandeered, the mason jar in the center of the table filled with gorgeous peonies. They remained silent while the reality of this crazy, sexy, fun situation settled around them and they understood it to be more heartbreaking than anything else.

It was wonderful to have these men vying over me. It

was a dream come true. But it was complicated and someone was going to get hurt. Maybe several someones.

And in the back of my mind, I worried I'd make the wrong choice. I worried I'd live my life wondering about the one I gave up.

I had to be certain. If I wasn't, I couldn't choose either of them. And that was just as painful.

Shannon cleared her throat. "You're going to need a killer dress but you're also going to need us. Bring them to Matt and Lauren's house on moving day. We'll help you." She shrugged. "Worst-case scenario, we send my husband to interrogate them. Or challenge them to some commando drills. They can do it shirtless and we'll go home and attack our husbands. It will be fabulous. Everyone benefits in that scenario."

Lauren hung her head. "Oh my god. Shannon."

Even though I wasn't in third grade anymore, I raised my hand. "I would enjoy that."

CHAPTER TWENTY-FOUR

Ben: Hey, girl. Any chance you have room in your shower for me?

Rob: There's a new poke bowl spot near my building. Interested in trying it out?

Magnolia: Greetings, friends.
Ben: Not the group text of death.
Ben: Please.
Ben: I'd rather the middle finger emoji.
Rob: Are you done yet?
Ben: I'm done with you.
Magnolia: Yeahhhhhhhhhh so I'm spending the night with my dog and Netflix. I'll catch up with you two later.
Rob: You know where to find me.

Ben: She knows where to find both of us, dickhead. The finding has never been an issue.

Rob: Thanks for clarifying that, Brock. Helpful.

Magnolia: Goodnight!

―――――

Ben: I know I said I wanted to work on the house tonight but I don't want to.

Magnolia: That's fine. No worries.

Magnolia: Is everything okay?

Ben: Yeah.

Magnolia: I'm not going to pull teeth, Brock.

Ben: My grandmother's headstone went up this morning and I've been parked in the cemetery since then.

Magnolia: Oh, honey.

Ben: No, it's nothing. I just don't want to do shit right now.

Magnolia: I understand.

Magnolia: The Sox are playing tonight. Want to order pizza and watch the game at my place? Gronk will be wearing his home game bow tie.

Ben: Don't you have tickets?

Magnolia: My brother is taking a client to the game.

Ben: What kind of work does he do? And which brother are we talking about?

Magnolia: Ash is an accountant. He and my dad work together. Linden is a tree doctor.

Ben: Which one has the tickets?

Magnolia: Ash. Linden will tell you his clients are trees, so…

Ben: Okay, let me get this straight. You're a landscape architect and one of your brothers is a tree doctor? How did you get so earthy-crunchy?

Magnolia: I hope you're typing earthy-crunchy with love.

Ben: Always.

Magnolia: We're the children of hardcore hippies. My parents kept chickens loooooong before it was cool and we all knew how to play the ukulele by the time we were 5.

Ben: That's special.

Magnolia: Yeah. I had a variety of opinions about it at the time but now I know it was a good way to grow up.

Ben: Okay, tell the truth. The accountant brother is the boring one, right?

Magnolia: I wouldn't say boring. He has different interests and priorities. Just like me and Linden, he's focused on his work and believes in what he does. Even if he takes himself a bit seriously.

Ben: Hey. Listen. I have to pass on the game. I'm not going to be good company tonight. Give my regrets to my boy Gronk, would you?

Magnolia: I'll tell him.

Ben: We'll connect after my next few shifts, okay?

Magnolia: Take care of yourself, Brock.

———

Rob: I read an article about some kind of gypsy moth invasion hitting the region. Does that sort of thing impact your work?

Magnolia: Um, yeah. Somewhat.

Rob: Is this an interesting topic for you?

Magnolia: lol, interesting? It's probably as interesting to me as rumors of a recession are to you.

Rob: Fuck, no, we're not discussing this.

Magnolia: It's bad enough to keep it in the back of your mind, right?

Rob: Totally. It's dangerous to even put those thoughts into consciousness.

Rob: I read an article about a new breed of hydrangea bushes. Is that safer?

Magnolia: Where the hell are you getting your news?

Rob: So, that's a NO on the hydrangea conversation?

Magnolia: Good effort, Russo. I'll give you credit for that.

———

Magnolia: How did you get that scar on your cheek?

Ben: Flew over the handlebars of my bike when I was 9. The bike pedal clipped my face in the wreck. Fucked me up real good. Broke my eye socket.

Magnolia: Eek. That sounds awful. I'm sorry.

Ben: No sweat. It was almost 30 years ago.

Magnolia: But you remember it vividly.

Ben: Like it was yesterday.

Ben: I guess some shit sticks with you, huh?

Magnolia: It does.

———

Ben: You're one of the most competent people I know so I figure you might have an answer for this.

Magnolia: Competent. That's a high bar.

Ben: It's a compliment.

Magnolia: Yes. As only you can deliver them.

Magnolia: How can I help you?

Ben: Do you know a lawyer who does wills and estates?

Because I don't know what the fuck I'm doing and I feel like I'm going to vomit every time I try to figure it out by myself.

Magnolia: I know a lawyer but she specializes in real estate. I'm sure she can give me some referrals.

Ben: Thank you.

Magnolia: Anytime.

Ben: Why do you do that? Why do you help?

Magnolia: Why not?

Ben: Because people are terrible and they'll fuck you over.

Magnolia: No matter what happens, I won't fuck you over.

Ben: Why not? You could.

Magnolia: Because I won't. Because I don't want to do that to you, to anyone. Because I've been fucked over and I won't repeat that.

Ben: You should be obnoxious with all your Helpful Hannah bullshit. You're just fucking precious instead.

Magnolia: …thanks?

Ben: Fuck. I'm sorry. I'm angry and I'm dumping it on you.

Magnolia: I know.

Ben: I am sorry.

Magnolia: I know that too.

———

Magnolia: I have a question with two parts.

Rob: Yes and yes.

Magnolia: Sadly, my dear, those are not valid answers but great job with the consistency.

Rob: I'll take the points wherever I can get them.

Magnolia: It's funny you say that.

Rob: Which part?

Magnolia: About the points. I'm not keeping score.

Rob: Yeah, I know. I didn't mean actual points.

Magnolia: I know. It's funny because I rarely think of you working for the points.

Rob: …if that's a statement about me being a rad guy, I'll take it.

Rob: If it's a statement about Brock working for his points, I'm going to pretend I didn't see it because I think it's better I know nothing more than the extreme basics.

Magnolia: You're a rad guy, Rob Russo.

Rob: You're fucking right, I am.

Magnolia: Do people say that? Rad. Is rad a thing?

Magnolia: Who cares. It's a thing for us.

Rob: I love it when you're decisive.

Magnolia: Hmm. That sounds like a statement on my indecisiveness.

Rob: Why would I do that?

Rob: Ugh. That sounded passive-aggressive. Sorry. I'm wiped out and I haven't packed for this trip to New York yet and I'm being an asshole.

Magnolia: Don't you leave first thing in the morning?

Rob: 6 a.m.

Magnolia: Go pack!

Rob: It sounds like you're worried about me.

Rob: I'd rather find out what you wanted to ask me.

Magnolia: Go. Pack.

Rob: Not until you ask me your two-part question.

Magnolia: No. Get your life together.

Magnolia: In fact, don't text me until you get through airport security tomorrow.

Rob: Why not?

Magnolia: You said it yourself. You're tired. You're traveling and working all day tomorrow. I'm sure you're stressed. Get

ready for your day and then go to bed like a grown ass
adult.

Rob: Come with me.

Magnolia: Where?!?

Rob: Anywhere but first, bed. I'll sleep if you're with me.

Rob: I was a perfect bedmate the last time we had a
sleepover.

Rob: How about this: I'll pack now and then head up to your
place. For sleeping. Promise.

Rob: Should I interpret your silence as disinterest in my
suggestion?

Magnolia: For your information, I was conferring with
Gronk. He gets a vote when it comes to sleepovers.

Rob: How did my furry friend vote?

Magnolia: As long as you don't mind him sharing your
pillow, he's open to the idea.

Rob: And you? Are you open to the idea?

Magnolia: I consulted the dog, so…yeah. Get your ass up
here.

———

Magnolia: I never asked my two-part question! And now I
have another question.

Rob: Wait. What? Which two-part question?

Magnolia: From last week! Before you left for New York! You
were procrastinating and I wasn't going to reward that
behavior.

Rob: I was not procrastinating.

Magnolia: Sounded like procrastinating.

Rob: Ask your three questions while I'm between meetings

and can't offend you with my procrastination or beg for an invitation to your bed.

Magnolia: Okay, let's do this.

Magnolia: 1 – when did you get your nose pierced?

Rob: When I was 19 and enormously stupid.

Magnolia: It was that bad?

Rob: Not the piercing, me. I was a self-absorbed jackass back then. I actually cringed thinking about that version of myself when you mentioned it.

Magnolia: Unlike the cringing you do when remembering how you introduced yourself to me by telling me your height, weight, and length?

Rob: Yes. Very much unlike that.

Rob: Next.

Magnolia: 2 – when did you take the piercing out?

Rob: Before I took the Series 7 exam to get my trader's license. That was a little more than 10 years ago. Seemed like the right time.

Magnolia: Do you miss it?

Rob: Was that the third question?

Magnolia: No, but you sounded sad.

Rob: I'm not sad. A little sentimental over my dumb fool youth but no, I don't miss the nose ring.

Rob: Neither do my parents.

Magnolia: 3 – I've been wondering about this since the first time we met in person. I'd thought RRRooster441 was just a derpy handle but your belt buckle had RRR engraved on it that day so...what's your middle name, Rob Russo?

Rob: It was really nice knowing you.

Magnolia: What? You won't tell me?

Rob: I'm concerned about the fallout, to be honest. It's a good thing I'm going to be on the West Coast all of next week. I won't be tempted to show up at your house and blast some Peter Gabriel.

Magnolia: It can't be that bad. You should tell me.

Rob: It's Richard.

Magnolia: Okay, so…?

Magnolia: Oh my god, it's Dick. Your middle name is DICK. That explains so much!

Rob: Yep.

Magnolia: The Dick. It's you.

Rob: I've been trying to tell you this since the start.

Magnolia: Yes, but this is next level, my friend.

Rob: Any other questions?

Magnolia: I'm fresh out of them. Thank you for indulging me.

Rob: Can I invite myself to your bed now?

Magnolia: No dick.

Rob: I'm going to spend the next 5 hours analyzing the fuck out of that response.

Magnolia: Have so much fun!

Magnolia: DICK! Oh my god. I can't believe how perfect that is.

CHAPTER
TWENTY-FIVE

MY DATE WAS AGONIZING OVER ORANGE.

"I just don't know," my mother said with an excessively long sigh. "Do these clash? I'd hate for them to clash."

She held up the nail polish bottles, one in tangerine and another in raspberry, for my review.

"I don't think you need to worry about your toes clashing with your fingers," I said. "They're far enough apart." I gave her the shrug born in adolescence and reserved for the mothers of daughters.

"I think you should worry a little more. Men like it when women are put together and that includes a coordinated mani-pedi."

"Do they now?" I asked, incredulous. My mother wasn't one to espouse such antiquated values.

"They do. It's the little things that matter," she said. "They also like when women wear heels."

"Do you own anything higher than a kitten heel? For the record, your gardening clogs don't count."

She tipped her chin up, murmured in agreement. "I have

some cute espadrilles. I wore them two weekends ago. If you were around, you would've seen them."

"Those aren't heels," I argued, skipping over the guilt trip entirely. Juggling Ben and Rob meant neglecting a number of things. Sunday dinners at home, steady laundry cycles, my sanity. "Not really. More importantly, if men don't like my nails and shoes, that's their problem."

"It doesn't have to be a problem at all," she replied. "Now, tell me what you think about these colors. Is it a crime against color wheel laws?"

"You should ask someone else. I'm not an authority on polish protocol."

She gave me the unimpressed stare that, even in my midthirties, told me to cut the sass and clean my room. "I don't know why I go to these lengths to have girl time with you when you can't manage a simple question about color coordination."

"Neither do I," I replied. "A manicure lasts two days on me, tops. Most of the time, I don't make it to my car without screwing the whole thing up."

My mother frowned, sniffed, and looked back at the rainbow of paint choices.

Goddamn it. Goddamn this bad mood. Goddamn this week of work disasters and weird dreams and man stress. So much man stress. I pressed my fingertips to my eyelids. "I appreciate that you demand I spend time with you on a regular basis."

Without glancing away from her fruit bowl of nail polishes, she said, "If I didn't do it, I'd never see you. It's been ages since you've shown your face at supper."

"I'm sure Ash and Linden are enjoying that," I replied. "They always wanted to pretend they were twins."

She picked up a bottle of pale blue, set it down with a wince. My mother lived by the treaty of seasonally inspired mani-pedis. Summer had to be a field of poppies, spring like an Easter egg, autumn a harvest festival. Blue had to wait for the frosty days of January.

"They've outgrown their twin antics, you know," she said. "They miss you too."

There was another sassy comment on the tip of my tongue but I swallowed it. Forced it down and reached for a better alternative because my mother didn't deserve my moody bullshit today. Our relationship wasn't fraught or complicated but we pushed and pulled at each other. We sniped and snarked. She meddled, I evaded. In the end, we always made up and moved on.

"I'm sorry I haven't been there recently. My weekends have been..." My voice trailed off as I searched for the right description of recent months. Hectic? Overscheduled? Over-whelming? All of the above. "Busy. I'm sorry. I've been busy and as I know you're aware, the drive from Beverly to New Bedford is a lot longer when you factor in all the traffic going out to the Cape."

"That's why I like visiting with you during the week," she replied. "Less traffic."

"Mmhmm."

She tapped a lemony yellow bottle against her palm before holding it up to the light. "If you don't want your nails done, you can sit there and keep me company while I get mine. Maybe then you can tell me what's happening in your life since I never hear from you anymore."

"Oh my god," I murmured to myself, sending an eyeroll skyward.

"I heard that." She stared at three bottles, shook her head, returned them to the shelf. Then she selected the original tangerine and raspberry shades and headed toward the technician waiting beside her station.

I grabbed the first bottle of dark red I spotted and followed. "I'm sorry. Again," I said, dropping into the pedicure chair beside her. "I've had a lot going on."

"Not that much. You haven't logged into your online dating accounts in months. I can tell because you haven't opened any of the new matches or messages you have."

I shouldn't have been surprised to find she was keeping tabs. "I should really deactivate those."

She shook her head, huffed out a sigh. "If you're giving up already then yes, I guess you should deactivate them. Better than misleading the men who match with you."

I blinked at her, ignoring the technician's question about the water temperature. After five or six million blinks, I finally asked, "Would you like to repeat that?"

She shot me a sharp glance before turning back to the dated copy of *People* magazine in her lap. "You *promised* me you were going to try this year. You said you were going to do it for yourself. But you're not trying if you don't even open the messages."

A laugh burst from my lips, deep and loud and unwelcome in the land of muted HGTV and hushed conversation and the illusion of relaxation. I caught a handful of indignant glimpses and plenty of side-eye action. "Believe me, I'm trying my ass off."

My mother stared at me then, her lips turned down in a frown and her brows pinched. "It's rude, Magnolia. For all you know, they're perfectly nice gentlemen and you don't even bother to acknowledge them. It's rude to ignore the messages—"

"They can fucking wait," I snapped.

A hysterical laugh followed, one that turned every head in my direction. This was where it happened. Right here in a strip mall nail salon, this was where I lost my damn mind. With adorably pretentious high school girls and exhausted suburban moms as my witnesses, that laugh turned into a wild, contagious giggle, and another, and then there was no stopping. I wasn't sure what invited the tears—the uncontrollable giggling or the suggestion I'd given up on this dating initiative. More likely, it was the men. The ones I cared for, the ones I wanted to hide from hurt.

But I went on laughing and crying and just fucking trembling through the enormity of these feelings. I was a boiling kettle, screeching and steaming while everyone watched. They offered tissues and water, and chocolate and even a Xanax at one point. But there was only one way to quiet a kettle, and I didn't know how to turn down the heat.

"Magnolia," my mother whispered. She looked at me, her eyes wide. "Magnolia, what's wrong?"

"You-you-you-you," I stammered between laughs, "you th-think I'm not trying but you have no idea what I'm going through."

"Then tell me." She held out her hands as if it was that simple. And maybe it was. Maybe I was too far down this path to see the light anymore but it felt far from simple. "Tell me what you're going through. Maybe I can help."

I shook my head, already feeling the heaviness of a cry-graine creeping in. "I stopped using the apps," I started with a sniffle, "because I think I'm falling in love and my life is a m-m-m-m-mess."

My mother's mouth fell open. She quickly recovered, asking, "Is he married? Please don't tell me he's married. You know better than to get involved in that kind of situation again."

Again.

I would've kept laughing if I wasn't busy seething over that word.

Again.

I'd made some mistakes. I knew that without the reminder. I'd made mistakes, and it took me longer to learn from some of them than others. But figuring it out was the sticky side of growing tired of your own bullshit. Learning to love your flawed, fragile self required a thick foundation of hard-packed mistakes and a ruthless devotion to never committing them again.

Again.

"That's not fair," I said. "I didn't know Peter was married. Sure, I missed some of the warning signs but I didn't knowingly get involved with a married man, Mom. I wouldn't do that."

"So, he isn't married?"

I rolled my eyes, barked out a laugh. "No. Not married."

She shrugged, waiting for an explanation.

I'd often thought about how I'd present the coincidence of Rob and Ben to my family. In my head, it always took place after the summer, after our arrangement ended. After I'd chosen.

But the reality of making a choice between Rob and Ben —crowning a victor—sank in my belly like a stone. This wasn't a season finale and these men weren't contestants and I wasn't taking long, contemplative walks on a deserted beach while a film crew caught my every frown and far-off gaze. This was my real life, and choosing one of these men meant building a relationship on uneven ground.

All the power sat in my hands. It'd been fun for a time. It'd been nice to feel adored, cherished, special. I'd never been special, not in the ways that it mattered. But I wasn't meant to keep this power.

"Is your period starting? Is that what this is about? You're feeling a little PMS-y?"

I lifted my palms to my eyes. "Oh my god. Mom. No. Just...no."

She huffed out a breath. "It's a fair question," she said. "You're not usually *this* dramatic and believe me—hormones can make you crazy."

"Thanks," I murmured. "That's really helpful."

She shifted toward me, her arm brushing against mine. "If he's not married, what's the problem?"

"There are two of him," I replied. "That's the problem."

"Okay. He's a twin," she mused. "There's no way you'll have less than two babies at once but that's nothing to cry about."

"That's the only way this could be worse," I said. "If they were twins." I shuddered at the thought of my brothers dating the same woman. Good god. "Not twins. Two separate men. I'm seeing two men who are not twins."

My mother arched both eyebrows. "Are you kidding me?"

"Does it look like I'm kidding?" I gestured toward my face. I didn't need to see my reflection to know I was a puffy, red mess. "Does any of this look like a joke to you?"

It didn't matter how loud I spoke because everyone was already tuned into this meltdown. Of course, they were. Nothing happened to me in private. Every critical moment in my life unfolded with an audience. It made me wonder— if I wasn't judged, did it even happen? I wasn't sure. I wasn't sure but I was completely certain I was done with this, all of this. The judging, the arched eyebrows, the *again*, the constant sense that I still wasn't doing it right.

Just fucking finished.

"No, Mom, I'm not kidding," I continued. "I've been seeing two men for"—I shook my head, trying to recall the moment it all began—"a few months now. Two different, unrelated men who are neither twins nor married."

She watched me for a beat, her eyebrows bent and the technician's repeated request that she return her foot to the bath ignored. Then, "A few months? It's been going on for— for a few months? And you didn't think I'd like to know that?"

"Yes, a few months and I'm not here for your complaints about it," I replied, still riding high on my righteousness. "I didn't set out with the objective of getting caught between two guys and I wouldn't wish this chaos on anyone. But most of all, I don't need anyone reminding me that once upon a time, I did foolish things. I did unbelievably foolish things and I ignored all the warnings in the world." I jabbed a finger at my chest. "Yep, that was me. But how many times do you think I needed to see my entire life ripped in half and sold for salvage before I burned the fool right out of me? How many times do you think I need my dog stolen from me or my business relationships fucked up or getting served with deposition summonses before I killed that stupid girl with fire?"

"Magnolia, I just—"

I held up both hands, cutting her off. "I don't need to hear it. I don't need anyone telling me I've made a bad habit of betting on the wrong horse. It's true. I've done it too many times and I've paid for each one. I've paid so much. Do you know how much it's cost me? Do you know how many of my friends got married and had babies and bought houses and succeeded in their careers and did all the things everyone is supposed to do while I wandered around, lost and confused, and hoping I'd get mine one of these days? That was all I wanted. But I was wandering and foolish and missed out on everything. Sometimes I wonder if I'll ever catch up. If I'll ever get my turn." I swiped a tear off my cheek. "But I'm not betting on horses anymore, Mom. I'm betting on myself now."

I shifted in my seat, staring out the salon windows. It was blindingly bright, the kind of sunny that bellowed *summer-rrrrrrr!* and dusted my nose with freckles within minutes outside. There were people walking on the sidewalk, driving on the road. Going about their lives. They weren't caught between a history of bad decisions and a desperate desire to get it right for once in their fucking lives. Or perhaps they were. Maybe they were suffering and struggling, failing and fucking it all up. Maybe we all suffered and struggled, but we couldn't see it until we got up close and really looked at someone.

"How do you like the color? It's good?" the technician asked.

I bobbed my head without looking. It didn't matter whether my toes clashed with my fingers or I wore heels or I did anything other than finding the right path through this —the one where I didn't choose a man but we chose each other—because I wanted my damn turn. I'd earned it.

"I'm sorry," my mother said softly. "What I said about you and married men, I—I'm sorry. I thought we'd laugh about it but now I see it wasn't very funny." From the corner of my eye, I saw her gesturing toward me. "You're strong, Magnolia. You're stronger than the boys. Always have been. I think that's why we give you a hard time. We think you can handle it. You can but that doesn't mean you should have to."

I glanced toward her. "It's fine."

"It's not fine," she shot back. "We've been teasing you about these hiccups of yours and I missed the fact it was hurting you so much you started keeping important things from us. From *me*."

"I didn't know what to say," I admitted. "I didn't think you'd approve of this situation and I couldn't deal with hearing that. It's stressful enough to find myself with feelings for two people. I needed time to sort it out by myself before getting hit with everyone's opinions."

She leaned forward, peered at the polish on her toes for a moment. "It's a mother's right to have opinions about everything her babies do. Even when they're not babies anymore," she said. "You'll do the same thing. Someday you'll call me up when your baby insists on wearing a party dress and rain boots to the grocery store and I'll tell you the best is yet to come."

I laughed, a bit less hysterical this time. "That seems like an incredibly distant and unlikely future."

My mother seemed poised to offer a cheeky reply but stopped herself. She glanced at my toes, remarking to the technician, "That color is going on too light. She needs another coat." Then, softly, "I can keep my opinions to myself for a couple of minutes. Longer if a new episode of the *Property Brothers* comes on." She speared me with a silly grin. "Tell me about them."

"I'm gonna need a minute." I reached for my bag, digging

inside that black hole for my water bottle. I guzzled it down as I checked my phone. Four messages.

Andy: Any chance you're free for lunch on Thursday? I want to talk to you about a few projects I'm scheduling for Q4.
Andy: I can swing Friday but I'll have Patrick with me. He's wonderful but he's no help when it comes to decoding text messages from boys and I love decoding text messages with you.

Rob: What do I have to do to see you tonight? I'm tied up until 8 but I want to see you tonight.

Ben: Hypothetical question: if someone spilled paint on concrete, how should they clean that up?

ALL OF THOSE questions could wait. I tucked my phone away and turned back to Mom. "I don't know where to start."

She tipped her head to the side, hummed. "Which one came first?"

I snorted at that. "Rob. Rob was first," I said. "He's an investment banker. He lives in the South End. He's really— he's thoughtful. That's what he is. Thoughtful. It seems like such a small, simple thing but I've never been with a thoughtful man before. And he's generous. He makes time for me when he doesn't have it and opens himself up even when it's difficult for him. We're a lot alike, me and Rob. We've been through bad relationships and don't know how to trust people and—and we're afraid of getting hurt again." I dragged my palms up and down my thighs, needing some outlet for the heat that sparked inside me every time I thought about Rob. Every time I thought about where we started and where we were right now. "I can tell him exactly what I'm thinking. I can disagree with him and I can tell him he's wrong and...he likes it. He's never once made me feel small or that my ideas aren't important." I gulped down a swell of emotion. "He's never made me feel like I'm not important and that—that's new for me."

My mother continued peering at her toes, her lips pursed. I couldn't read her expression.

Eventually, she said, "And the second?"

"Oh, right," I murmured. "Ben is a firefighter. He's the one fixing up the old Cape across the street from me. He bought it for his grandmother but she passed away before he could finish work on the house. That loss hit him hard. He's hurting and he's so angry at the world for taking his grandmother. I don't know if she went sooner than expected or he's just that devastated from the loss but he's in bad shape. I just want to swaddle him up and hold him tight and fix things for him."

"Mmhmm." She waved her hand. "Come on. Let's have it. I can't keep my opinions to myself if you don't give me the whole story."

I frowned. What more did she want? "If you think I'm giving you any naked details, you're wrong."

She looked me over the same way she did when I came home after curfew and she was figuring out whether I'd been drinking and fooling around with boys. But instead of asking me a dozen questions meant to trip me up, she only nodded and said, "Good for you."

"That's it?" I yelped. "You're not going to ask about their families or when you can meet them or generally pick apart everything I've said?"

"I promised I'd keep my opinions to myself," she replied with a nod toward the wall-mounted televisions streaming *Property Brothers*. "Now it's your turn to make me a promise."

"Oh, Jesus," I muttered.

"When the time is right, promise me you'll bring him to dinner," she said.

"Which one?"

She turned an indulgent smile on me. "You already told me which one, Magnolia."

CHAPTER
TWENTY-SIX

My date was in a bad mood. A terrible, no-good, *throwing bags of cement mix like they were softballs* mood.

I pushed my safety glasses up, dropped my hands to my hips. "What's the deal?" I asked, nodding toward the haphazard pile of cement mix. "What did they ever do to you?"

But Ben didn't answer. He stalked off, going around the side of his house and coming back with another bag over his shoulder. He threw that one on the pile with more force than the last few.

"Seriously. What's the deal, Ben?" I yelled. "If you're still mad about me not allowing you near saws of any kind then that's too fucking bad but—I mean, just tell me what's going on."

He stomped toward the side yard again but stopped, pivoted. "It's nothing," he called, the length of the backyard between us. "I'm just not feeling very friendly today."

I crossed my arms over my chest. "What? Why?"

He looked up, his gaze arcing from the bright summer

sky and trees to the roof. We'd made good progress on this place but it was slow going. Any renovation that received only a day or two of attention each week would be.

"I'm sorry, Magnolia," he replied, his tone thick and syrupy. "I forgot the part where I'm supposed to spend every minute fawning over you."

I peered at him. "You're not."

"Really? Are you sure about that?" he asked. "Because last I checked, the only objective here is kneeling at your feet and shooting sunbeams up your ass and reminding you that you have all the power here."

I yanked my gloves off, shoved them in my back pocket. "Yeah? Where are you checking? Because that seems fucking ridiculous to me."

He advanced on me in long strides, quickly closing the gap between us. "Does it? Or are you too busy enjoying all the kneeling and sunbeams to realize this whole thing is fucking ridiculous?"

I stared at him, not sure I understood which "whole thing" we were discussing. It could've been the work on this house. With just the two of us doing this on the weekends, it was tedious. I wanted to call in a crew to assist but Ben was dead set on doing this himself. He was proving some kind of point but I wasn't clear who was on the receiving end of that point.

It could've been the house but it was most likely us. Me and Ben…and Rob. With each passing day, the rope around us seemed to tighten, cinch us in closer. Make it harder to imagine walking away from one of them.

And yeah, I did have the power here. For once in my life, I wasn't being jerked around by a fuckboy or dealing with an asshole guy who set the shady terms. I held the cards; I was in control.

But unlike those jerks and those assholes who'd never cared a bit for me, Ben and Rob mattered to me.

"I know," I conceded, holding my hand out to him. He stayed rooted where he was, didn't reach for me in return. "It will be over soon."

"Yeah?" he snapped. "Is that supposed to be comforting? Or is it a threat? Like, I better get my shit together because judgment day is on the horizon? If I don't keep quiet, I'm gonna get cut. Is that it?"

I moved closer to him, curled my hand around his forearm. "No, not like that," I replied. "It's just—"

"I don't want to hear it," he said, looking away from me. "Not today."

I stared at him as he stared at the trees behind the house. His jaw was locked, his feet planted, his arms crossed. He was angry but that anger served as the shell. Inside, where he was tender and vulnerable, he wasn't angry. He was aching.

But I couldn't take full responsibility for that pain. Part of it, yes, but his grandmother owned the rest. He didn't say it but I knew he was struggling through that loss. I saw it every time he swept a bitter gaze over the house and mumbled to himself, "What was I thinking?" or "What a fucking disaster I've made out of this."

And he was allowed to struggle. There was no timeframe for grief. It took up residence in the dusky corners of our hearts, it grew, it swelled, and it stayed.

Then it occurred to me that he knew I was going to the engagement party with Rob tonight. I wasn't sure how—

hell, I could've mentioned it—but he knew, and he wasn't happy about that.

And that was the tough reality of dating two men. Two men who didn't play well with others. Two men who limited their sharing to cookies and beer. Two men who wanted to love me more than I knew how to accept.

I squeezed his arm one more time. "I'm going to go. If it's sunny tomorrow afternoon, we'll work on pouring the patio cement before I head down to New Bedford for dinner with my family."

I paused, debated whether I should say anything else. It wasn't the right move but I wanted to invite Ben to my parents' house. That urge wasn't a product of wanting to do a meet-the-parents dance but of wanting to give him a family. He needed that. It would complicate the shit out of my life but he needed some extra-strength mothering.

"Fuck the patio," he replied. "I hate this fucking project. It's nowhere near finished, it's costing a fucking fortune, and it's a shitty way to spend a summer. No offense, but this is fucking horrible."

I hummed to myself, nodding as I folded those comments into his overall mood. He wasn't insulting me or any of the free labor I'd offered. He was working out some issues. I was sticking with that story—and withholding the dinner invite. Maybe next weekend. "My mom dropped off a ton of food while I was at work on Thursday. Truly, a ton. There's a big dish of chicken salad in my fridge if you're hungry. I have lunch meetings all week so I know it will go to waste."

"I do like her chicken salad," he muttered, still staring at those damn trees. Why wouldn't he look at me? Why wouldn't he just tell me what was at the heart of this?

"Then come get it," I said. "I hate wasting food and I don't have time to drop any of this off at the Walsh Associates offices so you should take some of it."

He jerked a shoulder up. "Maybe."

"Okay. I'm going now." I pushed up on my toes to plant a kiss on his cheek. "The back door is open if you want to grab that salad."

I stepped back, expecting a colorful comment about back doors and grabbing and...I didn't know, salad? But he continued staring at the trees. He didn't take the opening I'd offered.

My chest ached as I walked across the street to my house. It was a real, true pain, one I'd experienced before but never in this way. Men had left me hurting plenty of times but I didn't think I'd ever been the one to leave someone raw and fragile and angry.

I tried to put it out of my mind as I stepped into the shower and washed off the day's work. I had several hours before the engagement party but I required extra time to sort out my hair and cram myself into Spanx and—

The shower curtain clattered against the rod and Ben was standing there, the fabric bunched in his fist, a scowl on his lips, his body as bare as the day he was born. "Scoot over," he ordered as he stepped under the spray and yanked the curtain back into place.

"All right," I murmured, mostly to myself.

A minute passed without a word from Ben. Not a grunt or growl. Then another minute. He didn't touch me either. But I felt him. Frustration—and hurt? I wasn't sure—radiated off him in waves. He couldn't hide any of it. We stood there, two separate souls sharing a shower while a fuckton of emotions choked the air between us.

Finally, I started, "Ben—"

"No." He shook his head, drove his fingers into my damp hair. Droplets streaked down his cheeks, over his chin. They weren't from the water. "No."

"Ben. Listen. I want—"

"No," he repeated, bringing his hands to my waist and backing me up against the wall. Goose bumps spread over my skin. The tile was cold despite the steam rising around us. "No."

He pressed his forehead against mine, closed his eyes while tears poured out. He stayed there, his thumbs on my pelvis and his fingertips digging into my ass cheeks, his breath on my cheek and his cock hot and hard on my belly.

He needed to hold me. He also needed to hate me.

"Ben, I want—"

He stole my words with a kiss, a thrust, a sob. He reached for my thigh, brought it to his waist. I was open to him now, in every way I could be. And he knew it because he looked me in the eye for the first time since I'd called out his moody cement tossing. He looked me in the eye while he pushed two fingers inside me, while I curled my hand around his cock. He stared at me, watching while I rocked and writhed against him, while I stroked him, while I begged for more, while we reached the edge and fell over together.

And then, when I was dizzy and warm and boneless, he pressed his lips to my neck and whispered, "Don't go. Please, Magnolia. Don't go tonight."

CHAPTER
TWENTY-SEVEN

My date was exceedingly stubborn.

I dragged a wide-toothed comb through my wet hair and caught a glimpse of Ben in my bedroom mirror. He had the balls to stand there with his arms crossed over his chest and a dark pink towel wrapped low on his waist, scowling. Scowling. At me. As if I was the one being unreasonable here.

"I'm just saying, you don't have to go."

And he just kept saying it. This had to be the third or fourth utterance. Thankfully, he wasn't busy thrumming my clit this time. That made it much harder to say anything but "Yesssssss."

"As I've told you, I do. I have to go," I replied, sparing him a glance in the mirror.

"As I've told you, that's not accurate," he argued. "You can get out of it. You can stay here." He ran his hand through his wet hair. "You can stay with me."

I pointed the comb at him. "This isn't fair. You aren't playing fair, Ben."

"None of this is fair, Magnolia. It hasn't been fair since the start." He untangled his arms to set his hands on his hips. I looked away. "Don't do that. Don't hide from me."

He needed me right now. Needed to hate me and punish me and then turn his grief on me. Needed me to gather up his broken pieces and put him back together.

He needed me to save him, to fix him.

And why wouldn't he want that from me? It was all I'd ever given him.

"I'm not hiding anything from you." I waved a hand at the inside-out robe I'd pulled on after dashing out of the shower as proof. Being inside-out, the ties were lost to me and it hung open. But remedying that would've required a lengthy process of taking it off, putting it to rights, and then donning it again.

"You're hiding," Ben said. "You don't want to do this. No more than anyone else. But you're hiding because you don't want to decide. You don't want to do anything because you're afraid."

I shook my head, stabbed my comb at him. "I'm not afraid of anything, thank you very much."

He made a sound, some sort of snarl-groan-sigh, and I heard the hardwood floor creak under his feet. I didn't dare glimpse in the mirror. I didn't want to watch him approaching me. I didn't want to spend any time with the sharp realization Ben expected me to heal him more than he needed anything else from me. More than he needed *me*.

But then his hands were on my waist and his body warm at my back and his words in my ear when he said, "Go ahead, sweetheart. Lie to me."

"I'm not lying. I have nothing to lie about. I've been completely forthcoming with you," I argued.

I felt him nod, his chin brushing the crown of my head. "Yeah, you have," he agreed. "With everyone but yourself."

I tossed the comb down, flattened my hands on the bureau in front of me. "Seriously, Ben. We're going to need to reschedule the soul-searching. Okay?"

He squeezed my waist. "How about tonight? About five minutes after you cut the suit loose."

There was absolutely no way any of that was happening. Aside from the fact I was planning on spending the night at Rob's apartment, I wasn't ready to end things with him. I didn't *want* to end things with him. But I wasn't prepared for the conversation Ben was intent on starting. And I wasn't ready to contend with the possibility that he was right about any of this. Not in the way he thought he was right, but those shades of difference didn't matter to him.

More than that, I wasn't interested in working through his weighty issues right now. I wanted the bad handyman, the tattooed firefighter, the guy who gave as good as he got. The sweet, sad boy who'd bought a house for his grandmother to live out her final days and invited himself into my shower to cry on my shoulder and confess his need for major emotional repair wasn't it for me. Not today.

That wasn't some new-found nihilism on my part but the reality I couldn't change or fix or save anyone else. I'd tried. I'd tried so damn hard. I'd poured all the energy in the world into others. Giving and giving and giving until I'd hacked myself straight to the stump. And I'd never once succeeded at changing or fixing or saving anyone else. But through all that failing, I'd learned how to save myself.

Finally, I said, "You're not playing fair. You can't come in here and make these demands. It's not fair to me." I glanced over my shoulder but didn't meet his eyes. "You wouldn't appreciate Rob making the same demands."

"I don't care what he wants," Ben replied. "It doesn't matter to me and I know it doesn't matter to you."

"Oh yeah?" I shot back. "How do you know that?"

He stepped closer, sandwiching me between him and the bureau. "Because you've never given him what he wants."

"And I give you what you want?"

He laughed. Chuckled, as if this was really entertaining. So damn funny that I was dating two men. Two wonderful, damaged, hilarious, *hot hot hot* men who wanted me. Really wanted me. Crazy super wanted me. Most of the time, I let myself believe they wanted me because they wanted to win. It was easier to make this attention about competition rather than the possibility two men wanted me enough to share.

"Not once," he replied. "Not once have you given me what I want. But I can't stop hoping my day will come."

"I'm sorry about that." *Motherfuck.* We were not doing this again. "I'm not trying to make this more difficult for anyone. I'm not trying to hurt you."

"I know." His hand shifted, sliding under my robe. Goddamn this inside-out mess. Why couldn't I pull off a good dramatic exit from the shower? "I know," he repeated, his hand still on my belly. "That's what I love about you."

"What?" I asked. "That while you're putting me in a completely unfair situation and making requests I can't possibly fulfill, I still want you to be all right? To walk away from all of this in one piece?"

"Yeah. That. That's what I love," he replied. "But there's only one situation where I'm walking away in one piece and you know it."

"Don't do that," I warned, elbowing him away.

"I can't help it," he argued. "But you can. You can make this better, Gigi."

I wanted to sink into this moment, drown in it. I wanted to wave the flag, drop my shield, and tell everyone the game was over. I didn't require any more fix-ups or setups. I didn't need the apps or matches. I was good now, I was done.

But I couldn't quit this game. Not yet.

It wasn't the mere knowledge that I was due to meet Rob in a matter of hours. It wasn't an overactive sense of obligation to Ben's emotional needs. It was more than that.

It was more. It was so much more.

CHAPTER
TWENTY-EIGHT

MY DATE WAS THREE SHEETS TO THE WIND.

Maybe not all the way there but he was on the road and making good time.

"Magnolia!" Rob bellowed from his kitchen island. "And her canine companion!"

I set my bags on the floor and released Gronk from his leash. He scurried off, intent on sniffling every corner and licking every wall. "Be good," I called after him.

Rob leaned against the stone surface with one arm held aloft, drink in hand. The other hand seemed to keep him steady. When we'd agreed to meet at his place before the engagement party—rather than him driving up to my house, only to turn back around and drive back into the city—I hadn't imagined he'd busy himself with pregaming. Although I wasn't sure I'd handle it differently if the tables were turned.

"How did you get more gorgeous while I was in San Francisco? That's not allowed. If you're going to be even more beautiful, I want to be here to watch while it happens."

I gestured toward the full-length dress, the one I never would've chosen without the insistence of Andy and Shannon. The dress was to blame. I was the exact same person I was when he left town for a business trip last week. "Nothing has changed. Fancy dresses and Spanx are optical illusions."

He stared at my torso for a moment, then cocked his head to the side and stared another moment. And then it was just awkward because I was certain he was wondering where I was hiding all my squishiness. Honestly, I was wondering the same thing. It seemed like heavy-duty shapewear worked by rearranging internal organs. I was no medical doctor, but I was fairly confident my liver and stomach were in my uterus—because why leave that space empty when I had a belly to smooth?—and my intestines and kidneys were packed away near my ribs. That worked out well because I wasn't visiting the ladies' room tonight. Once these things came down, they were staying down.

Then, "Nah. I didn't notice the dress until now." He shook his head, flattened his lips. "It's gonna look spectacular on the floor."

"As any pile of fabric costing upward of five hundred dollars should," I murmured.

Rob didn't catch that part, his brows knitting together and his forehead wrinkling while he leaned toward me as if he'd hear previously spoken words better that way. When he thought better of asking for clarification, he said, "Allow me to pour you a drink, love."

"I'll pass for now. Thanks," I said, stepping toward him. Goddamn, this man shouldn't be allowed in tuxedos. There should be a city ordinance banning such things because this was a safety hazard and he wasn't even fully dressed. The jacket was draped over the back of an island stool. His bow tie and collar hung open at his throat. Cuffs were rolled up his forearms. If he walked out in traffic like this, the city would grind to a halt. "One of us should stay upright at all times tonight."

He tipped his glass toward me, sending a splash of amber liquid over the rim. "You're a fuckin' babe, you know that?"

I held out both hands as if I was completely and thoroughly righteous in my fuckin' babe status. "I was just thinking you're not too bad yourself, Russo."

"No, I mean you're a *fuckin' babe,*" he drawled, smacking his free hand on the countertop. "How the fuck did I talk you into this shitshow?"

I held out my hands again but this time, it was a gesture of resignation. "I believe I talked you into this shitshow."

At the sound of Gronk's low growls, we glanced toward the living room. My pup was busy dragging throw pillows out from under the coffee table and constructing a nest for himself. I wagged a finger in his direction. "Don't even think about shredding those pillows."

"I don't care about the pillows." He spoke quietly as if he knew better than to let Gronk hear.

"He's not allowed to shred pillows."

"You're the boss here." He narrowed his eyes at me, smiling. "Yes, Miz Maggie, you are the boss and you are responsible for us attending this blessed event tonight." He considered his glass. "Why'd you do that? Why d'you want me to do this? Because it's making me fucking crazy."

I kicked off my heels and paced the length of the island. In all honesty, I was feeling that fucking crazy too. I did some social media stalking last week and discovered Rob's ex Miranda was all kinds of stunning. Sexy, sophisticated, put together. She looked like the kind of woman who knew how to take her daytime look to evening and had frequent occasion to use that skill.

"What part of it is making you crazy? Are you worried about Eddie?"

"He's dead to me," Rob said, waving away all thought of his former best friend. "He can suck my dick for all I care." He set his glass down, cringed. "Nah, I don't want that either. He's too self-absorbed to give a good blowie."

I ran my hands down my sides, over the thin fabric of my dress. It was a subtle choice, this plum-y purple sheath over-laid with superfine lace and tulle. It wasn't impressive on the hanger but it transformed into something magical on my body. I looked like I was intended to wear beautiful things, like this was my everyday style. And when I gazed at myself in the mirror, I believed it. I believed that I belonged at a black tie engagement party at one of the swankiest ball-rooms in the city. I believed I belonged on this man's arm.

More than that, I wanted to be the one on his arm.

"Then you're worried about seeing Miranda—"

"Nope," he shouted. "I don't give a fuck about her anymore. I realized I never loved her. Not really. I thought I did but no. No, that wasn't love. I turned that stone over"— he glanced down at his hand, wiggled his fingers like he was counting, then shook his head—"I don't know. Couple of days ago."

When I reached the far end of the island, I grabbed the half-empty bottle of bourbon and carried it to the bar cart in the living room. Inspected the pillow nest for signs of destruction and happily found none. "That's quite the devel-opment," I said, turning back to him.

"You know," he started, wagging a finger at me, "you're right. However, that's not the point."

I stared at him across the island. "And what is the point?"

"That I realized I love you," he said.

I barked out a laugh. "You're drunk, Rob."

"I still love you." His words came without strain or effort as if it cost him nothing to say them. "I do love you. I have since...you know, Magnolia, I think I loved you from the minute you wouldn't let me get my way. Just didn't let myself see it. Or something like that."

"Someone has to keep you in line," I muttered.

That's right, Magnolia. Dodge. Deflect. Do anything but focus on what he's saying.

I rolled my eyes at myself.

"You want to know how I realized this?" he asked.

I bobbed my head, eager for some explanation. "Please."

He glanced up at the ceiling, blinked at the exposed duct-work. Then, "I got back to my hotel room after being in meetings all day and then dinner with the same damn people I spent the day with. I flopped on the bed and I thought about you." He cleared his throat, shot a quick glance at me. His hazel eyes brightened, shedding the fog of liquor. "I thought about traveling with you. I wondered whether you'd been to San Francisco and which neighborhoods you'd like. Going places and—and being with you. I thought about that and I jerked off a couple of times while I did it—"

"A couple of times?" I interrupted. I knew he had some —*ahem*—staying power but Satan save us.

"Maybe three? Four? I don't know. It'd been a long day." He shot a shoulder up, let it fall.

Ladies and gentlemen, I give you Mr. Nine Inches and his amazingly short refractory period.

"Like I said, you're a babe. You give me plenty to work with." When I only blinked at him, he continued, "And as I was falling asleep—"

"I hope you tipped the housekeeping staff generously," I murmured.

"I always do," he replied. "As I was falling asleep, I realized I never once worried about you and the firefighter. You and anyone. I trust you, and I'm done holding Miranda's bullshit against you and...and I love you. I love you and I never loved her and this engagement party is making me fuckin' crazy because I can't believe it took me this long to see it. To know I was going through the motions, settling for someone because she was there and seemed...I don't know. Good enough." He grinned at me and the space between us seemed to dissolve. "I realized it because you've given me more than good enough and you make me give more than that too. You make me show up. You make me work for it."

I flattened my hands on the stone countertop, needing that solid surface to keep me anchored here. To keep me from allowing those words to wrap me up and warm me to the bone. To keep me from wanting to hear them again, wanting to take them and tuck them into a secret space where nothing would ever steal them from me. To keep me from believing that I deserved love—hot, sloppy, unflagging, imperfect love. That I had it, right here in a heart-stopping tuxedo.

All I had to do was accept it...and give it back.

"Say something," Rob urged. "Anything."

"You're drunk," I repeated, shooting a glance over his

shoulder at the microwave clock. "You're drunk and we're going to be late."

His lips pulled up in an easy grin as his eyelids drooped shut. He smiled, shook his head. His chin scruff rasped against his collar. Without thought, I leaned toward him, wanting to be closer to that sound. That sensation. "Not the response I was expecting but I'll take it."

"What were you expecting?"

"Not an update on my inebriation." Rob opened his eyes, rubbed the back of his neck. I wanted to stop him, bat his hand away, do it for him. Ease his tension. Ease everything.

So, I did.

I took a final step toward him and reached for the back of his neck with both hands. My fingers slipped beneath his starched collar, meeting warm skin. The scent of bourbon and Kiehl's olive fruit shampoo lingered on him. I leaned in, inhaled, brushed my lips over his jaw. He swayed toward me, a soft growl sounding in his throat as my thumbs kneaded his knots.

"Tell me something," I said.

"I've already told you the important stuff," he remarked.

My lips twitched into a smirk. "Why are you drinking?"

He cut his gaze toward the island and his abandoned tumbler. "Jet lag, I think."

"Since it's three hours earlier in California, that's pure bullshit." I smiled up at him. "Come on, Rob. Tell me what's happening with you."

"I was getting dressed and I thought about calling Eddie. For a minute, I forgot my best friend is gone. I forgot that he pissed away a lifelong friendship and I can't call him up to tell him—anything. I can't tell him anything. Not anymore.

And I can't be happy for him tonight. They deserve each other. They share the same views on loyalty."

He moved his hands to my hips but didn't stay there. He skimmed up to my waist and down to my backside, his touch gentle. Almost tentative. He swayed once again but this wasn't a drunken stumble. It was a dance to which neither of us knew the steps but we had a good idea how we wanted it to feel. We held each other, moving together in a waltz set to breaths and heartbeats.

Rob continued, "I guess I'm mourning the loss of my friend. I don't think I've allowed myself that yet. So, I poured myself a drink. And then, one more. I recognize this isn't the most well-adjusted coping mechanism for thirty-eight-year-old men but I've never once suggested I was well-adjusted."

"What did you want to share with him?"

He tipped his head to the side, a half-smile playing on his lips as he glanced down at me. "I wanted to tell him I met the game changer. That I fell for the game changer."

I stared at the freckled skin between his open collar. So much easier than meeting his gaze. So much easier than sliding all the way into this quicksand of his affection. "Is that so?"

An impatient growl sounded in his throat. "Stop fishing for compliments. I've already said you're hot as fuck and I love you. Don't make me confess my plans to steal you away and marry you."

I leaned back, touched a hand to my throat. If I was wearing pearls, I would've clutched them. "What was that?"

"Shhhh," he whispered, his index finger pressed to his lips. "It's a secret but I'm going to get you a diamond the size of an egg and you're going to make a husband out of me, love."

"What kind of egg?" We'd shuffled all the way across the room now. "Are we talking about chicken eggs or robin eggs? There's a big difference, Rob."

That was my incredibly mature coping mechanism in action. Give me an important moment and I'd give you some topflight sarcasm.

"Ostrich," he replied, serious as a stroke. "I might have to steal from a few monarchies to make it happen but they'll never notice it missing."

"Oh, good." I bobbed my head in agreement. "That's a good strategy."

"Thought so." He lifted his shoulders, let them fall. "I don't think we need to go to this party. I don't need to prove anything to them." He ran his knuckles down the line of my spine before wrapping his arms around my torso. He held me tight, almost too tight. I loved it. "I don't need to do it. Not when I'd much rather stay here and peel that dress off you."

"This"—I traced the fine detailing around the dress's v-neck—"is not hitting the floor until it's been adequately flaunted."

Rob's eyes crinkled as he laced our fingers together, brought our clasped hands to his chest. "Oh, love. I'll flaunt you. I'll flaunt the fuck out of you. And you know what? I won't even have to work that hard at it. You, just being all your you-ishness, is all it takes." He dropped his chin to the crown of my head, blew out a breath. "Eddie will take one look at us and he'll know. He'll know he did me a favor—a shitty one, but a favor. He'll know I never looked at Miranda the way I look at you."

"And how is that?" I whispered. I had to whisper. Had to pretend I didn't need every last one of his words.

He dragged his gaze up my body, taking forever to meet my eyes. "You're the only thing in the world I can see. Only thing I want to see."

My lips parted but I produced no sound. I couldn't explain it but those words hit me harder than his promise of love. They stole my breath, blurred my vision. I wasn't certain but it felt like my eyes transformed into cartoon hearts and throbbed right out of my skull.

Jesus Horatio Christ. I was falling for him. *This,* this was it. Falling was like this—a cartwheel and a jump from the high dive and tripping on a crack in the sidewalk and feeling the wind knocked out of your lungs as you crashed down. All of those things, all at once. Hot goose bumps ran down my arms and over my chest. A shiver sparked through my shoulders. My stomach—wherever it was—flipped, flipped again. Everything was warm and tingly.

He…loved me.

And I…oh my god. Oh, my god.

"You know what?" he asked. "We'll go. We'll drink champagne and toast this engagement because if those cocksuckers hadn't found each other, I never would've found you. I'm happy for it."

I tipped my head to the side. "Now we're thanking them?"

"Oh, fuck no," he roared. "Fuck. No. They deserve chlamydia and back-to-back tax audits."

"Rob. That might be a little severe." When he arched his brows, I continued, "The audits, not the chlamydia."

"Not hardly," he murmured. "But I would've been engaged—maybe even married—to a woman I didn't love and be best fucking friends with a guy who didn't have my back and I don't feel like they fucked me up anymore. I feel like—like one of those memes about the world working in mysterious ways and light coming after the dark and slogging through shit to see the sunrise."

"By that logic, they're the game changers," I said. "Not me."

"Erroneous," he yelled. It sounded like he was objecting in court. Gronk joined in with a howl. "Erroneous on all counts."

"You're drunk," I said with a laugh.

He shook his head once. "Not nearly as much as you think I am."

I peered at him then, wondering whether he was right. Whether I'd decided he was hammered and therefore everything out of his mouth was the product of loosened inhibitions and a slippery tongue. But I couldn't prevent myself from giving him a *yeah, whatever* eyeroll and head bob, and saying, "This would be a great time for me to ask if you want—"

"Yes," he interrupted. "Whatever it is, yes."

"Cool, cool," I murmured. "It's a good thing I brought my new strap-on, then."

That goddamn sarcasm of mine.

He gave me a bland stare. "For you, I'd do it. I'd ask you to go easy and use extra lube. Even more than you think necessary. The most lube ever. But I'd do it. I'd take whatever you had to give me, and who the fuck knows? Maybe I'd enjoy it." When a giggle slipped past my lips, he continued, "Ask the question, Magnolia."

I brought my free hand to my hair, stopping a second before I mussed the carefully messy bun I'd managed. I whispered, "Are you sure?"

I'd intended to ask him to help Matt and Lauren move

into their new house next weekend but I couldn't do it. I couldn't make this moment about anyone but us. And that was where Ben had me—I *did* know.

Oh, yeah. I knew. But I was a woman who lived in a cloud of doubt. Hell, there were instances when I didn't even believe these men liked me more than they liked the thrill of competition.

Rob studied me, his brow furrowed. He seemed confused, maybe annoyed. Maybe it was an annoying question. Maybe I was meant to take his words at face value and be happy I heard them at all.

I swiveled my head from side to side, shaking that nonsense loose. My sarcasm could stay but this uncertainty had to go. I'd come too far, worked too hard to let that noise drag me down.

"I'm sure I didn't love Miranda," he said. "I cared about her and I thought we were right for each other but we never loved each other. I know that now." His lips brushed over my temple as he locked his arms around my waist. "I know I love you and I know it has nothing to do with wanting to win. I realized something else this week."

I tipped my head back to meet his gaze. Stared, waited for him to continue. When he didn't, I said, "By all means, draw out the drama. I'm here for the suspense."

"You're so mean to me," he drawled. "How do you make it hurt so good, love?"

He was hard through his tuxedo pants, thick and throbbing. But that could wait. Sex was great but the sensation of every damn cell in your body colliding into a sharp arrow of affection for another human was better than any orgasm. "Because I know how."

"What else do you know?" he asked. I ran my hand up

his chest, pinched his nipple. He yelped, flattened me against him. "Why do I like it when you're mean to me?" He shook his head. "Never mind. Don't answer that."

His hands slipped over my backside. "What else did you realize?" I asked.

"That you could choose the firefighter," he said. "You could choose him and I'd bow out. I'd hate it. I'd fucking hate it. But I'd do it if it meant you were happy. If it was your choice, I'd wish you the best and step aside."

He watched me, his eyes wide and his lips parted as that same arrow of affection lanced through him.

I was *done*. Heart eyes and butterfly bellies and a lava cake heart. *Done*.

And I knew why I couldn't stay with Ben tonight, even when he begged. I felt things for Ben and I felt things with Ben but they weren't like this. Nothing was like this.

Because I knew.

I knew falling was like this.

———

WE WENT. We saw. We drank all the champagne.

Maybe not *all* of it, but when we stumbled into Rob's hired car later that night, my head was squishing like a fish-tail and the world felt like a sweet, bubbly sea. I was giggling for no obvious reason and my messy bun was falling apart, but I didn't want anything to change.

Rob pulled the car door shut behind him and fell back against the seat, his long legs sprawled out in front of him. His tie was loose and his collar open, his cuffs rolled up to his elbows. A wash of pink rode high on his cheeks. His eyes, that speckled blend of gold and green, bathed me in shimmering heat.

"That was," he started, gesturing toward me, "that was...interesting."

Another giggle burst from my lips, louder and more unchained than I'd expected. "Can I be honest?" He nodded, dropped his hand on my thigh. "I know I experienced this through a different lens than you, but I don't think it was bad-interesting. It was"—I bit my lip, hesitated—"weird. It was weird-interesting."

"So weird."

"Okay, okay." I scooted closer to him. That champagne and those fishtail thoughts, they stole all my caution, my care. "I think there's a weird element we've ignored up until this point. I think it's time we address it."

He swung my legs onto his lap, wrapped his arm around my torso. His hand slipped between my legs but the position we'd contorted ourselves into kept it chaste. As chaste as two drunk people in the back of a town car could be. "Is it complete and total lack of pigs-in-a-blanket at that party? I don't care where it's taking place, you need mini hot dogs."

"No, but now I'm hungry."

"Food. Yes. Let's do that." Right on cue, his stomach sent up a thunderous rumble. "We'll go home, get Gronk, and then walk over to that place on Boylston. The one with the dog-friendly patio."

"You want to get burgers and shakes in a tux, Russo? Is that what you're saying?"

"I want to take my contacts out before I scratch my corneas off," he answered. "But otherwise, yes. I promised to flaunt you tonight."

Rob in a tuxedo was bad enough. Add his sexy nerd

glasses with the thick, horn-rimmed frames to the equation and it didn't get much worse.

By worse, I definitely meant perfect. He was perfect.

And he wanted to feed me burgers and milkshakes, and bring my dog along too.

Perfect.

"I'm changing into flip-flops for the next portion of this flaunting. I really must get all the mileage out of this dress that I can. It's not like I can wear it to work."

Rob studied the neckline, traced it with his finger. "I would pay to see that."

"That can be arranged since your terrace is still a concrete wasteland."

He dipped his chin, sent me a stare that bit at my cheeks until I was flushed and grinning. "Send me a bill, love."

My lips parted as a gravelly breath sputtered out and that would've been confession enough, but then my belly gurgled. It was loud and vaguely odd—a product of organ rearrangement via Spanx—and it told Rob everything else he needed to know.

I was starving. For food, for him, for us.

And I couldn't hide it any longer.

He smiled, allowed me an exit from speaking the words crystalizing between us. "What have I ignored, Magnolia? Was it how Eddie gave Miranda the exact same ring I'd picked out for her? Or the swan ice sculpture, because that thing was unusual. I've already mentioned this but I think the mini hot dog issue is worth revisiting. I know for a fact that both of those motherfuckers love mini hot dogs."

"Those are valid concerns but the weirdest part is those motherfuckers invited you." Rob turned his attention back to my dress, now busy pushing the skirt over my knees. "Why would they do that?"

He traced the ball of my kneecap. "I don't know." He paused, lightly tracing an almost-healed scrape. "I think— maybe—they saw the gesture as an olive branch. A twisted olive branch from a fucked-up tree, but an olive branch. They probably thought they were earning some absolution in the process. Whatever their reasoning, I don't think they expected me to show up *and* show up with the most incredible woman in this city."

"They didn't expect to see you, no. They didn't hide their surprise too well." I dropped my head to his shoulder as another round of loose, silly giggles rolled through me. "I think we might've taken over their party. I haven't danced that much, ever."

"It's their fault. They hired a kick-ass band and your body was meant to move and—"

"—and you loved stealing some of their spotlight," I interrupted.

His expression softened, sobered. "I liked stealing it with you."

I reached for the open collar of his shirt, tugged his face closer to mine. "I liked it too."

Rob sucked in a breath. "I already love you. Stop making it worse."

I brought his lips to mine, offering a quick brush before pulling him in, demanding more. He tasted new, different. As long as I lived, I'd swear it wasn't champagne but the flavor of beginnings. It was hypnotic, like orange blossoms a minute before they bloomed.

CHAPTER
TWENTY-NINE

Ben: Hey, pretty girl.

Ben: I'm working nights every day this week so I won't see much of you unless you set something on fire. If you do that, stay away from the gas. You really need to know what you're doing to do it right.

Magnolia: Firefighter humor is…dark.

Ben: You don't know the half of it.

Magnolia: Does that concern you?

Ben: What do you mean?

Magnolia: I mean, I don't know much about you or your work. Does that concern you?

Ben: There's an emergency, I show up. There's a fire, I put it out. Not that complicated.

Magnolia: Okay, yeah, I get that but…we could still talk about it. We don't talk about a lot of things. You know?

Ben: Hadn't really thought about it.

Magnolia: No worries. It was just a random thought.

Ben: Yeah. It's all good.

Ben: Hey look I gotta go. Talk later.

Magnolia: Take care.

————

Rob: Hi, love. I'm just getting home but I hope you're in bed already.

Rob: I have a crazy early call with London in the morning. Morning for them, I guess.

Rob: I know I'm going to be tied up from that point forward but I wanted to make sure you got a good morning message before I stumble/sleepwalk into the office at 4 a.m.

Rob: I also wanted to mention your notable absence in my bed right now.

Rob: It is not the same without you.

Rob: I'm not the same without you.

Rob: In case you need proof, I bought a potted plant on the way home from that stupid long business dinner. There was a little flower shop I'd never noticed in the South End before. I didn't know they were open so late but I went in and picked out a green thing.

Rob: The lady working there said it was a peace lily but I don't see any flowers.

Rob: She also said it's toxic for dogs. I'm sure you know that. I don't know where to put it but Gronk can't climb so we'll find a good spot.

Rob: Right? He can't climb? I wouldn't put it past him though.

Rob: Anyway, yeah, I bought a plant.

Rob: Have an amazing day, love. Feel free to warm my bed and teach me how to deal with a plant tonight.

Magnolia: lol no, he can't climb

Magnolia: His vertical leap isn't bad but he also knows he's not supposed to eat plants so that helps.

Rob: Why are you awake, my love? Are you thinking about how much happier you'd be sleeping with me?

Magnolia: You do have central air and it is hot as balls so...yes.

Rob: That's fine. Use me for my HVAC. I'm good with it.

Magnolia: How was dinner?

Rob: Stupid long.

Magnolia: Other than that...

Rob: Fine. Closed some new business and picked up some good info that will keep the air conditioning on indefinitely. Had some nice roasted brussels sprouts with that sweet vinegar glaze stuff you like.

Magnolia: And you bought a peace lily.

Rob: Apparently.

Magnolia: It's a gateway houseplant, you know. First it's a peace lily and then it's a pothos and a spider plant and maybe an orchid or two. Soon enough you have 9 different types of ferns, a fiddle-leaf fig, and a rubber tree.

Rob: A rubber tree? You're making that up. That's a land-scape architect joke, right?

Magnolia: The sap is latex.

Rob: My mind is blown.

Magnolia: You've had a late night and you're looking at an early morning. Go to sleep. We'll talk about green things tomorrow.

Rob: Dinner?

Magnolia: Sure. I'll text you later.

Rob: Sounds good, love. Sleep well.

Magnolia: You too. Enjoy that air conditioning.

Rob: I'd enjoy it more with you.

Magnolia: Same.

————

Ben: I know it's the middle of the night and I really hope this doesn't wake you up.

Ben: You told me you've had your phone on silent for something like 19 years once so I figured this wouldn't make a sound but now I'm not sure if it will vibrate.

Ben: I hope you're not awake because this is a god-awful hour of the night.

Ben: I shouldn't even be typing this right now.

Ben: But I'm on nights so I'm up and I can't stop thinking about what you said.

Ben: We don't talk, do we?

Ben: We talk about paint colors and your dog and my complete inability to hammer a nail straight but we don't talk about anything important.

Ben: I was trying to figure out why that is and I don't think I can talk.

Ben: Right now. I can't talk right now.

Ben: I think I'm really fucked up and the deepest thing I can handle is bashing the shit out of a nail and then yanking it out and doing it all over again because you won't let me fuck up.

Ben: Maybe that's what I'm supposed to get out of this. You won't let me fuck up the only good thing I ever tried to do.

Magnolia: I'm sure you've done plenty of good things.

Ben: Fuck I woke you up.

Ben: I'm so sorry.

Magnolia: I'm awake because Gronk had to go out. There was a squirrel taunting him.

Magnolia: Or a ghost. I'm not sure which one.

Ben: Do you believe that? Dogs can see ghosts?

Magnolia: Ummm…I think so? There are times when he barks at empty rooms and I refuse to believe he's hollering at the termites.

Ben: I like that.

Ben: I wish I could see ghosts.

Magnolia: I know, sweetie. I know. I'm sorry you're going through this. That house isn't the only good thing you've done. I'm sure of it.

Ben: I didn't do anything. That's the problem. I had this big idea and thought I was going to pull off this whole remodel in a goddamn weekend or something and I could've spent that time with my grandmother. So, now she's gone and I didn't give her a nice place for her last days and I didn't even spend those fucking days with her.

Magnolia: Did she know you were working on a house for her?

Ben: Yeah.

Magnolia: I'm no expert on the matter but I think that gesture probably spoke volumes to her.

Ben: Maybe.

Magnolia: It's okay if you can't talk right now. There was a time when I couldn't talk.

Ben: When? What happened?

Magnolia: I made some bad choices a few years ago. I thought something was real but it really, really wasn't. I ruined a dear friendship, one I'll never get back.

Ben: I don't believe that.

Magnolia: lol which part?

Ben: I don't believe that you ruined anything.

Magnolia: Believe it. I've ruined more things than I've preserved. Ruined myself once or twice or a dozen times.

Ben: I don't believe that.

Magnolia: Well…it's true.

Ben: What happened?

Magnolia: Which time? There's the time I dated a guy for YEARS even though he stole absolutely everything from me.

Magnolia: Including my dog.

Ben: First of all, he ruined that situation.

Magnolia: And I let it happen. I saw it, I knew it, and I just let it happen.

Ben: I'm gonna call bullshit on that.

Magnolia: Your second point?

Ben: Oh yeah. I'm gonna need his full name. An address if you have it. I have a rubber hose and I'm in the mood to teach some manners.

Magnolia: Don't bother. Not worth your time.

Ben: What else? What else have you ruined? Because I don't think you have it in you, pretty girl.

Magnolia: Ha. How about flunking out of college two times? Mostly because I just didn't show up or do shit.

Ben: You know what they say. Third time is the charm.

Magnolia: Uh, not really. I just got tired of my own bullshit and didn't like working the drive-thru line at Starbucks and found something I actually wanted to learn.

Ben: I'm not sure I could get tired of my own bullshit. I kinda like it.

Magnolia: Yeah. I know.

Ben: What else? Give me your worst.

Magnolia: There was a guy who helped me when I was first starting out in landscape architecture. I misunderstood a few interactions and signals. Or, I took those interactions and signals and I invented something that wasn't there.

Magnolia: Then I truly strangled the shit out of that relationship with both hands. Mentorship, gone. Professional relationships, gone. Business engagements, gone.

Ben: I will also need his name and address.

Magnolia: I would've given you both a few years ago but the best recovery from shitshows like that one is moving on and doing well.

Ben: All right. Listen. You're pretty and nice and I like the hell out of you and you have worked more than your share of shitshows but you haven't spent your grandmother's last days on earth fucking around with a house that needed months of work.

Magnolia: You're right. I haven't experienced that.

Ben: You're not carrying that kind of regret around.

Magnolia: No. Again, you're right. I'm not carrying that specific regret.

Ben: Not trying to be a dick.

Magnolia: I don't think you're being a dick. I think you're hurting. A lot.

Magnolia: And I wish there was something I could say to make it better but I'm not sure I can do that for you.

Ben: It's okay. It's not your job to make it better.

———

Magnolia: Any interest in an espresso martini lunch?

Magnolia: Because I could use an espresso martini today.

Andy: Your Wednesday is going that well, huh?

Magnolia: My Wednesday started at 12:45 a.m. when I got up to get a cookie and found a bunch of texts from Rob.

Andy: Is he losing his shit?

Magnolia: Actually, no. He was perfectly charming. But we talked about plants and air conditioning for 20 minutes. Then we made dinner plans for tonight.

Andy: Okay…

Magnolia: But I woke up 4 hours later to a fuckton of texts from Ben and he was losing his shit.

Magnolia: I made an offhand comment to him earlier in the day about how we don't really talk about things. I said something about not knowing anything about his work. Like, I know he's a firefighter and I understand the basics of that but…there's gotta be more, right? Or anything? Or doesn't he want to tell me about his daily life?

Magnolia: He stewed on that for approximately 12 hours and then opened up about losing his grandmother and his regrets and how he's just super fucked up right now.

Andy: Which we knew…

Magnolia: We did.

Andy: Regardless, you had a tough night.

Magnolia: Yeah. A lot of feels.

Andy: So many feels.

Magnolia: Espresso martini lunch?

Andy: Sorry I thought the answer was obvious.

Andy: Yes. We need to sort you out before dinner.

CHAPTER
THIRTY

MY DATES WERE TOO MUCH OF A GOOD THING.

It seemed unlikely. It seemed impossible. How could one person find herself with both cups running over after years with no running, no cups? But here I was, crouched behind a boxwood bush, creeping on Ben and Rob while they argued about sports.

"This is what I've become," I murmured to myself, gripping my trowel tighter. "I'm the crazy lady hiding in bushes."

This hadn't been my intention. I didn't imagine I'd spend Matt and Lauren's move-in day ducked down in the shrubbery but when I pulled up this morning, the boxwoods and the periwinkle beneath them caught my attention. It was nothing major but I couldn't think about unpacking the house until the landscape looked right.

And then Rob and Ben walked up the quiet suburban street together, bullshitting and ball-busting the way men do. I scrambled behind the bush, no longer concerned with the half-exposed root ball, and eavesdropped on their conversation.

Because that was normal. Totally normal.

"None of this is normal," I whispered. "And now I'm talking to myself. Awesome."

"I don't know, man. I don't know about the depth charts. If QB takes a bad hit, we're in survival mode. I hate to say it but this dynasty is winding down," Ben said, shaking his head as he folded his arms over his chest.

He shouldn't be allowed to do that. It should be illegal and there should be a police force tasked with eliminating gratuitous arm crossing. There should be a fine too. A huge fine. Equivalent to the size of those damn forearms.

"I couldn't disagree more," Rob replied, mirroring Ben's stance.

Hipshot, arms crossed. Shorts, t-shirt like a second skin. *Fuck me.*

"A dynasty isn't built on the back of one coach or one quarterback," Rob continued. "It's a broad, deep foundation with layers of institutional knowledge and leadership. Coaches and defensive coordinators will come and go. QBs and wide receivers too. The dynasty has never been stronger."

"Listen, I want to believe as much as you do," Ben said. "The last thing I want is five months of shitty football but I want to be realistic here. It's better to exceed low expectations than deal with another fucking disappointment in my life."

Rob peered at him. Eventually, he said, "Dude, it's just football. It's gonna be okay."

From all the way across the front yard, I saw Ben's full-body eyeroll. "And here I thought you believed in the dynasty."

Rob shrugged. "I mean, yeah. I do. But I can deal with a

rebuilding season or two. I'm not about to cry over it. We've had a good long run, you know?"

"That's convenient," Ben muttered. "Didn't peg you for a fair-weather fan."

"Oh, come the fuck on," Rob replied. "I'm here for winning seasons and I'm here for losing seasons. You're the one with all the end of days talk."

"You're a fuckin' drama queen," Ben shot back.

"I'm the drama queen? You were the one pissing and moaning about all the off-season trades. I mean, that shit happens. Good players get traded but the game goes on."

Ben glared at him. "Is that supposed to be some kind of spiritual lesson? If it is, I'm not here for it. I'm in no mood for any millennial meditation horseshit."

Rob's shoulders bounced as he chuckled in response. "Listen, man. My firm has some preseason game tickets. You wanna go?"

Ben bent down, picked up a twig fallen from the maple tree overhead. He swiped it through the air like a tiny sword. "Fuck yeah, I wanna go. When?"

I blinked hard and fast as they pulled out their phones and murmured over schedules.

This wasn't cups running over. This was unfuckingbelievable. They—they were turning into friends. If I hadn't witnessed this, I would've doubted the shit out of it.

"What the hell are you doing?"

I lost my balance when I heard those words over my shoulder. I ended up on my back in the dirt, glaring up at Sam Walsh.

He held out his hand to me, and since I was awkwardly wedged between the house, the bush, and the dirt, I needed his help.

I didn't want to accept it. Not because of him but because of me. Even now, years after I imagined a flirtatious relationship between us, I didn't want to need anything from him. I wanted to be competent without him, even when I was sprawled on the ground.

"Come on, Gigi," he said, thrusting his hand toward me again.

I dug my elbows into the dirt, pushing up on my own. "I'm fine," I replied, still crouched behind the boxwood. "Thanks though."

"At least tell me what you're doing," he said, dipping his hands into his pockets.

Before looking at Sam, I shot a glance over the bush at Rob and Ben. They were huddled together, pointing at their phone screens. "The root ball wasn't level," I replied. "That led to the groundcover settling in uneven patterns."

We'd talked out our issues years ago. Apologies accepted, hatchets buried. But even when you glued the shards back together and made the plate whole again, the cracks remained.

"Did we run a rainwater irrigation system?" he asked, turning his attention to the roofline. "This seems like the perfect property for that kind of setup."

"Yes," I replied softly, glancing back to Rob and Ben. Rob was gesturing down the street now and Ben was leaning in the same direction. I couldn't hear their conversation anymore.

"Why do I get the impression I have no idea what's going on here?" Sam asked.

I wasn't certain I was meant to answer him. He always loved a good rhetorical question but I wasn't the person who could do that with him anymore. We were relative strangers, even with our apologies accepted and hatchets buried. With all that acceptance and burial came distance, a yawning gap between who we used to be and who we were now.

"You don't," I murmured, mostly to myself.

Sam swung a glance between me and the men on the sidewalk. "Those guys aren't with the transport company."

"They're not," I whispered, still watching them.

"Friends of yours?" Sam asked. I murmured in agreement and he continued, "And why are we watching them?"

"Because I'm not ready to—to—I don't know," I stammered. "Because I am. Because this is where I'm sitting and it's fine. I'm fine. You don't have to be part of this. You can go because it's fine. I am fine."

Sam considered this for a moment before saying, "All right." He sanded his palms together and dropped down beside me. "It's nice back here."

"Oh my god, just shut up," I whisper-hissed. "What are you doing? Why are you here? Can you please go back inside or wherever it was you came from?"

He let out a gentle chuckle as he folded his arms on his bent knees. "Lauren and Matt are arguing about something irrelevant. Andy is in the attic but don't ask me why. Shannon is yelling at walls and Tiel is trying to rein her in. Will and Patrick are building something. God only knows what. Riley and Alex aren't here yet. Not surprising. I think Nick and Erin are headed here but I haven't seen them yet. Or they're hiding somewhere."

"Which leaves you..." My voice trailed off as I rolled my hand in his direction, expecting further explanation. "Stalking me in the bushes?"

"Tiel told me about your—uh—"

"Don't try," I interrupted, holding up a hand. "She told

THE MAGNOLIA CHRONICLES 267

you I'm seeing two guys. Right? And I was bringing them today? That's what she said?"

Sam nodded. "Yeah. Basically."

I couldn't stop myself from saying, "You two tell each other everything."

He nodded again, an affectionate smile pulling at his lips. "Pretty much."

He really loved that woman. Really fucking loved her. You could see it radiating off him like steam rising from the road after a summer rainstorm.

"And that's why you came looking for me?" I asked.

He glanced up at me with a quick shake of his head. "No. No, I was trying to avoid Matt and Lauren's argument about sponges and silverware and other tragedies." Another head-shake. "I just wanted to avoid all of that."

"You decided talking to me was the way to avoid another tragedy? I suppose there's a first time for everything."

He shifted then, meeting my gaze and holding it. "I saw the work you did on that Louisburg Square project with Matt. It was incredible."

With an eyebrow arched and more skepticism than I knew I possessed, I replied, "Thanks?"

"And your design for the North End project Riley and Andy are handling, it's flawless."

"Mmhmm." All skepticism.

Sam and I hadn't talked business in years. Actual years. We stopped collaborating after I climbed into the handbasket and drove our professional relationship straight to hell. I did a ton of work with his family's firm and I had brunch with his wife most weekends and we saw plenty of each other, but we saw each other in the way Saturn sees the sun: distant, aware of one another but only in presence, never getting closer than that comfortable orbit and barely above freezing.

"And then the Bay Village job you're doing with Patrick is —well, it's fascinating," he continued. "I wasn't sure how it would work out but you had five brilliant solutions ready to go."

"I'm going to stop you right there because why the fuck are you telling me this, Sam? Seriously, what's the point? I don't have a punch card and I'm not working toward a free frozen yogurt here so why are you rubber-stamping my recent work?"

He held up his hands. Let them fall. Blew out a sigh. Dug his sneakered heels into the dirt. Then, "Because I hate that you won't work with me anymore. Patrick, Matt, Riley, Andy—they all work with you and can't stop talking about your amazing designs and I'm stuck trolling every green-house and garden center for a landscape architect who has ideas on xeriscaping in zone six." He pointed at me, all jabby and rude. "I found you at that spec home showing and I was the one who convinced them you and your roof gardens were awesome and then I fucked everything up and I don't even get to talk to you about those roof gardens anymore."

"That's right," I said, touching my fingertips to my lips. "You did this."

He gave me a sharp, wide-eyed glare. "Yeah. I know." He snickered. "I partnered with a fucking fool a few months ago. An idiot who didn't know how to design for city rooftops but said he did. I'm honestly surprised I didn't give myself an aneurysm dealing with that shit."

"Because you don't get to talk to me anymore," I said, staring ahead. Ben and Rob stood in my line of sight but I couldn't see them. Just their shapes, their gestures. Always with the gestures. And those damn forearms. All right, I could see those. But not much else beyond the tidal wave of shock from this conversation.

"Can I fix that?" Sam asked. "Can I change it? Because it's been years and I'm happily married." He wiggled his wedding band at me. "And you're here with two men and that's gotta be serious because they're helping people move. People they don't even know. Moving is the highest level favor in the echelon of favors. I have to believe we're both in places where the mistakes of the past are ancient history, and we can work on some gardens again. Listen to me, Gigi, I cannot have Patrick walking around with better landscape designs than me. I can't do it. And dammit, I miss working with you. You're talented and you don't get enough attention for it and my work has suffered from not having you as a collaborator."

"Mmhmm," I managed. I continued watching Ben and Rob as tears clouded my eyes.

Why was I watching them? Why was I here, lingering in the shadow cast by the home and the earthy comfort of the dirt and green? Why didn't I approach Rob and Ben when I first saw them?

Because I know.

I knew, and I was afraid that knowledge would paint itself up and down my face if I had to share space with them both. I was afraid I'd overcorrect for that knowledge and make everything more confusing in the process. Right now, the only option for me was watching from a distance.

I didn't want it this way. I didn't want it to be like this anymore. I wanted to walk up to the man I was falling for and let him fold me into his arms without also worrying about the one I wasn't falling for. Worry—that was such a huge part of this. I worried all the fucking time.

I wanted to stop worrying, stop hiding, stop agonizing over a choice I'd made—when was it?—forever ago. But the tricky thing about me and decisions was that I didn't trust myself. Not all the way, not yet. I couldn't. Not after thirty-odd years of fucking everything up.

Perhaps the toughest peak to climb in finally being okay with myself was realizing I hadn't spent thirty-odd years fucking everything up. I'd spent those years learning to listen to my instincts and unlearning the societal garbage about how I was supposed to think, act, dress, eat, talk, be. Shedding the layers of skin I'd grown in frantic attempts to be a thousand different iterations of the person I thought I was supposed to be. Hating myself for everything. For no good reason. Even if it never looked like thorough and proper hate, it was. You couldn't love yourself when the list of things you wanted to change was longer than your arm. Never knowing how to love myself just as I was and working hard at repackaging myself until I was right and good and—and loveable.

Years ago, I read an account of climbing Mount Everest, and one of the random bits of information that stuck with me was how climbers often abandoned their things along the route to the summit. They realized they had to drop the things they'd believed necessary or were told they required in order to keep going. In order to survive the climb.

I'd made mistakes, sure. I was profoundly, irrevocably human and I didn't have to hold on to those mistakes anymore. I didn't have to apologize for them again.

And I didn't need any of that shit to survive the climb.

CHAPTER
THIRTY-ONE

SAM NUDGED MY ARM AND ASKED, "ARE WE GOOD?"

I bobbed my head in agreement, still staring at Ben and Rob through the boxwood. I'd have to go out there eventually. I'd have to see them and talk to them and be…normal. Whichever version of normal I passed off as my own.

It wasn't that I meant to avoid them. I enjoyed both of them in separate and distinct ways, and if I was required to choose between Sam Walsh and either of my boys, well… Sam wasn't winning. To be fair, I didn't dislike Sam. I wasn't angry at him. I wasn't holding on to a grudge. I lived with a bit of contempt and a slightly larger bit of resentment. Maybe those were the primary ingredients in a grudge and I couldn't be bothered to read the recipe. Regardless, I'd allowed myself to believe that was behind me.

But I did resent him. That was the bare bones truth of it. I was a terrible train wreck of a flirt and there was no way in hell he'd mistaken my advances for anything but. He was a smart guy and he let me embarrass myself. So, yeah. I resented him for never, ever, not even once mentioning that he was in a relationship. For never making an offhand remark about his girlfriend to tip me off. To save us both from the events that followed.

I didn't let that resentment rule me and I didn't lead with it either. How could I? My best friends were Sam's sister-in-law and his younger brother and I worked with his firm on a daily basis and I was here, helping his brother move into a new house. I adored his entire family—his wife included—but there was bad blood in the water. It was always there, lingering in the background like the memory of Ruby Sharpe's announcement to our entire sixth grade class that I was going to be a gorilla for Halloween on account of my as-of-then unshaven legs.

And the contempt, that came later. It stewed in the weeks and months that followed my spectacular crash-and-burn demonstration with Sam. It boiled over but then I pushed it to the back burner, left it there to simmer. It cooled every time Riley or Andy or Tiel—or anyone in Sam's orbit—worked at bringing me in and making things right. Every time someone else stepped in to patch the tear. I was certain Sam had a good reason for steering clear of that conversation until just now when we found ourselves wedged between a hedgerow and the house.

Underneath all the rubble, Sam was a good guy. I knew it because I'd known him. Ages and ages ago, I'd known him. We'd been such good friends. We'd talked shop like there was nothing else in the world worth discussing and he'd connected me with clients who turned into my biggest, most important jobs.

He'd thought he was doing the right thing then and now —finally—with both of us plunked down in the dirt, he was.

"Yeah. I'm booked up for the remainder of the summer," I

said. "But let's get something on the calendar. Shoot me a message later in the week. I'm sure we can sit down and look at your project horizon."

Just like that, the resentment and contempt I'd been clutching for years started to loosen. Letting go was strange. Not especially pleasant. For the same reason I kept jeans that didn't fit comfortably, I wanted to take back the hard, worn leather of that emotional armor.

Because I might need it again.

"I'll call you. There's a project coming up that's perfect for you. Even better, it has a huge landscape budget."

"Now you're speaking words I understand," I replied.

"You're saying I should've led with budget and then begged for your time?" he asked, laughing. "That would've worked better?"

"It's been a few years since we've collaborated, Sam," I said, my words cool and deliberate though I felt none of that chill vibe. "I don't accept small money projects anymore."

He made a sound in his throat, some kind of rattling sigh. "Yeah," he murmured. "I know. Riley's mentioned it two or three hundred times."

Ah, Riley. He was the best of friends. Just the best of them.

Sam pushed to his feet and brushed the dirt from the seat of his shorts. "Sitting behind a bush is great and all but why don't we get up before we meet a colony of fire ants or something? Introduce me to your friends, will you?"

He stepped away from the boxwood and I acted on my brain's first impulse, one still reaching for all of that resentment.

It wasn't a good impulse.

It wasn't a wise impulse.

It wasn't the right impulse.

But it was the first. And only.

I lunged toward Sam and caught him around the calves. The impact sent him stumbling to the lawn and my hold on him meant I followed him down.

My torso hit the ground first, pushing an indelicate grunt from my lips in the process. The inertia yanked my t-shirt down but the essentials stayed covered. Thank god. I couldn't add a wardrobe malfunction to today's list of tragedies. Not after whatever it was I just did to Sam.

Until right now, I'd believed my worst moments were behind me. At the very least, my worst Sam Walsh moments were behind me. But no. *Nooooo.* Dragging him to the ground was somehow worse—substantially worse—than slamming my lips to his all those years ago. I'd had a rationale for that. This…this defied all reason.

"What the hell was that, Gigi?" he yelled as he pushed up. "What the actual hell?"

I dropped my forehead down, sedating myself with the scent of green grass. When was I going to learn? When was I going to stop getting in my own way? Was that even possible? Was there a world where I wasn't literally falling down and scraping myself up all over again?

That world didn't exist. Not for me. I was always going to do all of those things but maybe—just maybe—there could be a world where Sam Walsh wasn't involved in my relationship with Rob and Ben. Even if I had to tackle him.

"Gigi, any explanation would be awesome," Sam continued. "I really fucking hope you were saving me from a possum or something."

Thanks to Sam (and a few other truly unpleasant men), I could handle damn near anything. I could pick myself up, dust myself off, and pretend I hadn't fallen into a home-grown sinkhole. I could be nice and cheery and not give a fuck about any of it. I could fake it. Oh, I could fake it the best. Wasn't that what I'd been doing for—for years?

But I couldn't fake it with Rob *and* Ben *and* Sam. Not all at once. Not after that weird and necessary conversation in the bushes. Not anymore. I couldn't.

Rob and Ben called to me but I stayed there, my hands pressed to my face and head down in the grass. I heard footsteps and then felt hands on my shoulders, my back, but I didn't move. I needed another minute to recover. Before I had to fake it one more time.

"Magnolia?" Rob said to my back. "Magnolia, honey, say something."

"Who the fuck are you and what the fuck happened here?" Ben snapped. "What did you fucking do to her?"

"This was—it's all good, gentlemen," Sam replied.

"What kind of fuckin' predator are you?" Ben continued.

"Excuse me?" Sam answered.

"Sam? Sam, why are you covered in grass stains and why is Magnolia on the ground?"

Oh my god. That was Lauren. Due any day pregnant, moving into her new house fourteen seconds after the paint dried, dealing with all this mayhem Lauren. *Oh my god.* I'd just tackled Sam to the ground like a lunatic and I was flat on the lawn in front of her house, adding to the damn mayhem.

"Seems like something I'd do."

That was Riley. *Oh, shit. Just…shit.*

It was true. Nothing happened in my life unless I had an audience around to judge me while it happened.

"We just tripped," Sam replied. "It was nothing. If I know

Gigi, I know she's dying of embarrassment and waiting for the lawn to swallow her."

If I know Gigi.

I snorted at that. He was right. But we didn't know each other anymore.

"I know you think you can be left unsupervised, Sam"—*oh, god, that was Shannon*—"but that's not the case if you're tripping on flat, unobstructed grass and taking Magnolia down with you."

"Is there not a better use of your time?"

That question came from Patrick and I was now convinced the entire Walsh family was staring at me, face-down in the grass. I should've picked myself up by now but I needed another minute. To put myself back together and find the right blend of joyous indifference necessary to stand up, shake the grass from my hair, look these people in the eye, and go forward without explaining my inexplicable desire to physically prevent Sam from approaching Ben and Rob.

A hand squeezed my shoulder, ran down my spine. I wasn't sure whether it was Rob or Ben. Right now, I was content with that show of support coming from either man.

"Thank you for that brilliant question, Patrick. I appreciate you and everyone else coming out to evaluate the current state of affairs. Helpful. Extremely helpful." Sam continued, "And it was probably my fault. You know, as I reflect on it now, yes. It was my fault. I'm the responsible party here. I am—I'm deserving of the blame. Gigi did nothing wrong."

Finally. Finally, an apology I believed. Perhaps it was a product of Sam speaking it to everyone else. Maybe it grew from the conversation we had behind the boxwood. What-ever the reason, I believed it this time.

I believed it, and I believed I didn't need the emotional armor anymore.

"Thank you for that," I mumbled into the grass.

"And who the fuck are you?" Ben seethed.

Ben was good at that. The snapping, the seething. Angry suited him even if it wasn't a healthy way to live. And I didn't have to look up from my earthy meditation spot to know he wasn't the one kneeling beside me and rubbing my back. His words were too far away for that. If I had to put money down on his location, I'd bet he was busy edging into Sam's space and shooting glares hot enough to cut steel.

"I'm Sam Walsh and this is my brother's house," he replied. "Who might you be?"

"Let's not do this," I said, finally pushing up from the grass. I was right about Ben glowering at Sam. A-plus effort on that front. I was right about Rob keeping a hand on my shoulder too. And I was right about the entire Walsh family plus a few new faces watching this delightful exchange. "Let's go unpack some boxes instead."

"Are you the one who took the dog?" Ben asked, jabbing a finger in Sam's direction.

"No, sir, I am not. I was on the dog rescue squad," Sam replied, hands up in surrender. "I'm not—I'm not any of them. I'm tangentially involved at best."

"What the fuck does that mean?" Ben snapped.

That earned him a snort from me as I settled on my knees and scanned the yard. "I told you not to ask." I couldn't place the new faces in the group. Six of them, five women and one man. They looked slightly younger and somewhat confused. That was fair. "You really shouldn't have asked."

"Well, I did," Ben replied, pointing an impatient frown at me. "I don't know what's up here but I don't like it."

I stared at him but I knew the Walshes were closing in around us. They never missed the rowdy stuff and this definitely qualified as rowdy stuff. "Let's just forget this. Okay?"

Ben tossed his hands up. "Whatever you want," he replied as he took an exaggerated step back from Sam.

Lauren's husband Matt approached, a hammer in one hand and roll of painter's tape in the other. "Do you want me to throw him out?" he asked, pointing the handle end of the hammer at Sam. "I will. He's shirking his responsibilities and picking fights in my front yard. Maybe that's acceptable in Fort Point but this is suburbia. We don't put up with that shit here."

"No worries. It was an accident," I said, laughing. "Please don't kick him to the curb on my account."

"Then I'll do it," Shannon called. "Make yourself useful and go get some lunch for everyone, Sam." She marched toward us, a mobile phone pressed to her ear. "Whatever it is you broke, you can fix with food."

"I don't believe I broke anything," Sam replied. "But rather than debate that with an audience of this size, I'll pick up lunch. Maybe then I'll get something I can actually eat."

"Stop it with your sob stories," Shannon said.

"I would argue they are less sob stories and more real accounts of me foraging for food on a regular basis," he said.

"You haven't foraged a day in your life," Matt added.

"What are we talking about? Foraging? Like, for mushrooms?" Patrick asked.

"I've been known to forage a mushroom or two in my day," Riley said.

"Not that kind of mushroom," Andy said to him.

"And that's enough of the Walsh Family Theater for today," Lauren announced. "Matthew, my dear, please stop using that hammer as a pointer. I know you can manage your tools and all but we don't need any additional accidents." She glanced between me and Sam. "Sam, you're in charge of catering. If you can find me some of those little clementine oranges, I'd appreciate it. I'm pretty sure the Whole Foods near MIT had some last week. It's a bit of a trek, but..." Her voice trailed off as she rubbed her belly. "Like I said, I'd appreciate it."

"I'll see what I can do." He hooked a glance at me over his shoulder, offering a tight smile before breaking away from the group. He waved at Ben as he passed him en route to the sidewalk but Ben only scowled back.

Lauren continued, "Andy, I need you to take Patrick and Riley inside. I need them to work on plotting out locations for bedroom furniture before it arrives and we have mass chaos." She pointed toward the house as Andy narrowed her eyes, clearly confused by the request. If I had to guess, I'd say Lauren was putting hands to work and tearing eyeballs off me. She was an angel. "Shannon, my mom is going to be here any minute and I need you to figure out the baby's room before she does. Go. Make it happen. Run like the wind."

Rob kept his hand moving along my spine, each sweep loosening the tension coiled there. God, I was tired. I was tired of trying so damn hard. Tired of being one step to the left, one minute too late. And I was tired of constantly stepping into that joyous indifference and pretending everything was all right. Everything was always all right.

"What do you need right now?" Rob said, his words low enough to stay between us.

I shook my head and let myself lean against him. "This."

"Yeah?" His lips brushed the shell of my ear. "Are you sure you don't want to fake a sprained ankle? I'll get you out of here. You won't have to deal with him anymore."

Exhaling slowly, I let my eyelids fall. One of the many problems with concurrently dating two men was losing track of the information I'd shared with each of them. It was never more evident than right now as Rob knew all about my history with Sam. Ben knew the rough sketch but Rob knew the details and he knew who Sam was—and wasn't—to me.

He knew and he stayed right here with me.

He knew this weird, tenuous, strained but polite but also distant situation called for a calm response. That goddamn indifference. He understood how swagger only widened the chasm. He knew I needed this to be better but that I couldn't do the fixing. I couldn't be the one apologizing this time.

And he knew I needed someone to stand with me rather than someone to stand for me.

"How did you know?" I asked. "How did you know I needed this?"

He chuckled in a quiet way that vibrated through his chest and straight into me. "I didn't know so much as to repay the favor."

I turned my head to glance over my shoulder at him. "Which favor is that?"

"You had my back at the engagement party."

I frowned, shook my head. "I didn't do anything. I was there with you but I didn't do anything."

He wrapped his arm around my waist. "And I'm not doing anything but being here." His lips landed on my temple, stayed there long enough to chase away some of my lingering embarrassment. Some of it. "What about that ankle? Should we get it checked out? I know a beer garden not too far from here with brews perfect for treating imaginary injuries."

"Maybe later," I said, patting his hand. "It wasn't terrible, with Sam. I think we patched a few things up. There was that awful moment where I tackled him but it was nice of him to own that one."

"It's about time," Rob said under his breath.

I glanced up to find Lauren smiling down at us. "Sorry about all this," I said to her. "I didn't come here with the intention of instigating anything."

She waved her hand. "Don't mention it. Some people exercise, the Walshes yell at each other." To Rob, she said, "I'm Lauren Walsh and you're supremely tolerant of both this day and those shenanigans you just witnessed."

"Not at all. I'm Rob Russo," he replied. "I heard there were boxes to unpack and things to assemble, and I'm happy to do it."

She laughed, shaking her head. "And we are thankful for every hand on deck today," she said, shooting a glance across the yard at Ben. "If you don't mind, I have a perfect project for Mr. Brock. Can I steal him?"

"Take him," Rob replied quickly. "Keep him. He's all yours."

"You're just adorable, aren't you?" Lauren murmured. "Stay there for a bit, Gigi. You've been running around fixing trees and plants and god knows what else before Sam went all…you know, Samish. I hope everything is all right on that front. I hope you're all right."

"I am," I said, and I meant it. I was all right without the resentment and contempt and burned bridges. Without the indifference. I was better. "I might have space in my schedule to take on a few of Sam's properties."

"Make him work for it, girl." She glanced to the group of twentysomethings congregated near the front door and then eyed Ben again. He was having a conversation with Matt that seemed largely composed of hand gestures. "It's truly the perfect project. If I can convince him of it."

The magical intuition of Lauren Walsh was not to be underestimated. The woman noticed things to which the rest of us were blind. And in this moment, I was certain she saw me and Rob and Ben and all the things we didn't say out loud. She saw and she knew, and now she had a plan.

"I've never doubted you before," I replied. "I'm not about to start now."

With a nod, Lauren stalked toward the group near the door. She peeled off a man and woman and led them toward Ben and Matt. She was quick to gather the men but Ben wasn't going without a spirited discussion as always.

He pointed at me, asking, "Are you good? I can stay. I'll do whatever you want, Gigi."

"Oh, sweetie," Lauren cooed. "You have such a good heart, worrying after her like that. She'll join us in a few minutes."

Ben blinked at Lauren, his irritation melting by the second. "Okay." He nodded, glanced back at me. His lips tipped up in a smile. So unlike him. It lasted all of ten seconds before his gaze stumbled onto Rob and he went full glower. "I'm watching you, Russo."

"As always," Rob replied.

Lauren allowed none of this, quickly directing him into the garage with the rest of her crew, leaving me and Rob alone on the grass. He ran his hand over my knee, thumbing away the streak of green.

"I'm not sure what's happened here," he said. "But I feel like it's a lot."

For the second time today, tears filled my eyes. This wasn't about finally crossing a threshold with Sam or letting go of all my grudges—because yeah, they *were* grudges. It wasn't about the Walshes rallying around me. It wasn't Lauren taking Ben into her care. It was none of this but also all of it.

That climb, it never ended. Not really. There was no singular point of getting it or being all the way there. But there was a big difference between taking the first step and having the summit in sight.

And I could see it now. I didn't know everything and I was certain I'd get lost again but the air was thinner up here and my bags were lighter and now I knew there was more ahead of me than behind.

I nodded, brushed away a tear. "I feel like it's everything."

CHAPTER
THIRTY-TWO

I didn't have a date today. Not tonight, tomorrow, or the day after. My week was wide open, and for the first time in months it belonged to me.

I needed it to be this way. I needed to get a few things straight with myself before seeing Rob or Ben again.

Two days ago at Matt and Lauren's new house was the last I'd seen my boys. *My boys*. Ha. That was such an over-simplification of the matter. They were good men. Good to me and good for me.

A handful of months ago, my only wish in this romantic life of mine was being wanted. To be someone's first and best choice. Back then, I'd thought there was nothing better than belonging to someone, fully and irrevocably.

But it took a shove from my mother, a hot, hot summer, and the affections of two very different, very precious men to realize I belonged to myself. I didn't need Ben. I didn't need Rob. I needed me and nothing more. And that was the *ah-ha* moment of all this—the delicate space between needs and wants. I needed to know and love myself and I wanted a man who knew and loved me as I was.

After two decades' worth of rejection, it was difficult to take up that mindset. Part of me was compelled to binge on the affection Ben and Rob offered. Take it all and squirrel it away because they'd snatch it back soon. But the other part knew that wasn't necessary. It wasn't going anywhere and even if it did, I loved myself.

The best part—and yeah, there was a best part of dating —was I had a man who knew and loved me in all my part-time hot mess ways.

And I was enough.

CHAPTER
THIRTY-THREE

I HAD A DATE WITH AN OVERGROWN MESS.

I stood in my kitchen early on Saturday morning, cold brew coffee in one hand and my phone in the other, and stared out at my backyard.

The phone vibrated in my hand but I set it down without glancing at the screen. The messages would keep.

I wasn't avoiding anything. I was spending time with myself and my thoughts. This past week, I'd worked, walked Gronk, and slept alone. It wasn't entirely fair to disappear but I needed this. I needed to be certain.

With certainty came a shiver of dread. That certainty meant saying goodbye to someone, to altering our relationship forever. I'd never been the one to initiate the goodbye. I'd always been on the receiving end of those goodbyes and I didn't enjoy this side of the exchange any better.

But just as my mother had predicted I would, I knew. I knew, I'd known for longer than I cared to admit, and I was ready to take the next step. But first, I had a date with my garden.

It was hot today, just as the tail-end of summer was meant to be. Hot, hazy, humid. Unpleasant, uncomfortable air, the kind that swaddled your skin and brought sweat to the strangest of places. Behind the ears, the backs of the knees, the crease of the elbow.

Rather than taking refuge from this heat, I pulled on my gloves. Gronk was sprawled on the floor, his tongue lolling out the side of his mouth. He didn't react when I opened the back door.

"Are you coming?" I called to him. He lifted his head, stared at me for a moment, and returned to his sprawl. "Don't you dare scratch on this door to come out in five minutes. And don't think about barking at me from the bedroom window. I'm not having it."

He replied with a single tail wag and a lengthy snore-sigh.

I stepped out into the morning sun and assessed the condition of the yard. It was a strange parcel of land, jagged and asymmetrical, the kind deeded in the time of farmlands and horse-drawn carriages. It was a rarity in this area. An old rock ledge marked the property lines on either side and a pocket-sized forest formed the back boundary. The neighborhood surrounding my aunt's land was nothing like this, each plot carved up into orderly rectangular boxes, symbols of postwar prosperity and order.

My aunt's aesthetic veered toward flowering wild and it showed. When she'd purchased this home forty-odd years ago, the yard had been a failed experiment in English rose gardening. She'd hacked it all back and replaced the roses with every colorful bloom she could find. But after a few years of careful tending, the roses pushed past the new plantings, edging themselves back into prominence.

Now, the garden lived on like an old memory book. English roses from a time before any Santillian women lived here. Lilacs, irises, gladiolus, zinnias, dahlias, hydrangeas from my aunt. Ferns and creeping rosemary from me. There was a magnolia tree out front, one planted the year I was born. There was an ash and linden too but the pink flowering magnolia was Aunt Francesca's favorite.

It took me all of my thirty-four years to figure it out but now I knew I'd always been wanted. My parents, my brothers, my friends, my aunt—they'd circled around me right from the start. It wasn't the same as wanting to be loved and desired but I'd learned being the object of desire wasn't the great accomplishment of my life.

Sharing love with someone who'd earned a spot in my life, that was an accomplishment. That was worth working for. Being desired was the first step in a miles-long hike.

I attacked the weeds first. With this heat and frequent summer showers, it was no surprise they were taking over the yard. I was waist-deep in unwelcome shoots and vines. Invasive species adored these conditions. I plunged my fingers into the earth over and over, tracing the line of the root all the way down and tearing it out. I was too focused on ousting the weeds to notice anything but the next obstacle in my path.

I definitely didn't notice Ben until he shouted, "Take a break, would you? I'm tired just watching you."

From my hands and knees position, I lifted my head to find Ben near the back door, his fists balled on his waist. "And how long have you been watching?"

"About ten minutes." He shoved his hands in his pockets, shrugged. "Maybe more. Maybe less. Figured you'd see me eventually but it looks like you have the crazy eyes going."

I pushed to my feet and dusted the dirt off my knees and gloved hands. "I did not have crazy eyes."

"Uh, yeah, you did," he argued. "If I was in there"—he pointed at the section I'd cleared—"you would've yanked me up too."

"Likely story," I muttered as I picked my way through the garden toward him. "To what do I owe this surprise visit?"

He stared at me through his dark sunglasses, silent while I pulled off my cap and mopped the sweat from my brow. "Where's your guard dog? Shouldn't he be out here, warning off trespassers?"

I waved my hat toward the house. "Too hot for him. He requires a temperate climate."

Ben whistled. "That pup has the life." He shook his head, smiling at me. "Let's go inside. Your shoulders are getting red."

I glanced at my bare arms and found he was right, I was heading toward a sunburn. "The sun's more intense than I thought."

"Yeah," he replied, dragging the word out. "Or maybe you shouldn't be doing yard work during a heat wave."

"If I waited for good gardening days, I'd get seven or eight a year." Ben followed me into the house, stopping to pet Gronk while I washed my hands at the kitchen sink.

"Hey, buddy," he said, crouching down to meet the dog at his level. "Having a snoozer? Good day for it."

"Want a drink?" I looped my fingers around the refrigerator door handle, watching while Ben loved all over my dog. Giving affection came easily to him. The rest of his emotions were less clear. "I have beer."

"I'll pass on the beer." He scooped Gronk up, cradling

him in his arms, and settled at the kitchen table. "Water, please."

Carrying two glasses of water, I joined Ben at the table. His attention belonged to Gronk as he scratched the dog's head, patted his flanks, and carried on a hushed conversation as if he'd get a response any minute now.

I was guilty of all the same things but it was curious to see Ben focused only on Gronk. "If you wanted a playdate with my dog, you could've asked." The remark was mostly sarcastic. Mostly.

He glanced up at me, his expression rigid. "I need to talk to you."

Even the most stable, secure people in the world wobbled against those words. "Okay."

He returned his attention to Gronk, stroking the space between his ears. "I need to talk and I need you to not say anything."

"So," I started, lifting my glass, "you want me to sit here? Without responding?"

"Yeah, pretty much." He shrugged as if this was a common request. "I would've texted you but that seemed like a chickenshit choice and I'm tired of making the chickenshit choice."

Another wobble. Even if it didn't make sense. That fear of rejection, it never went all the way away. Not even when I wanted the rejection. When the rejection saved me from delivering the same blow. "Oh," I murmured. "Oh. That kind of conversation. Okay."

"Nothing bad. Not for you."

He kept his gaze trained on Gronk. He didn't even want to look at me. Didn't want to or couldn't? Was there a difference? Did it even matter?

Ben continued, "I've been thinking this week. I've been thinking a lot."

My eyebrows arched up. "That's not like you."

He slapped his palm on the table, grinning at me for the first time today. "What did I tell you about keeping quiet?"

"All right. I'll be quiet. As much as I can."

He shared an eyeroll with Gronk that suggested I couldn't be trusted. "Like I said, I've been thinking a lot. And like you said, that's uncommon for me." He forced a brittle laugh. I didn't reciprocate. "I've been thinking and I want to say a couple of things to you. First, I want you to know you're one of the best people I've ever met. You yelled at me and you wouldn't let me fuck up and you did the exact opposite of everyone else in my life and I—I appreciate that. I appreciate everything you've done and everything you've put up with because I've been a whole fucking lot to put up with recently."

"Are you firing me? As your home improvement mentor? Because that's what this sounds like." I pressed my fingertips to my lips. "Oh. Sorry. I'm not supposed to say anything."

Ben held Gronk up to meet his eyes. "What is wrong with her? I don't know how you put up with this, buddy. I really don't." He looked up at me. "I'm not firing you. For fuck's sake, Gigi."

"You're not paying me either so I suppose it's a moot point."

"You're making me think twice about doing this in person," he grumbled.

My belly flopped once, then again. I reached across the table and squeezed his hand before pulling back. "Just tell me, Ben. Whatever it is, just tell me."

He traced the stripe of white running down Gronk's

head. "When all of this started, with you and me and Rob, I justified it to myself. I told myself we wouldn't have had a connection if Rob was right for you. If you really wanted to be with him."

"Yeah, but I hadn't even met Rob in person back then. Technically, I met you first and—"

Ben held up a hand, his eyelids snapping shut. "Things have changed. That's obvious to everyone. We had different connections for different reasons and that's—that's okay. But things have changed." He ran his hands down Gronk's back, prompting the dog to stretch in his lap. "You showed up in my house in the middle of the night and you saved me. I know you wouldn't tell it that way—"

"Not unless we're talking about saving you from unpermitted construction fines," I added under my breath.

"—but you helped me through the hardest time of my life. Just by being there and kicking my ass and forcing me to do things the right way. I didn't know it was going to be this difficult, and I didn't know I was going to need help but you showed me the way from one point to another. I appreciate that."

"You're welcome." I glanced down at the table and trailed my index finger through the condensation ringing my glass. "What is it you need to say, Ben?"

I watched as a storm cloud drifted over him, quick like summer thunder. It was over just as fast as it rolled in. "I like you. So much. So fuckin' much. You don't take my shit and you know the right thing to say at the worst moments and you're a cool lady when you're not preaching about building codes."

"But?" I prompted.

Here I was, walking straight into rejection. The fear was

there, irrational as it was. The anxiety too. But I was ready for this. I welcomed it.

He looked up at me, Gronk cuddled against his chest like a wiggly, squishy shield. "But I'm not for you and you're not for me."

"I know." I nodded, offering a small smile. I prayed my expression wasn't painted with relief. Ben didn't want to see that. "I know."

He pressed his fingers to his temples. "You could've mentioned this before I ripped my guts out and dropped them on the floor in front of you."

"And miss out on this fun? No. Never." I folded my arms over my chest. "Aside from the fun, I didn't want to hurt you. I know how much you're going through and I didn't want to add to that. I didn't want to make things worse for you."

"Oh, right," Ben drawled. "Allowing me to slow-walk myself to that conclusion with the help of a cutthroat teacher was much better. Thanks for that, Gigi. Really, I appreciate it. Thanks."

I leaned forward, clasped my fingers around my glass. "Tell me about this teacher."

Ben ran his hand through his hair, over his scruffy chin. He huffed out a wry chuckle as the inklings of a smile softened his face. It started in his eyes, gradually reaching his lips and pulling them up into a craggy grin. "Is this how it's gonna be with us now? I'm supposed to tell you about my feelings and shit? And I don't even get the benefit of naked showers?"

"Come on, Ben. All showers should be naked," I replied. "But yeah, let's do this. Let's be disgustingly mature and cleave our relationship into two separate and distinct segments."

He gestured toward me. "The shower segment and the not-showering segment?"

I tapped a finger on my chest. "I'm still showering."

"But not with me," he replied.

"It seems like I'm spending a lot of time explaining when and how to wash," I said. "Perhaps you could find a YouTube tutorial for that and leave me out of it."

"I'm just saying, I wouldn't mind a shower with you."

"Here's a small suggestion." I tipped my head toward him. "This person, the cutthroat teacher? I'm confident she won't enjoy these references to bathing with me."

He bobbed his head in solemn agreement. That was, I interpreted it as solemn agreement. The goings-on of Ben's mind still eluded me.

"I can see that," he said eventually.

"About this woman," I said. "I need more details, Brock. Who is she, when did you meet her, how much of your shit does she tolerate?" I ticked off each question on my fingers. "You know, the important details."

"Her name is Grace, and I met her last weekend. She was helping out at that house, the one your friends moved into." He blew out a breath and pressed his palms to his eyes. "I don't know how to explain it," he continued, "but the woman is a villain and I am obsessed with her."

I leaned back, considering this. There were several things I'd expected from a conversation with Ben Brock that terminated our romantic relationship. I'd anticipated his trademark bluster and some request for a sex-on-the-side arrangement. Not that I'd wanted it but I'd also expected him to fight for me, insist I couldn't possibly choose Rob.

None of that involved him announcing he'd met another woman. Not only met another woman but already possessed big, confusing, obsessive feelings for that woman.

And I was ecstatic. There wasn't even a twinge of betrayal.

"What kind of villain?" I asked.

He dropped his hands and stared at me wide-eyed. "The best kind. The *best* kind," he repeated. "I've talked to her every day this week and I am—"

"Smitten?" I interrupted. I couldn't help but beam at Ben. I'd never seen him twisted quite like this. It was fabulous. "Because you're smitten."

He jerked a shoulder up, shrugging off my response. "You said something recently. Something about getting tired of your bullshit. This woman, Grace, she was tired of my bullshit before she met me and she has no problem telling me that."

"I'm a fan," I replied, both hands up in praise. "When are you seeing her again?"

Ben stroked Gronk's coat for a moment, silent. Then, "I don't know. I had to do this first. I had to do right by you before I could do anything with her. Hell, I don't know if she's interested. She ignores my texts for eleven hours and then tells me to unfuck myself and I don't know what to do about any of it. I just want—I don't know—I want her attention." He shot an apprehensive glimpse in my direction. "That's about as lame as it sounds, isn't it?"

I felt a rush of warm affection for Ben. It wasn't romantic or sexual, not at all. It was the kind of affection reserved for the special people who came into your life and changed the course for the better. He'd changed my course and I'd needed him to do that. I'd needed him to push me, to hem me in and force me to take charge of our complex relationship. But more than that, he'd forced me to make choices.

I couldn't sit back and wait for love to find me. I couldn't expect it to come in the exact dimensions I required. I couldn't cross my fingers and hope to find someone better than my shabby roster of exes. I had to orchestrate that magic for myself.

And now it seemed Ben had to orchestrate his own magic.

"Assuming she wants to see you again, I'd love to meet her," I said. "I want good things for you, Ben. You're not getting rid of me. I'll be checking in on you and asking about this scary villain teacher and making sure you're doing well even if we don't share showers anymore." I pointed over his shoulder, in the direction of his house. "And I'm not letting you screw up those renovations."

"Yeah?" he remarked. "What's Rob have to say about that?"

Another rush of affection hit me, this one tighter, more urgent than the first. I loved Rob. I could say that now and I could believe it. I could keep it without worrying after it leaving me.

I loved him and he loved me.

He loved me when love was the last thing he wanted.

He loved me when I couldn't choose him, when I wouldn't.

He loved me exactly as I was, requiring no more, no less.

He loved me and I loved him, and now, we both knew it. We could say it, we could live it.

I sucked in a breath to keep myself from crying because *goddamn*, this shit was hell on my emotions. "I'll mention it to him tomorrow. We have a couple hours in the car to talk through it."

Ben gave Gronk a vigorous head scratch and set him down on the floor. The dog turned, perched his paws on Ben's leg. "Where are you going tomorrow?"

I beamed, incapable of hiding the nervous excitement inside me. "I'm taking him home for Sunday dinner with my family."

CHAPTER
THIRTY-FOUR
ROB

Rob: Any chance you'd be interested in me swinging by a few hours earlier than planned before dinner with the family?

Magnolia: Of course I'd be interested in that.

Rob: Would it be presumptuous to swing by a day earlier? As in this afternoon?

Magnolia: I can't imagine how being presumptuous could get in your way.

Rob: So…is that a yes? I need a clear signal here. I want to show up in the middle of your Very Serious Talk with Brock like I want a broken nose.

Magnolia: Good news for you—I've already had the Very Serious Talk.

Rob: How did the old boy take it?

Magnolia: You sound exceedingly smug.

Rob: Me, smug? Noooo.

Magnolia: Yes.

Rob: Back to the early arrival…

Magnolia: I've been weeding all day and I need a shower. The back door is open.

Rob: You're giving me too much to work with here, honey.

Magnolia: Your mind is a dark and depraved place.

Rob: If you only knew the half of it...

Magnolia: I've estimated pretty well, thanks.

Rob: Would it be presumptuous for me to ask you not to get dressed after this shower?

Magnolia: You're asking me to...what? Lounge around the house nude?

Rob: That sounds divine.

Magnolia: Gronk doesn't account for clothing or lack thereof. He'll jump on my lap regardless. I love my dog but not enough for that.

Rob: Can't blame me for asking. I'll see you soon, babe.

———

I SHOULD'VE MENTIONED I WAS ALREADY ON THE ROAD.

I should've mentioned I'd left my apartment two hours ago or that I was now driving in circles around one of Boston's assorted suburbs, waiting for some sign she'd had the official sit-down with Ben.

I should've also mentioned I was a raging ball of neediness, at once rough and tender and just fucking anxious because there were no guarantees here. It was like working out way too hard and waking up with aches that made it impossible to pull a shirt over my head or hold a cup of coffee without my hand shaking—all while wondering if the ground beneath me was about to give way.

Should've.

Didn't.

That was how I found myself parked in Magnolia's driveway not more than twenty minutes later.

Twenty one minutes later, I found myself staring across the street at Ben Brock. I should've anticipated running into him here but that concern sailed away right around the time I'd said "Fuck it" and jumped in my car.

"Hey," he called as he shoved a box into the bed of his truck.

"Hey," I replied.

With that comfortable distance between us, he said, "Congratulations to the victor."

I shook my head. "It's not about winning. It was never a game."

"And yet you still won." Before I could argue that point, he continued, "You know I'm only busting your balls, you fuckin' fragile prick. Calm down, would you? *Jeeeeesus*. Not that it matters but I've moved on. Actually, I met someone."

I dipped my hands into my pocket, jerked my chin up. "Is that so?"

"Yep." He glanced at his truck, his yard, down the street. Then, back at me. "Is this going to be weird? You and me? Because I don't want to have uncomfortable moments every time we see each other and I'm gonna get hosed if I try to sell this house right now."

Note to self: convince Magnolia to move in with me immediately.

"Nah, man. Of course not. And you know Magnolia wouldn't allow that," I said.

Ben scuffed the toe of his shoe against the pavement. "That's the damn truth."

A silence settled between us, not awkward but not enjoyable either. It was like the stillness that stretched on the way a drawbridge lowered—slow and crucial, and achingly long yet nothing could make it any faster.

Then, "I gotta get to Home Depot," Ben said, his hands in his pockets. "I have to return this stuff. I got the wrong—well, I don't even know what I did. It's just fuckin' wrong."

"Right, right," I murmured. I jerked a thumb over my shoulder, in the direction of Magnolia's house. "I should—"

"Yeah," Ben interrupted, stabbing a finger toward her door. "What the hell are you doing out here? Get in there. Do you have treats for the dog? Sometimes, I'll hide some bacon biscuits in my pocket and he's my best friend."

I reached into the back seat, retrieved a bag of toys and snacks from a pet boutique I'd visited earlier in the week. Back when I was really losing my cool. "All good."

"Smart man," he replied with a fleeting glance at her house. "Good luck with the family tomorrow. They can't be any tougher than her friends."

"That's what I'm hoping," I replied, backing up the driveway. "Good luck at Home Depot—and with the person you met."

I wasn't afraid of Magnolia's family, not when Magnolia was the only one who actually mattered in this equation… and she was probably naked *right now*. Why the hell was I still talking to this guy?

"Grace. You wouldn't like her," he called. "We'll have to get together some time."

"Yeah. That all makes sense."

He lifted his hands up. "Does to me."

I waved as he hopped into his truck. Since I had no

interest in watching him drive away or doing anything that didn't involve going inside and just *being* with Magnolia, preferably nude, I hiked around the side yard toward the back door. Gronk was waiting for me there, his bottom on the floor and his tail wagging just inside the door.

"Here's the deal, buddy," I said, reaching into the bag. "If you give me and your human some alone time, you can have all these toys and treats."

His ears perked up at the mention of *treats*. I opened the package of ridiculously expensive jerky and offered him a small piece, nearly losing a finger in the process.

"It's good, right?" He held the dry meat between his paws and went to work, making some noises that sounded strangely similar to *nom-nom-nom* in the process. "It was fourteen dollars a pound so I need you to really appreciate this. It's the high-quality shit, okay?"

Gronk ignored me, which was fine. We didn't need to have conversations. Not today. Not when I didn't have to hold back anymore, didn't have to share. Didn't have to *wait*.

While Gronk nommed all over his snack, I hid the toys and treats around the kitchen and living room. A knotted rope under the coffee table, a small tennis ball on one of his many beds. I was on my hands and knees, tucking the jerky into places he could reach on his short legs. It wasn't my finest moment but I'd watched Magnolia do that once and learned it gave Gronk something to do when she needed him occupied. He'd go hunting for his loot and stay too busy to notice she was on an important call or painting a wall or something non-dog like that.

"If you leave much more of that out for him, you'll learn what it sounds like when a Boston terrier vomits," I heard from behind me.

And it meant I was too busy to notice the bathrobed beauty watching me from the hall.

I gained my feet and brushed my hands together. Her hair was wet and her eyes smiled. "Hi there." Several feet and a sofa separated us. "Question for you. Is it wrong to bribe your dog to get your undivided attention?"

She shook her head. "Not at all. Just keep in mind his stomach is very small and he doesn't stop eating when he's had too much. Also, he'll always expect goodies from you now."

"I can accommodate that." I shrugged. "His approval is critical to this."

"*This*," Magnolia repeated as she wrapped the robe's thin belt around her finger, unraveled it, and started over the process again. "We're really doing *this*, huh?"

"I think we are." Skirting the sofa and closing the distance between us, I continued, "Though I'm wondering about something. If I hadn't asked to come here today, would you have come to me? Or would you have made me wait to see you until tomorrow?"

"I needed to wash up," she started with a shaky breath, "before inviting you over. I was a mess from working in the yard. I had brambles in my hair and dirt all the way up my arms. I was filthy—"

"You haven't seen filthy yet, sweet pea," I interrupted.

"I wanted to be ready for you," Magnolia replied. "Not all garden gross."

I lashed my arms around her waist, skimming my hands over the soft, torturously thin fabric of her robe. "So, I beat you to it."

"You have a way of doing that, Rob," she said with a laugh. "You come right out and ask for what you want."

"Speaking of which..." With both hands on her waist, I speed walked her toward her bedroom.

She laughed, braced her hands on my biceps as the backs of her legs hit the side of the bed. "Yes? Something you were saying? Don't tell me you're all talk until it's go time. That would be a major disappointment after months of verbal foreplay."

I pressed the heel of my palm to my fly but it alleviated none of the pressure there. Made it worse if anything. It had been *months* of foreplay. No wonder I was a wreck. "I love that mouth of yours."

Reaching for the belt holding the robe in shut, I tugged until the fabric parted and a delicious strip of skin was revealed. After a quick glance up at her to confirm this was okay, this was what she wanted, I trailed my lips from her collar bone to the valley between her breasts. "Magnolia," I said, her name heaving out in a growled sigh. "I've been thinking about this for so long, I don't know what to say right now."

"Don't say anything," she replied. "Just show me."

I slipped my hands under the robe and over her shoulders, sending the garment to the floor. For a moment, I stared, drinking in her luscious curves, her dusky brown nipples, her smooth, glowing skin. Then I drove my fingers through her damp hair and sealed my lips to hers.

By some gift of muscle memory and teamwork, we unfastened my belt, popped the buttons on my shorts open, pushed my boxers down, and wrenched the shirt over my head. It wasn't pretty but it was effective, and that was all we required today.

"Right here," I said, trading places with her. I sat on the

edge of the bed, caging her between my legs. "I want you right here."

She hesitated a second before settling on my lap. My shaft was tucked against her belly and that first feel of her core, hot and ready as she rocked against my thighs, made me wild. I kissed her neck, her jaw, her dark nipples. Everything. Everything I wanted, I took.

"You're ready this?" I asked, my hands holding her hips steady because I couldn't take much more of her perfect little rolls and wiggles.

Magnolia reached between us and took my bare cock in hand. God, there was nothing better in the world than having the perfunctory health-and-safety convo *before* getting naked. She stared into my eyes as she pumped me like she was daring me with each stroke to stop her. Like she expected me to draw the line here and reclaim control.

My opinion on that was much like my dick—hardly.

"You're not going to be nice or polite, are you?" she asked.

She dragged me through the warm pool of her arousal and I had to grit my teeth to respond, "What gave that away?"

"You're looking at me the same way I looked at the weeds in my garden." Magnolia positioned me at her entrance but didn't move, didn't sink down. "Like you want to tear me up."

"I promise I'll always be nice to you, my darling," I said, my hips bucking up despite every effort to the contrary. "I'll be as polite as I know how to be. I'll respect you and admire you and I'll treat you like my equal in every way." I dug my fingers into her ass, holding her steady. "And I promise I'll always fuck you like I own you."

"Oh my god, Rob, *yes*." She sank down and dropped her head back on her shoulders, raked her nails over my scalp and released the kind of deep, satisfied groan I wanted to hear every day for the rest of my life. Then, "You weren't lying about this cock."

If there was a formula for measuring for male pride, it was that groan plus those words. "I'm happy this is good for you."

"You know it's better than good," she said on a shuddering breath. "I hope you're going to last because I want to savor this. I haven't had sex in ages."

"Going to last?" I repeated. "That's it. That's enough commentary from you, precious." I held her still and slapped her ass before lifting her from my lap. I dropped her on the mattress and pushed to my feet. "And you know you could've had sex with me *months* ago."

Crawling backward on her elbows, Magnolia snapped, "I know. You mentioned it at least six million times."

I curled my fingers around my cock, stroked it while she settled against the pillows. God, she was so fucking beautiful and so fucking *mine*. "Spread those legs for me. I want to see you."

Again, she hesitated but then parted her legs and glanced at the hand shuttling over my length. "This is fun to watch though I'd really prefer getting that thing inside me again."

"Why I thought for one minute you'd be less challenging in bed than you are everywhere else is a mystery to me," I murmured to myself as I edged between her legs.

She reached up, skimming her hands over my chest and shoulders. "And here I am, wondering why you spent months selling me on your big, bad cock but now refuse to use it."

I leaned down, my lips ghosting over hers as I stroked myself against her core. "Quiet now, honey. This cunt is mine. *You* are mine."

We stared at each other as my crown thumped her clit, as she gasped and shivered, as she arched up to meet me. She gave the tiniest of nods and a whispered "always" as I pushed inside her.

Magnolia cried out, I buried a moan-turned-growl in her neck. She rocked up into me, I nearly blew it all right then. It was so right, terrifyingly right because this was *it*. This woman was *it* for me.

"You're rowdy," I said, sliding an arm around her waist to hold her still. "I fucking love that."

"You're rearranging my organs with that cock," she replied, her ankles locking at the base of my spine as her body moved with mine. "I believe you're the rowdy one here."

I sucked in as much oxygen as I could but it wasn't enough. My body was diverting all resources toward holding out as long as humanly possible and if I could manage that, nothing else was necessary.

"I'm just practicing for when I put a baby in you," I replied because I wasn't doing any of the things I should've done today. I wasn't keeping it to entry-level dirty talk but at the same time, there was no reason to censor or sanitize. Was it a little fucked up to get off on this? I didn't know. I didn't care either. As long as we knew we were safe together and we could draw lines when needed, nothing was off-limits, nothing was taboo. On a different, less needy day, I could call her a slut while she sat on my face or bite her nipples while we watched porn. No limits. No taboos. No reason not to lean into the forever we were building as a filthy fantasy, the one we'd claim for ourselves when we were good and ready. "Will that be after I marry you? Or before?"

"*Oh my god*." She clawed at my back and I could already feel the places where her short nails left welts and scratches. Loved every one of them because I'd earned them from her. "You actually said that."

I slammed into her like I was trying to prove a point. Which I was. I wanted her to know I was as serious as death do us part right now. "Answer me. Before or after?"

Magnolia thrashed underneath me, sending the pillows flying off the bed and something on her nightstand to the floor. None of it mattered. We didn't care. "After, after, after," she gasped.

I pulled back, the head of my cock lingering only barely inside her. "We'll have a significant amount of time to practice unless you're running away with me to elope tonight."

"Rob," she cried out. "*Rob,* if you don't move right now I'm going to die."

"I won't let that happen." I thrust inside her against and I knew this was almost over for both of us. The way her thighs locked around me and she fisted her hands in my hair, the way she clung to me while I fucked her mindlessly, it was all too much to experience while also trying to last for hours.

Her lips found my shoulder and stayed there as she whispered "oh, oh, *oh, yes*." I drove into her, too over-whelmed by these sensations to respond with more than my body's instincts. Everything hurt, it ached straight down to my bones. My body was twisted tight, my blood pounding hot in my veins. My muscles were working hard, pushing as I held myself off, spasming as I surrendered to the glorious ache of it all. I couldn't hold on another minute without splitting right in half.

In some other part of the house, Gronk started barking like a maniac at the same moment I came with a roar. I went rigid, every last inch of me, as I emptied myself into her. It was like a downpour.

"Gronk," she called, her voice sex-drenched. "No barking! None of that."

For his part, Gronk didn't give a shit and I knew Magnolia would keep on chastising him until he stopped. So, I did the only reasonable thing I could think of and pressed my palm to her mouth. "Come for me, filthy girl," I said. "Let me feel you clench and shiver deep inside. Let me feel you working every last drop out of me."

If I was the downpour, Magnolia was the thunder and lightning, climaxing in loud, jolting bursts that made my heart squeeze and my cock pulse. It was better than anything I'd imagined, anything I'd ever wanted.

When the last spurt pulsed through me, I dropped my head between her breasts and closed my eyes. I was brain numb and half delirious and didn't think I could peel myself from this heaven for anything, not when I was still half hard inside her. Not when I was busy thinking up all the ways we could do this again.

"You're making some sounds," she said, her fingers drawing lazy circles on my scalp. "Little grumbles and growls. What are those about?"

"Thinking about fucking you again."

"Again," she repeated.

"Mmhmm. All night, filthy girl. All night."

She traced the tendons in the back of my neck, smoothing

every ounce of tension stored there. "I could get down with that."

Yes.

I was going to marry this girl.

I was going to put babies in her.

And I was going to keep covering her mouth during sex if she insisted on hollering at the dog.

CHAPTER
THIRTY-FIVE
ROB

"So, here's the thing," Magnolia said as she merged onto the highway.

I stroked Gronk's back. We'd made it one block from the house before his panting and whining in the backseat became too much. That was how he came to be perched on my lap and checking out the scenery on I-93. "There's a thing?"

"There's always a thing," she replied. "That's the thing about me. There's always a thing."

"I'd never thought to put it so succinctly." I glanced over at her but she didn't notice. She was busy driving like she couldn't spare a glimpse and that seemed like a fine reminder that Magnolia went deep. She might have fourteen different thoughts going at once but she was *deep* in them.

There was always a thing.

I was coming to find I quite liked that about her. "Okay," I said. "What's the thing for today?"

"Well, there are a few of them," she said under her breath.

KATE CANTERBARY

"First of all, my brothers." She gave a great sigh. "They've been known to have some fun at these family dinners."

That didn't sound so bad. "What kind of fun?"

She snickered. "Remember how I told you my mother invited some dude from an online dating app to Sunday dinner once?"

"Yes," I murmured. That was either an expert level move or the definition of feral, and I was still split on the difference.

"Well, my brothers had *a lot* of fun with that guy. He didn't know what hit him."

"Are we talking about a flag football game with some unnecessary roughness or what? Just tell me what I'm walking into and whether the dog will protect me."

"The dog barks and that's the extent of his protective response. He'll also scratch at shins and ankles."

I peered at Gronk. "Sounds like I'm on my own."

"You're not," she said quickly. "And I doubt this will be anything like it was when—dammit, what was his name?"

"I'm taking it as a good sign that you don't remember."

"No—I mean, yes, sure—but it's that my brothers were... god, how do I explain this? They were messing around, calling him Titus or Targaryen, and I'm not sure I caught his actual name in that mess. I was also busy glaring at my mother the entire time so I was only half-listening."

I gave a strangled laugh but I wasn't worried. I'd survived in a frat house with sixty abysmally behaved brothers for three years and worked with hooligans cut from the same rowdy cloth every day. Hell, I *was* one of those hooligans. I could hold my own with Magnolia's brothers. I'd be fine.

"What else? What's the other thing?" I asked.

"Oh, right," she murmured to herself. "My mother can be a little—" Magnolia paused, her lips parted and her head tipped barely to one side as she passed exit after exit. Eventually, she continued. "Much. She can be a little much."

"Yeah, so can I. Have you forgotten how we met? How I started things?"

With a shrug, she replied, "It could be said that the way I continued things was a little much."

"And thank god for that."

Had it been literal fucking torture to carry on a relationship with this woman while Brock did the same? Yep. Would I have wanted it any other way? You could bet your ass I wished Brock had never entered the picture. All of that was true and at the same time, I knew this was the way it was meant to be. This was how I was supposed to fight and fall for Magnolia. This was how it was supposed to go down for all of us.

So, yeah, I was thankful as fuck that Magnolia was a little much.

"I'm looking forward to it," I said.

"Okay, that's very polite and all, but I need you to know my mother can get carried away. She'll invite you to one event or another at her church and by *invite*, I definitely mean she'll corner you and make it impossible to say no."

"Sounds like every private wealth manager I know." I scratched behind Gronk's ears. "You know I'm not fresh out of the sandbox, right? I've been known to close a deal or two in my day. I dare say I closed you, Miz Maggie."

She laughed. "I think I closed *you*."

"If that's your version of the story, I can stick with it. But don't worry about your family, love. I've got this."

"I just don't want you to run screaming."

"That's not going to happen," I said with a quick glance in her direction. She didn't notice. Her concern was adorable. Really adorable. As if it was possible for her hyper-involved family to scare me away. If her friends—and the other fucking guy she'd been dating—hadn't accomplished that, nothing would.

I could handle this. A mom who operated on meddle level one hundred. Some ball-busting brothers. I had this under control.

And I had the dog. That had to count for something.

* * *

Magnolia's parents lived in an old house in a section of New Bedford that treasured its old houses but unlike all the other manicured homes on the street, this one had a slightly different feel to it. There was no single thing that made it stand apart but a collection of small things that added up.

An overabundance of blue hydrangeas hugging the house. They seemed determined to block the windows and choke the front walkway. A pair of long, raised garden beds packed tight with tomato cages and zucchini trellises. A few too many trees and rosebushes along the perimeter, too many flower pots around the front door. And then there was the older Subaru wagon with no fewer than twenty bumper stickers on the back end, all in the vein of "Save the Bay" and "Follow Me to the Farmers Market!" and "Water is Sacred" and "Feel the Bern."

When Magnolia noticed me reading them, she said,

"Yeah. Like I told you earlier, my mom can be a little much but at least she's upfront about all of it."

I couldn't explain why all of this—the bumper stickers, the tomatoes, the overgrown bushes, the promise of a family certain to give me a hard time—was so damn charming but I couldn't hide my grin.

"What's that about?" she asked, pointing at my smile.

"Nothing at all." After setting Gronk on the ground and twisting his leash around my wrist, I grabbed the wine and flowers I'd brought along. Like I'd said, I knew how to close a deal or two.

"Something," she said as she turned toward the walkway.

"Wait a second," I said, tucking the bottles under my arm and beckoning her closer. She shifted back, her gaze questioning, and that moment of confusion was just enough for me to pull her in and seal my lips to hers.

I'd been doing this for months—dragging her close, shutting her up with a kiss—though it felt different today. It wasn't about stealing moments with her anymore. It was about keeping them.

As I twisted my hand around her hair, I was fractionally aware of passing cars and slamming doors. Aware in a completely unconcerned sense, one that allowed absolutely no room for thoughts or propriety or decency or—

"Uh, Maggie. The neighbors are staring."

"Mrs. McCafferty has her rosary beads out."

Brothers.

Magnolia pulled away from me with a surprised gasp and when I pivoted toward the voices, I found a pair of men eyeing us. The resemblance between them was clear though they were as different as their vehicles—the vintage Porsche and the gleaming black truck.

"Oh, hey," she said, tucking her hair behind her ears. "Linden, Ash." She gestured to each. "This is Rob."

The men traded a glance.

"It's a pleasure to meet you," I said.

Linden stared at Magnolia. "Mom didn't say anything about this."

With a sheepish look, Magnolia glanced to the ground. "That's because she doesn't know."

Oh, shit.

"What was that?" I asked.

"I really need to understand the logic behind this," Ash said.

"I didn't want Mom going nuts over this," she replied defensively. "I just wanted it to be a regular Sunday dinner." When the three of us only blinked at her, she continued, "And, honestly, it's only fair considering some of Mom's shenanigans." More blinking. "And she told me last month to bring Rob home whenever I was ready."

Linden studied the six pack in his hand. "I did not bring enough beer for this."

I held up the bottles. "I brought wine."

Ash nodded. "Smart move."

Linden pointed to the house. "Can I go in first? I want to get a good seat."

Magnolia glared at her brothers. Triplets, man. They were a hoot. "Yes. Fine. Go. You should only hope I am this kind and accommodating when you two bring people home."

Ash scoffed. "Like I have time for that."

Linden clapped his brother on the back. "Like I have any interest in that."

They marched inside, leaving me and Magnolia alone

once again. I ran my hand over her hair. "You could've mentioned this was a surprise."

"I was going to. It was on my list of things to explain."

"Ah. Another thing."

Her eyes crinkled at the corners. "Are you upset?"

I smoothed the crease between her brows with my thumb. "No. But you gotta let me be a co-conspirator. We'll have more fun that way."

"Fun," she repeated. "Yes, let's hope this is fun. If it isn't—"

"There's a cute dog and booze. We'll manage."

We entered through a side door around the far end of the driveway, and stepped into the kitchen. Ash and Linden were tucked into the breakfast nook while an older woman who looked astonishingly similar to Magnolia chopped a cucumber at the countertop.

The door banged shut behind us and Mrs. Santillian glanced up with an expectant grin—until she spotted me and her eyes popped wide.

"Hi, Mom," Magnolia said. "I want you to meet Rob Russo."

There was a split second where I didn't know which direction this was headed. The lady had a knife and I didn't doubt she could debone me if given the chance, and if *I'd* brought someone home without proper notice, my mother would've sent me out back to dig myself a grave.

But then the shock wore off and her eyes turned warm. She dried her hands on a dishtowel and came to me. She plucked the flowers and wine bottles from me, dumping them into Magnolia's hands with little care, and took me by the shoulders.

"Rob," she said, staring at me intently. "I've heard so much about you. It's about time I put a face to the name."

"Don't think I told you his name," Magnolia murmured.

"All the same," Mrs. Santillian said. "You're here now. Do you like halibut? Of course, you do. You're a growing boy."

"And all growing boys who are also in their late thirties like halibut," Magnolia said under her breath.

I shot her a teasing grin before saying, "I love a good halibut. Thank you for having me, Mrs. Santillian."

"Oh, please call me Diana. Only my students call me Mrs. Santillian and we're not in school today."

"Diana," I said with my winningest smile.

"Now, how did you two meet?" She tapped her forefinger to her lips with a glance between me and Magnolia. "I can't seem to remember Magnolia telling me that little detail."

"She wants to know whether she can claim credit for this match," Magnolia said. "And the answer to that is no, you cannot, Mom."

"This was worth the drive down here," Linden murmured.

"It really was," Ash agreed.

"We met several months ago," I said, searching for the most palatable way to explain that I'd wanted to use her daughter as a fucktoy to burn away all memory of my last relationship but had since evolved from that viewpoint. "We started out talking. Just as friends—"

Linden rubbed his palm over his face. "If he says *with benefits*, I'm not going to be the one to explain that to Mom."

Magnolia threw a dishtowel at her brother. "Shut the hell up."

Diana wagged a finger at her. "There is no need for language like that."

"We started out as friends," I repeated, "even though I was very impatient and didn't want to wait. Somewhere along the line, things changed and I'm happy I made the cut." With an easy shrug, I added, "I have been bribing Gronk with some primo dog treats so I can't say I've been playing it entirely fair."

"I'll allow it," Linden said.

"Isn't that precious!" Diana cooed. "If you're on Gronk's good side, you're on mine too."

Magnolia busied herself with putting the flowers in a vase and filing the bottle of white wine away in the fridge, occasionally glancing over at me with a knowing grin while her mother peppered me with questions. She wanted to know about my family, where I was from, how I liked New England compared to New York.

When those matters were suitably addressed, Diana hooked a glance at her daughter, saying, "I wish I'd known you were bringing a guest, Magnolia. I would've had an extra place set at the table."

Magnolia pointed at the pile of plates and cutlery on the countertop. "You haven't set the table because you make the boys do that and I didn't get any notice about Trevor—"

"Troy," Ash interrupted.

"Are you sure? It's not Truman?" Linden asked him.

Ash shook his head. "Troy."

"Troubadour," Linden replied.

"Telemachus," Ash said.

"Tommy boy," Linden said.

"Toulouse," Ash said.

"*Enough of that,*" Diana snapped. To Magnolia, she said, "I would've appreciated some notice, if for no other reason than making sure I had enough for an extra guest."

Magnolia folded her arms. "Enough? Really? Not sure that one holds up, Mom, seeing as you always cook enough to send the three of us home with several days'-worth of leftovers."

"No leftovers for me, thanks," Ash said. "I'm traveling for an audit all week."

My ears perked up at that. "You're in auditing?"

Ash shrugged. "Financial accounting, audits, taxation."

"Investment banking," I said. "You're based out of Boston, I assume?"

Behind me, I heard Diana whisper to Magnolia, "He's a *banker*?"

Ash nodded. "Yeah. My office is near Copley. Where are you?"

"Financial district," I said. "State Street."

Linden glanced between me and Ash. "Oh. What a wonderful development. Another money guy at the table. Thank the gods for beer."

Ignoring his brother, Ash studied me for a thoughtful moment before saying, "Any ideas what the Fed will do to interest rates next month?"

I dropped down to unclip Gronk's leash. "I have a few ideas, yeah, but most of them are wishful thinking."

Diana snapped her fingers at us. "We don't talk business at dinner."

Ash gestured to the breakfast table. "It's not dinner yet."

"It will be soon enough. Go set the table," she ordered. "We'll use the nice glasses tonight. Okay? From the china cabinet. And the nice cloth napkins too. Take your brother with you." Gronk chased after Ash and Linden as they exited the kitchen. "Magnolia, set out a bowl of water for the dog. He must be dying of thirst after the drive down here."

"Already did," she replied as she came up beside me. "Where's Dad?"

"At the golf course," Diana said. "Something about getting in an hour at the driving range. That was two hours ago."

Magnolia met my gaze with a cheeky grin. "Anything I can do to help?" I asked.

"Heaven's sake, no," Diana said.

"I don't mind being put to work," I said. "I'm sure there's something I could do for you." Magnolia rolled her eyes at me. I gave her a wink. "Closing the deal," I mouthed to her.

"You could help Magnolia pick some parsley from the garden," Diana said. She pointed to a basket by the door. "I'm not sure if there's any more Mexican oregano but if you see any, grab a few sprigs."

Magnolia looped the basket's handle in the crook of her elbow and gestured for me to join her outside. I followed as she meandered through the garden, watching as she studied the leaves and flowers in the beds. My gaze traced the line of her legs as she walked, the curve of her hips as she kneeled down to snip some greens.

She reached back, her hand waiting for mine. I took it, stepped closer to her. "What should I be looking for, love?"

"Some privacy," she said with a laugh.

I leaned in, pressed my lips to the back of her neck. "We'll get enough of that later tonight."

"That doesn't mean I don't want some right now," she replied. "This is stressful for me, you know? You're amazing and they adore you, and everything is great, but this whole thing is a lot."

I wrapped an arm around her waist, nestled her backside against my front. "How can I make it less stressful?"

"You can't," she said, laughing again. "But there's a spot in the back there, behind those trees, that's almost completely hidden. If you wanted to—"

"If you think I can fuck you behind a tree and then take you inside to sit through a meal with your parents and brothers, you are very confused about several things. I don't know how to fuck you politely, my love, and it will show."

A deep throat clearing sounded behind us. Then, "I don't believe we've met. I'm Carlo Santillian. Magnolia's father. And who are you?"

Where was the dog when I needed him?

"Oh my god," Magnolia whispered. "*Oh my god.*"

With a resolute nod to myself, I stepped forward and extended my hand in the man's direction. "Rob Russo, sir." He regarded me and my hand with an impatient glare that suggested I really shouldn't talk about my carnal knowledge of his daughter while on his property. Not unless I wanted to see what he could do with his nine-iron.

Fair. That was fair.

With a slight eye roll, he took my hand and gave it a quick shake. "Walk inside with me," he said. "My wife won't holler about me being late for supper if she's busy being polite to you."

I shot Magnolia a tight smile as I marched back into the kitchen, Mr. Santillian hot on my heels. As expected, Diana was this close to railing at her husband but choked it down in favor of asking me whether we found any of the oregano she wanted.

Magnolia entered the kitchen behind us, the basket filled with herbs and her cheeks flushed and her eyes bright. She swatted my ass as she passed by, mouthing over her shoulder, "You're trouble."

I nodded because she was right. I'd been trouble from the start. Instead of copping to that, I whispered, "I love you."

EPILOGUE
ROB

The next year.
Early spring.

"I'M TELLING YOU, DUDE. THIS YEAR IS GOING TO BE THE rebuilding year. They can't keep it going," I said, tipping my beer bottle toward my companion. "I was wrong about this past season. I'll give you that much—"

"You'll give me that much," Ben scoffed. "You're such an asshole."

"Calling it like I see it," I replied. "Even the best players age out of the game. The smart ones get out early and invest wisely. I know a guy who manages investments for several former NFL players and—"

"Oh my god, nobody cares," he said, groaning.

I grinned at him from across the table. Ben Brock was one surly son of a bitch. I wasn't certain but it seemed as though he was made entirely of salt. Salt that, at one point, might've loved my fiancée. And here I was, bullshitting about ball games with him while we knocked back a round of beers.

The world was fucking weird.

"All right," I murmured, gesturing to the waiter for our check. "Are we doing this or what?"

He lifted his beer bottle, shooting me a narrowed glance across the table. "What's the rush, Russo? Are you trying to hustle me off the market?"

"Man, you're already off the market," I said with a laugh. "Don't try to deny it."

He shook his head, sipped. "Too right," he said, mostly to himself. He glanced at his phone. "A little more than three months until you walk down the aisle. Not taking any chances between now and then, are you?"

I stared at him, a stiff smile pulling at my lips. I trusted Magnolia. Through and through. I trusted Ben—about as far as I could throw him. Our shared history aside, I knew he didn't want Magnolia. I knew he belonged to another woman. I knew this, and I knew he wasn't pulling any shit at our wedding. However, no one was talking me out of caution.

Goddammit, I was getting married.

Fifteen months ago, I swore I'd never love again.

Nine months ago, I broke that vow.

Six months ago, I put a ring on Magnolia's finger.

Three months from now, I was making a new vow. One I intended to keep the rest of my days.

I couldn't fucking wait to marry her on the beach in New Bedford.

"Yeah, let's do this," Ben said, interrupting my thoughts. "I can't deal with the ambiguity anymore. I gotta lock Killer down."

I winced. "Do you have to call her that?"

He shrugged. "It works for her."

I could grant him that much but it didn't make Grace Kilmeade's nickname any more palatable and I worked with guys who went by Booch, Mad Dog, and Mole Sauce. "Whatever, dude," I said. "What's the plan? You said you have a hookup. Is this legal or should I text my attorney in advance?"

"You're such an asshole," he muttered. He rubbed his hands on his thighs as if he was working out some nervous energy. I smirked. Even though I'd been there and done that, I smirked. "What if she says no? That's a possibility, isn't it? I'm sure Gigi said no to you at least four or five times."

I dropped some cash on the table and stood, pulling on my coat. "In on the first shot."

That was always the way with Magnolia. She was the first woman I'd approached on the dating app, the first woman I'd shared my brokenhearted story with, the first woman I loved all the way through and back again, the first I'd asked to marry me, the first I knew better than I knew myself.

Ben led the way through the tavern, stopping outside on the sidewalk. "She's young," he said, shoving his hands into his coat pockets. "Haven't you seen the stories about her generation? None of them want to get married."

Magnolia and I had joined in on too many group dates with Ben and Grace over the past few months for me to doubt that she bested him on the maturity scale. "Millennials don't like home ownership, American cheese, or movie theaters either." I gestured toward him. "If we're to believe any of that applies to Grace, we should probably skip this activity altogether because they don't care for diamonds either."

"You're not helping," he replied.

"All right." I shrugged against the howling wind. "She's not that young. Have you talked about getting married? The future, where things are going, all of that?"

He pierced me with a sharp glare. "Yes, Dr. Phil, we have."

Seriously. Salt to the marrow with this one.

"Then what are you worried about?" I asked. "You've got five, maybe six years on her. Right?"

"Closer to nine," he replied.

I hadn't expected that but kept the surprise off my face. "So what? She's clearly made up for it in maturity. Has her age complicated things yet?"

"No," he grumbled.

"Then why is it a problem now?" I asked. "Despite the fact she enjoys your company, I'd say she's wise beyond her years."

"Truth," he murmured, rubbing his hands together. This late March cold snap was dreadful. "I don't want to do this only to get shot down." He hit me with a pointed glare. "I'm not interested in repeating that experience."

I blinked at him. We both knew that wasn't how it shook out with Magnolia but he was always on the hunt for sympathy. "I'm not following you to an underground gem dealer unless you're sure about this. Get there or buy me a beer because it's too damn cold to stand out here much longer."

He stared down the street for a long moment then turned an impatient glare in my direction. "Why the fuck did I bring you along for this?"

I lifted my shoulders, let them fall. "Beats the shit out of me. Don't you have other friends? I can't be the only person you'd call to chaperone a shopping excursion."

That was the kick in the ass Ben needed because he said, "Okay, then. Let's do this. Let's buy an engagement ring." He coughed and sucked in a breath as if he was choking. "Jesus Roosevelt Christ, I'm asking Killer to marry me. I'm—I'm gonna *marry* this woman."

I clapped him on the back. "It's great when it hits you, huh? It's like a near-drowning."

He continued coughing and sputtering. "When did this happen? *How* did this happen?"

"By my count, you have Lauren Walsh to thank."

He hit me with an unimpressed glare. "Can't believe we got roped into moving people we didn't even know. What kind of bullshit was that?"

That earned him another smack on the back. "It worked out for the best. You met Grace, right?"

He gestured down the street and we started in that direction. "Correction. I did not *meet* her. I was caught in her motherfuckin' force field."

I shoved my hands into my coat pockets, a smile forcing its way across my lips. "Yeah. It's exactly like that."

I followed Ben to a building on the far fringe of Boston's Theater District. After being buzzed in, we climbed two sets of stairs and waited on a narrow landing. I pulled my phone from my pocket and shot off a text to Magnolia.

Rob: This is not what I'd expected but it's 100% on-brand for Brock so I probably should've expected everything.
Magnolia: Sounds about right.

Magnolia: Promise me you won't let him make any excessively odd choices. Odd is fine but not excessively odd.
Grace does have a tiny mustache tattoo on her ring
finger so...
Rob: I believe that's the entire reasoning behind my invitation to this event.
Magnolia: He invited you because you're his friend and he trusts your opinions.
Magnolia: He likes you. Even if he doesn't act like it.
Magnolia: But also, you have done this a few times.
Rob: You are so rude to me.

"HEY." Ben slapped the doorframe, snatching my attention away from the screen. He tipped his head toward the open door. "He's ready for us."

A man wearing a black apron covered in dusty handprints introduced himself as Syleski as he ushered us into the office. He pointed at the chairs in front of his desk, asking, "Rings, yes? That's what you want?"

Ben glanced to me, an *oh fuck what am I doing?* look on his face. I pulled out a chair, pushed him into it. "Yes," I answered. "He's looking for an engagement ring."

"Nothing traditional," Ben added. "It has to be different. Really unique."

I nodded but said to Syleski, "Not too different."

The jeweler ducked into the back section of the office while I shucked my winter coat, hung it over the chair. "Loosen up, Brock. You're going to survive."

He snapped off a response but I ignored him in favor of my phone.

Rob: He's not drunk enough for this.

Rob: Neither am I.

Magnolia: You can drink later. With me.

Magnolia: I want to see this ring and I don't think Ben has visited since before we finished work on the kitchen.

Rob: I am not bringing him home after this. I have other plans for our evening, love.

Magnolia: Are we talking plans or Plans?

Rob: Plans.

Magnolia: Maybe you should send me a dick pic so I know what to expect from these Plans.

Rob: You're going to remind me of that on our wedding day, aren't you?

Magnolia: Anything is possible.

SYLESKI RETURNED with a velvet-covered tray and launched into a rapid explanation of each cut, style, material. The options seemed endless. At one point, I was certain Ben went cross-eyed.

"This is modern but also elegant," Syleski said, holding up a slight platinum band with a round diamond winking from the center. "Unique, yes?"

Ben shook his head. "No. That's not right for her." He glanced at me, his eyes wide and hair sticking in every direction after running his hands through it every forty seconds. "I need something as dark as her heart."

The jeweler's brows pitched up. "What he's saying," I jumped in, "is he'd like to see some colored gemstones."

"Do you have black diamonds?" Ben asked.

I swallowed a groan as Syleski answered, "A few, yes." He glanced at me for approval. I shrugged. "You want to see them?"

I glanced between Ben and the jeweler. "How about some black and some colored gemstones? More options."

When Syleski stepped away, Ben shifted to face me. "Am I fucking this up?"

"No, not at all. It's fine. These things take time. Lots of back and forth." I studied my phone for a second. "When are you planning to ask Grace? Do you have an idea how you want to do it?"

He huffed out a sigh and dropped every random proposal plan in the world on me. I smiled and nodded because it was evident he needed to work these options out, but my mind wandered back to the autumn morning Magnolia and I had closed on our new home.

We hadn't gone looking to buy a house together, but it seemed the house went looking for us. The brownstone sat adjacent to Hayes Park in the South End, not far from my apartment. We'd passed it while walking Gronk on several occasions, each time admiring the stained-glass windows, the dedicated parking, the neighboring rose garden. It wasn't until Magnolia's friend Riley mentioned he was considering it as a restoration project and wanted her input on the landscape design that we'd realized it was available.

And we wanted it. There was no shortage of work needed but we were up for those challenges. That, and her friends jumped at the idea of helping us fix up the house. Those were friends worth having.

Within two weeks, we'd made an offer, plunked down the cash, and had ourselves a home.

And when we'd pulled up in front of the house we'd bought together on that October morning, I asked Magnolia to get the keys from the front pocket of my laptop bag. She didn't see that pocket, instead reaching into the one where I kept an extra set of earbuds, some paperclips, and the engagement ring I'd been carrying around for more than a month. She pulled out a small manila envelope, one identical to the envelope containing the keys, and dropped a diamond into my palm.

She blinked furiously. "That's not a key."

"Nope," I replied.

"That's not a key," she repeated. "It's something very different from a key and I'm not sure whether this is a fun setup where I was supposed to find the thing that isn't a key or I went in the wrong pocket and this is a really big mistake."

I licked my lips. "Which do you want it to be?"

She kept blinking, her lips parted and her gaze fixed on the ring. "I think I know what you want it to be because you wouldn't have this thing that is not a key otherwise." She pushed her hair behind her ears, took a sip of her iced coffee, glanced at the brownstone. "And I think I know what I want it to be too but there's this little part of me"—she held up two fingers, barely an inch apart—"that doesn't believe you really want it. Doesn't want you to want me. That part is wrong and I know that but I have to mentally climb over those rocks first."

"What do you see when you climb over them?"

She hesitated, tapping a finger against her lips. "This wasn't how I imagined it would go."

"What did you imagine, love?"

She pursed her lips to fight off a smile. I loved it when she did that, as if schooling her mouth could hide her smiles when they blossomed in her eyes more than anywhere else. "I imagined I'd ask you." She tipped her chin toward my palm. "I thought I'd beat you to it."

I barked out a laugh, closed my fingers around the ring. "That's not how this is going to work, Magnolia."

She reared back. "Excuse you?"

"No, my love. I'm sorry but you don't get to propose to me."

Her eyes narrowed, brows furrowed, lips parted. I loved the look of outrage on her face. It was adorable. "And why not?" she asked.

"Because I've waited," I replied. "I've waited since—since the very start. Then I waited all summer and into autumn. I've wanted to do this so many times and I've waited. I wanted it to be right for you, for me, for us."

She dragged her teeth over her bottom lip. "How much longer did you intend to wait?"

I slumped back against my seat, rubbed my forehead. "Not long. Your mother told me I wouldn't be welcome in her home if I didn't hurry up."

"Oh my god," she whispered, bringing her fingertips to her temples. "My mother."

I reached for her hand. "Do you remember how I researched magnolias when you first told me your name, MizMaggie? I was sure I'd seen one but I didn't know off the top of my head what a magnolia looked like and I had to see for myself. I found photos but I also learned magnolias are nothing like other flowers. They blossomed before bees appeared on earth. They waited a long time for the world to understand them and that time made them tougher. More independent. So much stronger." I pushed the ring past her knuckle. "You don't have to wait any longer, Magnolia."

She blinked down at her hand. "We've both waited."

"Hey. Russo, hey."

"Yeah?" I asked Ben, shaking off the memory of that morning. "What's up?"

He held out a slim platinum band with a rough-cut blue stone seated at the center. "What about this one? It's a sapphire. It's kind of pretty and small, but it's also gnarly. Maybe a little scary. Just like Killer. Right?"

I peered at the ring. Not unlike Grace, it was delicate but undeniably gnarly. "For once, we agree."

EXTENDED EPILOGUE
ROB

A LETTER. SHE WANTED A LETTER.

It was my own damn fault, if I was being honest. I'd asked Magnolia what I could give her as a wedding gift and she wanted *a letter*. From *me*.

I'd expected something straightforward. Purchaseable. Like, earrings.

A letter was…neither of those things. I was no expert but it seemed less risky to drop several grand on sparkly earrings than committing words to a page and giving them to my future wife on the day of our wedding.

But here I was, sixteen hours from the ceremony and the only doubt in my mind was whether I'd fail to meet my bride's one request of me.

And that was why I was drumming my fingers on the hotel's front desk at one thirty in the morning as I waited for paper. Because I was writing a letter and the small notepad on the nightstand wasn't going to cut it.

When I made it back to my room with a full ream of paper tucked under my arm, I dedicated a solid minute to scowling at the bed. The *empty* bed. I couldn't remember why I was going along with this tradition when we'd shared a bed the past ten months. The night before our wedding shouldn't have been any different.

Oh, right. Magnolia wanted that too and fuck me if I didn't live to give her everything she desired. Including this letter.

Dear Magnolia,
I am marrying you today. We are getting married. It is our
wedding day. I am very happy and I love you.

"What the fuck is that?" I grumbled to myself. I balled that page up and shot it across the room, disgusted with myself. "Take two."

Dear Magnolia,
As you're aware, we're getting married today.

"Oh, no. Fuck this," I cried, trashing this attempt as well. "Not an interoffice memo, Russo. A letter. To the woman you happen to love very much and one who doesn't require a briefing on the events of her wedding day."

Dear Magnolia,
Your eyes shimmer like precious gems and your hair reminds me of
molasses. Not because it's sticky, but because it's dark and smells
nice.

"Oh my god. Oh my *god*, what is wrong with me?" I said to myself. "She's going to leave me at the altar if she reads this."

I picked up my phone, the urge to call her intense. I wanted to. I wanted to hear her voice and listen to her as she told me everything she'd done since we parted a few hours ago. I wanted her to remind me how to exist. I hadn't existed like this—without her—in over a year.

Instead of calling, I scrolled through months of text messages from Magnolia. There were the ordinary ("Are you still at home? Can you check if we have almond milk?") and the ridiculous ("There's a chipmunk singlehandedly destroying my backyard remodel project in Winchester and I'm not happy with that little fucker.") and the extraordinary ("I hope you know your ass looked especially yummy this morning. Wear that suit more often. Also, I plan on giving that ass a good squeeze tonight. Feel free to be naked when I do it!").

It took more than an hour to find the beginning, the first messages we'd shared back when we were two strangers matched on an app. When I was an absolute jackass undeserving of her attention.

Rob: Good morning.

Magnolia: Hi! Happy Monday!

Rob: How was your weekend?

Magnolia: Fine. I'm glad it's a new week. Looking for a fresh start on many things.

Rob: Same. Yeah, I'm in the exact same boat with you.

Magnolia: Awesome.

Rob: Let me be blunt. I just got out of a long relationship and I'm fucked up in the head right now but I'm 6'3, 210, and my dick is a solid 9 inches.

Magnolia: I'm sorry about your breakup.

Rob: Thank you. You want to help me fuck away the memories of my ex? No strings, no expectations, no emotional baggage?

Magnolia: I understand what you're going through, I truly do, but I don't see how this could be free of emotional baggage. And I don't really want expectation-less sex. I'm into strings and expectations and emotions. I want all of those things.

"I WANTED THOSE THINGS TOO," I said to the empty room. I put my phone down, glanced out the window at the saturated darkness of Narragansett Bay. "I just didn't know it."

Dear Magnolia,

It's strange to be writing you like this, on paper and without the benefit of receiving a response or an emoji reaction four seconds later. It's strange, although it reminds me of the beginning. Our beginning. Back when the only way we knew each other was text messaging.

I thought I had it all figured out. I thought I could shut off, shut down. You let me try but you knew it wouldn't work. Somehow, you knew me better than I knew myself, and you knew it within a handful of texts.

I'm not arrogant enough to say I knew you that quickly but I had one hell of a good idea by the time I met you.

Did you know I saw you through the window before I reached the bakery? Did you know I watched you for a minute, probably more?

You were rearranging things at the table and texting your friend and just being fucking adorable. Did you know you were devastatingly gorgeous that day? You were and the only reason that was different from every other day is it was my first time being devastated by you. I'd tried to tell myself that reaction was the product of all the other problems in my life. I did a halfway decent job of convincing myself too. Whenever that conviction faltered, I filled in the gaps with completely perverted thoughts about you.

I probably shouldn't mention that but you've heard worse confessions from me and it's the goddamn truth, Magnolia. I sat across that little table from you and wondered what it would take to get you on the table. Or in my lap. I wanted to touch you, taste you, tell you all the filthy, delicious things in my head. Tell you that I was devastated by you and it meant something, even if I didn't know how to process it at the time. I didn't think I could live another day if I didn't drag my tongue along the underside of your breasts while I had you under me. I wanted to tear you apart and consume you—and you weren't giving me any of it. Not at all. No, I had to work for it and wait for it.

Here we are, hours away from exchanging vows and I know I'm really lucky you responded to my first message…and the other ones too. You picked up the mess of me and somehow put the pieces back where they belonged, even when I didn't deserve that kind of generosity from you.

And I still want to run my tongue along the underside of your breasts. Still want you in my lap and on the table of your choosing. If I'm being honest, I want you here with me right now, traditions be damned. I want to turn off the world and bury myself in you. I want to wear your thighs as earmuffs and I want scars on my shoulders from your nails. I want entire days to pass while the only thing I do is you.

Since our weekend is booked up, we're not getting entire days locked inside a hotel room. Just like you making me work for it and wait for it didn't deter me, neither will an insane wedding weekend schedule.

While you read this, I'll be sneaking into your dressing room and talking you out of that sweet little Mrs. Russo robe. You'll walk down that aisle with wet, wet panties and shaking legs, and I'll shed a tear over that glorious sight.

After I get my ring on your finger, I'm bribing our driver to take the long, slow route to the reception and spending every single minute of that drive with my head under your dress.

Some time between cocktail hour and cutting the cake, I'm stealing you away and we're finding a room with a locking door and the kind of sofa that will allow me to sit back with your perfect ass in my hands. I want your dress all around us while I fuck you slow and quiet. I want every reminder in the world that you married me.

After that, when your panties are safe and sound in my pocket, we'll celebrate this crazy thing we found in each other until we drag each other to back to the hotel. I don't know what will happen then but I know I can't wait to have good old-fashioned bed sex with my wife...the one who wanted me to write her a letter.

I love you for that. For everything. Not simply because you devas-

tated me while putting me back together, but because you make me work for it. You make me wait.

About the earrings…you don't have to wear them today. I'm sure you have something picked out already. But I'd like to see you wearing only those earrings at least once during our honeymoon.

I love you, Magnolia. Today, tomorrow, and always.

Rob

I RESISTED the urge to read through the words I'd written and folded the pages in thirds, stuffed them into the hotel-branded envelope. I set it beside the velvet jeweler's box on the bureau and stared at the bed once again. I didn't want to sleep alone but the thought of seeing Magnolia in a matter of hours—marrying her—filled me with contentment.

No risks in sight.

———

Thank you for reading! I hope you loved Magnolia's journey.

Look for Ash's story in Boss in the Bedsheets **and Linden's in** The Belle and the Beard.

AN EXCERPT *from* **Boss in the Bedsheets:**

I studied the thick stubble on his jaw and above his upper lip as I considered this. "I hate to break it to you, Ash, but we're past the point of requiring permission to ask personal questions. This is all one big personal question."

"Is that a yes or a no, Zelda?"

"Yes, go ahead," I replied.

He dragged his hand from between my shoulders to my waist, slow slow slow like he wanted me to record the feel of his fingertips all over my skin. "What are you wearing?"

"It's a shirt."

He fisted his hand around the fabric. If he gave the tiniest of tugs, it was bound to rip. "Is it really?"

"Yes," I snapped, failing to keep a laugh out of my voice. "And shorts."

He released the shirt, then traced his knuckles along my vintage waistband. "I'd really like to know whose boxers you're wearing."

"Who? What? Oh, they're mine," I sputtered. "Yeah. These are mine."

He stared down at the boxers, frowning. "I can't decide if I'm surprised or relieved."

"No?"

"No," Ash replied. "And that's not the greatest complication in this matter."

"What would that be?"

His frown morphed into a grimace, his brows gathering. "There's the issue of me being irrationally troubled at the prospect of you sleeping in some other guy's underwear."

Boss in the Bedsheets is available now!

ALSO BY KATE CANTERBARY

The Magnolia Chronicles — Magnolia
Boss in the Bedsheets — Ash and Zelda
The Belle and the Beard — Linden and Jasper-Anne

Talbott's Cove

Fresh Catch — Owen and Cole
Hard Pressed — Jackson and Annette
Far Cry — Brooke and JJ
Rough Sketch — Gus and Neera

Benchmarks Series

Professional Development — Drew and Tara
Orientation — Jory and Max

Brothers In Arms

Missing In Action — Wes and Tom
Coastal Elite — Jordan and April

Get exclusive sneak previews of upcoming releases through Kate's newsletter and private reader group, The Canterbary Tales, on Facebook.

ABOUT KATE

USA Today Bestseller Kate Canterbary writes smart, steamy contemporary romances loaded with heat, heart, and happy ever afters. Kate lives on the New England coast with her husband and daughter.

You can find Kate at www.katecanterbary.com

facebook.com/kcanterbary

twitter.com/kcanterbary

instagram.com/katecanterbary

amazon.com/Kate-Canterbary

bookbub.com/authors/kate-canterbary

goodreads.com/Kate_Canterbary

pinterest.com/katecanterbary

tiktok.com/@katecanterbary

ACKNOWLEDGMENTS

This book is nothing like anything I've ever written and I have to thank the people who loved it every step of the way. Everyone who loved Magnolia all the way back to *Necessary Restorations*. All the early readers following Magnolia's story in serialized form on Book+Main Bites and all the readers who chose to wait until Magnolia's story was complete to read.

Thank you for loving my characters and their stories. Thank you for waiting until they are ready to be told. Thank you for trusting me to tell them the way they deserve to be told.

And thank you to the people who help me turn the loose pocket change that I call my ideas into big, beautiful stories. Without your cheerleading and support—and the occasional "I told you so"—I'm not sure I'd ever finish a book. You know who you are and you know you're dear to me. Thank you for everything you do.

CPSIA information can be obtained
at www.ICGtesting.com
Printed in the USA
BVHW041656180723
667437BV00003B/54